JEANETTE BAKER

The Delaney Woman

MIRA®

ISBN 1-55166-696-0

THE DELANEY WOMAN

Copyright © 2003 by Jeanette Baker.

Visit us at www.mirabooks.com

Printed in U.S.A.

"Will you find who killed my brother and his son?"

Cecil Marsh leaned back in his chair. Lines of weariness etched his cheeks. "Honestly?" He shook his head. "It's doubtful. These people are clever and the situation complicated. It isn't likely one person acted alone. The odds aren't good, Miss Delaney. They never are. I'm sorry. Can you help us at all?"

They wanted her help, these men who treated murder as blandly as they did the morning weather report. Rage loomed in her chest. Connor and Danny were dead, killed by assassins, and it was merely *an unfortunate circumstance.* Kellie bit down on the inside of her cheek. Her eyes were blank, her words expressionless. She had a single name, a common name. It was all she would give them. "Tom Whelan," she said quietly. "My brother was communicating with a man named Tom Whelan."

"There are thousands of Tom Whelans. Do you have a location?"

"No," she lied. "All I have is his name."

Marsh stood. "Thank you for your information, Miss Delaney. We'll let you know if anything develops." He had his arm under her elbow, leading her toward the door. "These things take time. It's best to get on with your life and let us do our business. Connor would have wanted that. He understood how things worked."

Kellie stood outside the door closed firmly shut against her. The interview was over. She had been swatted aside, an annoying fly in the path of a steamroller bent on moving in the opposite direction.

There was nothing left to do but take matters into her own hands and go to Banburren, check into Tom Whelan's guest house and find out what she could. There was no time to lose.

ACKNOWLEDGMENTS

The vision of this book changed a great many times and took longer than usual to write. For those who suffered with me through the rewrites, the plot changes, the name changes, the various beginnings and endings, many, many thanks for your unconditional support.

Specifically:

My fellow authors, Pat Perry and Jean Stewart, for their words of encouragement.

My sister, Vicki Riley, for her pragmatic, no-nonsense advice.

My agent, Loretta Barrett, for always calling me back, and for understanding when to leave me alone and when not to.

My editor, Valerie Gray, for being such a trooper, for not giving up on me and for making me laugh when I wanted to cry.

My brand-new husband, Stephen Farrell, for uncomplainingly giving up evenings and weekends to help me rethink and rework this book, and for teaching me how to Zip up files over and over again until I finally got it right, without ever questioning my Intelligence Quotient.

One

"Fast forward," shrieked four-year-old Danny, his hands covering his eyes, "fast forward."

Kellie Delaney, familiar with the procedure, pressed the forward button on the remote control and counted to ten. Then she gently squeezed her nephew's arm. "It's over, Danny," she said gently, "the scary part is over."

Danny removed the hand from his left eye, opened it to a mere slit, and glanced at the telly. Convinced his aunt and beloved godmother was telling the truth, he settled back into the couch and concentrated on the story before him.

Kellie stroked the blond curls. All the Delaneys were cursed with curly hair, so fine and thick it couldn't be controlled. She kissed his cheek. Comforted, the little boy curled into her side, never removing his eyes from the screen. It was always the same. Danny insisted on his favorite video, Walt Disney's *Bambi,* and yet the point where the fawn lost his mother continued to terrify him. Ridiculous as it sounded, Kellie wondered if it wasn't a subconscious notion emblazoned in him from infancy.

His own mother, Kellie's sister-in-law, had given up her life for him. Lizzie Delaney's cancer wasn't diagnosed until her pregnancy was in its second term. The doctors advised aborting her fetus but Catholicism and a mother's protective instincts prevailed and she'd refused. Danny and the cancer had grown together. She had given birth to a healthy baby but for Lizzie it was too late. The babe and Lizzie's husband, Connor, were left behind to fend for themselves. Kellie had come down from Derry City for the christening and fallen in love with the tiny, motherless infant.

Dazed with grief, her twin brother had asked her to stay. It wasn't terribly difficult to find a teaching position. Somehow the three of them had managed to muddle through the last four years, Kellie standing in as aunt, mother, confidante and sister.

She loved her role. She loved the charming university town of Oxford and she loved her job teaching English at a private girls' academy near the river. She loved the drive down the tree-lined streets of the walled city. She loved the parking lot with its broken pavement and blades of grass persistently growing between the cracks. She loved the old brick buildings, the polished wood and the smells of dust and books and age and chalk. She loved the staggered rows of student desks in her classroom and the long oval windows, gleaming and diamond-paned, facing out over green lawns.

The very idea that she, Kellie Delaney of the Falls, could have come to this place in her life never ceased to amaze her. She didn't want to think about growing up in a family all but the most tolerant would call dysfunctional, but the memories intruded on her whether she called them up or not.

Her father, Brian Delaney, the family patriarch, hadn't seen a sober moment in four decades. Mary, her mother, had her hands full with seven children, a drunk for a husband and never enough money to feed her family all at once. She took in washing and mending and the only time her eyes weren't red was the first hour she opened them in the morning. Because there was always another baby on the way and too much to do, the older siblings found ways to fend for themselves.

Bridget, the first born, was thrown out of Saint Theresa's Catholic School for Girls when she arrived late one morning with one side of her head shaved and her skirt rolled up to her fanny. Sean was kneecapped for joyriding down the Ormeau Road in a car he'd lifted from the car park behind Dempsey's Pub. The car belonged to Father Donnelly who'd stopped to wet his thirst on the way to say Mass for the political prisoners in Long Kesh. Another brother, Liam, a self-proclaimed member of a paramilitary group, had turned him in. The two youngest Delaney brothers, Michael and Gene, were already heavily involved in the drug culture that had swept through West Belfast at the first sign of a halting of hostilities between Protestants and Catholics. And then there was Connor, her twin, her soul mate, a university graduate working for British law enforcement in Oxford, England.

There were times when Kellie, one of the pair of the only serene, goal-oriented, academic children in the bunch, was sure the wristbands proclaiming which babies belonged to whom had been switched when she and Connor were born and her mother had brought home someone else's twins. She would dream that somewhere she had parents who lived in a well-ordered house with a piano and bookshelves, people who read and discussed world events and spoke in soft voices, people who were never red-faced, never pounded the table with their fists and never, ever fell in the gutters too overcome with the drink to care where they spent the night.

Of course, when she looked into the mirror, her argument went the way of a too thin rainbow on a day of smattering sunlight. She was the image of her mother in Mary's younger, less dragged-out days and only a fool or an idiot would believe that Mrs. Delaney had ever cuckolded her husband.

Automatically, Kellie crossed herself and mumbled a quick but heartfelt Hail Mary. The ugly image of what she'd escaped never failed to bring on a shuddering prayer of thanksgiving and fervent appreciation for the blessings she'd been given.

The cushy job offer from Silverlake Academy came as a wonderful surprise. She'd been in Oxford for less than a month and had only the one interview. She'd connected immediately with the headmistress but hadn't counted on the job. There were few openings, most of them occurring through attrition when a teacher retired. No one wanted to leave Silverlake but the English teacher's husband had been unexpectedly transferred. The salary was excellent and the perks more than competitive. Kellie could actually afford to live within the city of Oxford. Connor had offered to supplement her salary, a gesture of appreciation for leaving her position in Derry, but she didn't need it. Not that her brother hadn't done well for himself. The lovely old home with its hand-carved moldings, polished oak floors and beveled-glass windows was a find. Kellie still didn't understand how a police officer, even if he did have a degree in criminology and wore a suit and not a uniform, could afford to live the way he did. She wasn't complaining. Connor was extremely generous and Kellie benefited from his circumstances as if they were her own.

Life was so perfect it frightened her. Kellie's superstitious tendencies, although buried deeply, were definitely Irish. The sense that all was progressing too well to continue had been highly developed in her Catholic childhood. It was only natural for her to assume in the deepest recesses of her consciousness that someday soon the ax would fall. *The way of the Shiia* the Irish called it. *Beatrice's Law* was the English translation.

The final *Bambi* scene was winding down. It was time for dinner. The ritual was always the same when Kellie was in charge. Danny was allowed his favorite, bangers and chips, foods Connor religiously avoided. She stood and held out her hand. "Come on, love. It's time for tea."

Obediently, the little boy took her hand, slid off the couch and trotted beside her down the hall with its plush, jewel-bright runner into the kitchen. Kellie groaned as she lifted Danny to the counter to watch her cook. "You're a very big boy. Soon you'll be too heavy for me."

The child nodded and reached for a handful of popcorn from the half-empty bowl. Kellie tickled his tummy, loving his distinctive chuckle. "Watch," she said, grabbing a kernel and throwing it into the air. She opened her mouth and caught it between her teeth. Danny laughed. She did it again.

"I want to do it, too," he said.

"You shall." She picked out another kernel and held it over his head. "Open your mouth," she said, "and tilt your head back like this."

Danny imitated her. She dropped it neatly into his mouth. He clapped his hands and laughed. "Again," he said.

"Just once and then dinner." Once more she held the kernel barely out of reach and dropped it into her nephew's mouth. He chewed, swallowed and smiled sunnily. A wave of tenderness washed over her. This small, lovable tyrant, adorable and slightly spoiled, was as dear to her as if he were her own child.

If anything marred the satisfaction of Kellie's existence, it was her inability to settle down with a family of her own. She knew she was reasonably attractive, not a great beauty, but cute in a wholesome sort of way, and she cleaned up well. Opportunities came her way fairly frequently, but she couldn't seem to connect with anyone. Her roots betrayed her. From a small isolated Nationalist enclave in Belfast, she wasn't comfortable with the cosmopolitan attitude toward sex. Even discussing it was embarrassing to her. Not that she had ruled it out completely; it was just that she thought it should be done with someone who meant more than a brief interlude. All good Catholic girls grew up believing that sex was sinful, that the act was only for benefit of procreation and that boys were beasts with disgusting appetites. By the time they learned differently they were safely married and well on the way to agreeing. Kellie had outgrown the attitudes of her childhood, but she wasn't ready for the casual promiscuity all around her.

Her sole sexual experience had left her raw. She'd met and fallen in love with an American attached to the embassy. Gregory Charles Hampton Bennett was a Bennett of Beacon Hill, a blue blood whose ancestors had arrived on that ship everyone who was anyone came over on. Not that his pedigree had meant anything to Kellie. She was weak in American history. After all, America had only been a sovereign nation for a bit over two centuries. It was a country settled by Englishmen and her own country, Ireland, had been at war with England for eight hundred years. Still, Greg was a darling man who'd adored her, temporarily. It was the temporary part that had bothered her. He hadn't made that quite clear and by the time he did, there was nothing to do but end it and wish him well when he returned to America.

Connor had helped her through it; Connor, her twin, who thought she was perfect in every way. He'd reminded Kellie that she had quite enough of her own to bring to the table, that she was something unusual in her own right, that she had a high-boned, clear-eyed, creamy-skinned Irish loveliness, despite her hated riotous curls that resisted gel, mousse, blow dryers and flat irons, and that everything was better and brighter when she was around. "Not to worry," he assured her. "Thirty-five isn't too old. You'll find someone much better in the end." Kellie's innate sense of honesty refused to accept his observations completely. He was her brother after all. Still, it was uplifting having a brother like Connor. Especially considering her other five disappointing siblings. She loved them desperately, of course. Family loyalty was as inbred in the Delaneys as were their large distinctive gray eyes, their love of words and music and the direct uncompromising way they had of expressing their opinions.

Kellie shook off her reverie, refusing to dwell in even the barest hint of darkness. Connor was always telling her she was too serious, to stop thinking of what might be and try to focus on the pleasure of the present. She concentrated on following his advice. She'd even come to the conclusion that romantic love was highly overrated. She'd thought seriously about the gamut of emotions she'd run when she was with Greg and decided that love could be described in stages.

In the beginning it is all consuming. The very idea of one's beloved not returning love with the same intensity is so painful it becomes unbearable. Edges are sharply defined and every word, every nuance and gesture is analyzed with the clarity and definition of a slide under a microscope. Later, when the gloss and newness fade, when one becomes more secure in the relationship and steps back with a bit of detachment, when a touch of realistic skepticism is attached to the face of love, one relaxes a bit, able to go about the business of living without the ever present consciousness of wondering what one's lover thinks or how he feels. In short, lovers begin to take each other for granted which is, she thought, a very good thing because such an intense level of emotion could never be permanently maintained with any degree of sanity.

Danny pointed out the window. "Da's home."

Sure enough, Kellie heard her brother's car in the carport. She lifted her nephew to the floor and together they walked outside.

"Hello, lad," said Connor, swinging his son into the air. "How's my favorite son?"

"I'm eating chips and bangers," confided Danny. "Aunt Kellie made some for you, too."

Connor laughed and tousled his son's curly head before setting him on his feet "Did she now? Bangers and chips, my favorite." He leaned close to Kellie's ear. "Is there anything else edible in the house?"

"I made some pasta and a salad. It's in the refrigerator." She tucked her hand in his arm. "Are you set for tomorrow?"

"Nearly. Are you sure you won't come with us?"

Kellie shook her head. "I'm going home for the rest of my holiday. Mam called me and you know how she rarely does that. She's having a hard time of it, Connor."

"Tell me something I don't know," he said bitterly. "When hasn't she? Living with an unemployed drunk takes its toll."

"Stop it. He wasn't always that way."

"Just our whole lives."

Kellie shook his arm in protest. "Do you remember how he used to play the pipes? Wasn't he wonderful?"

"Aye, if only one could make a living as an average musician."

"What has he done to make you so unforgiving? I'm not and I lived the same life you did."

"Where shall I begin? With his not coming to my wedding, or to Lizzie's funeral?"

Her voice softened. Connor was rarely bitter. "Is that why you do what you do? Work here in England for the British authorities because of what Da was?"

"Don't go psychoanalyzing me, Kellie."

"I'm simply asking you a question. You've chosen an odd profession for an Irish Catholic from Belfast."

He kissed her cheek. "I'm here because it's a lovely town and it's not Belfast. Say hello to Mam for me and tell her she's always welcome here."

The following morning Connor Delaney strapped his son into the child's restraint in the back of the car and took his place in the driver's seat. "We're on our way, lad," he said cheerily and pulled out onto the tree-lined street. He turned left, negotiated the roundabout onto the Coast Road and settled into the slow lane for a leisurely drive. Danny's head was already nodding. He would nap most of the way. Connor turned on the radio. Classical music filled the cab. It wasn't his normal preference but he left it there anyway. Today it suited his mood. The car was comfortable, tuned and packed for his vacation.

He stopped for petrol in a small town near the Welsh border. For the remainder of the journey the roads would be winding and narrow. Danny munched on crackers. Connor began singing the first verse of

"Old MacDonald Had a Farm." Somewhere in the middle of the third verse, Danny joined in.

The sharp, rugged beauty of the mountains rose on the right side of the car. Connor, intent on the descending road, spared no more than a cursory glance at the soaring peaks of the Swanseas on one side and the slate-gray ocean slapping against jagged cliffs on the other. He maneuvered the car around a hairpin curve, downshifted and applied the brakes. Instead of slowing down the car picked up speed. He depressed the brake pedal once again. Nothing happened. He pulled at the emergency brake. The car shuddered. Connor watched the lever on the speed dial creep up to seventy kilometers per hour. Solid rock rose on one side. "Hold on, Danny," he muttered. "Hold on, lad." His last conscious memory was the wide eyes of his son as their eyes met in the rearview mirror.

Kellie was well into a thorough cleaning of her flat when she heard the doorbell ring. Wiping her hands on a towel, she opened the side window. Two police officers stood on her front stoop.

"Yes?" she inquired politely. "May I help you?"

"We're here to see Miss Delaney," the older one said.

"You've found her."

"May we come in, miss?"

"Of course."

Kelly opened the door. "Pardon the mess. I'm cleaning."

"I'm sorry, Miss Delancy, very sorry, but there's been an auto accident. It's your brother and his son. There were no survivors."

Two

The granite headstones marking the plots were varying shades of gray, a pale color, thick and uniform whether the stone was new, or dark and thin, covered in mildew proportionate to its age, or weathered by the centuries. It seemed to Kellie that the entire world was shrouded in gray. Gray heads bent over prayer books, gray clouds hanging heavily over the treetops, gray coats absorbing the color of the day. Rain pounded sideways on the grassy hillside, mixing it up with wind in uneven spurts so that even those who'd come prepared with golf-size umbrellas were drenched to the skin.

Kellie had the vaguest memory of her mother saying something absurd, something like, *It's God's will, after all.* She hated her for that. Other voices murmured words of sympathy. What was it they said? Something about how terribly sorry they were. *Sorry.* Where had such a pitiful word come from? It conveyed nothing of the magnitude of their loss. Connor and Danny were gone from her forever. She couldn't bear to think, could barely muster the effort to breathe. Her bright, sunny-headed nephew was dead. How could such a thing be? How could a being powerful enough to arrange the events of the universe have allowed such a mistake to take place?

It was fitting that it should rain today, that the world should be dark and wild and angry. What had the priest said? Kellie couldn't remember. What did it matter? Nothing mattered, not the people gathered here today, not the Mass, nor the reception that would follow at home. She wanted it all to be over, the grave-side ceremony, the wake, the mourners, the entire day. Then she could take the pills the doctor had prescribed, crawl beneath the bed covers and sleep. Sleep brought peace. The hours of drug-induced unconsciousness were worth the ache of waking, the initial discomfort of knowing something was wrong followed by the heartbreaking awareness that nothing would ever be right again.

Tears froze on her cheeks. She looked around at heads bent against the wind and hands stuffed deeply into overcoat pockets. It must be cold. She shifted slightly, turned into the wind and waited. Nothing. She felt nothing but pain. It consumed her, this emotional awareness, devouring all thoughts of such minor physical discomforts as cold or hunger or pain or exhaustion.

Somehow, it was over. The mourners were disappearing in groups of two and three. Perhaps something was expected of her. She looked around, confused. Gillian Chambers, a friend from her earliest days in Oxford, wrapped both arms around her and led her in the direction of the car.

"We're going to get through this," her friend muttered, "and then you're coming home with me for as long as it takes."

Kellie stared at her blankly, neither arguing nor agreeing. It simply didn't matter.

A man in a dark wool coat approached them. He had no umbrella. "I'm very sorry, Miss Delaney. My name is John Griffith. I'm a colleague of your brother's. I need you to verify some information for me."

Gillian's arms tightened protectively. "Are you mad?" she snapped. "Not now."

"I understand," he said immediately. His accent wasn't quite British. "I'm terribly sorry for your loss." He handed Kellie a card. "Please ring me when you're feeling up to it."

"Idiot." Gillian's grip on Kellie's shoulder guided her toward the car. "Where do they find people like that?"

Kellie didn't answer. She couldn't. It was enough to simply cling to her friend's arm and move forward. Later, much later, when she could think again, if she could ever think again, she would attend to John Griffith.

Gillian sliced open the muffin and slathered white mayonnaise on both sides. Then she carved two sandwich-size pieces of ham from the bone, added several slices of cheese and tomatoes and popped them into the microwave. "It isn't much but I've the lecture to attend tonight."

Kellie sat at the table, staring at the newspaper.

Gillian turned to look at her. "Would you care to come with me?"

"No, thank you. I'm tired tonight."

"What else is new?" muttered Gillian under her breath.

"Did you say something?"

The microwave beeped. Gillian removed the sandwiches, took another plate from the cupboard, divided the food evenly and set both plates on the table. She took a deep breath. "Kellie, love. Life goes on. I don't expect you to dance jigs on tabletops, but you've got to go on, too. The term starts next week. Are you ready for it?" She sat down and reached out to take her friend's hands. "What about your job? How long will they wait for you? It's a good position. You've worked hard to get where you are."

Kellie stared at her. "Where is that, Gillian?"

"You're a respected teacher in the community. Doesn't that mean anything to you?"

Kellie thought a moment, testing the question. "I suppose so," she answered, as if she hadn't really understood the question.

Gillian sat back in her chair, defeated. "I don't know what's to become of you," she said. "What will you do all day if you don't work?"

For the first time since she heard the dreadful news, some of the glaze left Kellie's eyes. She pushed back her hair. "Of course I'm going to work. I certainly don't expect you to support me and I'm certainly not going back to my mother."

"I worry about you."

"I know. You've been a grand friend." Kellie bit

into her sandwich. "This is very good." She smiled. "I'm going home, Gilly. It's been a week and you're right. I need to clean out Connor's house before I can sell it."

"Did he leave you everything?"

"Yes, but I'm not taking it. There are enough at home who can use the money. I don't need it and I'd never hear the end of it if I left them out."

"They'll canonize you, Kellie. Why not keep a bit for yourself?"

"I don't want anything that came of this awful tragedy."

"Sorry." Gillian bit her lip. "I didn't think."

"Never mind. Eat your sandwich. I'll be gone when you get back."

Kellie threw the overnight bag into the back of her Rover and drove the three miles to her flat. Everything was as she had left it. The plants were a bit droopy, the newspapers stacked up and the mail had collected in a pile on the floor, but otherwise all was as usual. How odd. Pre-Connor and post-Connor and nothing had changed. Nothing but her life. What would she do with herself now that Connor and Danny were gone? There was her teaching, but that was over every afternoon. Her life, her real life, began and ended with her family. Tears welled up and spilled down her cheeks. She wiped them away.

Dropping her bag on the floor of the entry, she walked into the kitchen, poured herself a glass of wine and sat down at the table to sort through her mail. The peal of the doorbell startled her. Kellie looked at her watch. How odd. Who could it be this late? She wasn't expecting anyone. Kellie made no move to leave her chair. Again the bell sounded. She waited, arms and legs tense and immobile. It rang a third time. Stubbornly she tightened her lips and closed her eyes. She would not answer the door.

The windowpane rattled. She opened her eyes. Framed by the moldings were a man's head and shoulders. Another stranger. The last one brought disaster. At least this one wasn't wearing a police uniform. He beckoned her to the window. Annoyed and more than a little embarrassed, Kellie rose from the table, walked to the door and opened it. "May I help you?" she asked icily.

He walked back to the door, pulled his wallet from his pocket and flipped it open. It was something official. A license of some sort.

"Perhaps you remember me," he began. "I'm John Griffith. We spoke at the funeral."

She looked at him blankly.

He stepped into the kitchen. "I worked with your brother at the station. He was investigating a special assignment. We were hoping to look through some of his files."

"Why are you asking me?"

"There isn't anything on the computer at the office. We've checked it thoroughly. We're in a bit of a bind here or we wouldn't ask. We need to see his home computer." He glanced around. "You wouldn't by chance be storing anything for him here?"

"What exactly are you looking for?"

"We don't know really, names, references."

She had the typical Irish suspicion of the British police. "There's nothing of his here. I'll be cleaning out the house tomorrow. You can come around there if you like. I'm not really comfortable having you take the computer. There are personal items on it. I hope you understand."

"Of course."

"If you could be more specific, I might be able to help you if I find anything."

He hesitated. "I'll let you know." He smiled. "When shall I meet you?"

"Ten o'clock."

"I'll be there."

Kellie locked the door behind him. The wine no longer appealed to her, nor did the unopened mail. She was edgy with an anxious, unsettled feeling that tied her stomach into uncomfortable knots.

Where was the fairness? Not that Kellie had been raised to believe life was fair or even supposed to be. She could still hear her mother's voice explaining that life wasn't meant to be enjoyed. Fun was superfluous. People were put on this earth to create more people, to serve God, to withstand hardship, to endure. Catholic women, Irish Catholic women, were raised on the principle of endurance. The more one endured, the shorter one's time in purgatory. The rewards of heaven came to those who endured.

Kellie had resolved that Catholicism was not for her. She hadn't the strength or the conviction for it. Let women like Mary Delaney bear the burden of the church on shoulders frail from too much childbearing, too few vitamins, too little of everything except perpetual poverty.

Kellie had known from the time of her first communion when she was seven years old that something wasn't quite right with the church's stand on women. Lizzie Delaney's early death was proof enough. If her sister-in-law had agreed to an abortion and gone through the prescribed radiation and chemotherapy she would be alive today. Danny wouldn't have survived but there might have been other children. Perhaps Connor would never have driven the Coast Road the day his car veered off the cliff. Perhaps he and Lizzie would have vacationed elsewhere. Perhaps they would be waiting for her at a cozy pub near the Thames and she wouldn't be sitting here wishing she had the stomach to get thoroughly, painlessly drunk.

Kellie grabbed her jacket. She needed answers. With the exception of the funeral, it had been a very long time since she'd been inside a church. Perhaps the Anglo-Saxons had a different interpretation of mortal sin than the Celts.

Saint Paul's was a relatively modern building without personality. An English priest manned the confessional. *English priest.* The two words together were outrageous, never to be heard in Belfast. The door clicked shut enclosing her in semidarkness. "Bless me, Father, for I have sinned," Kellie whispered into the grate. "It has been three years since my last confession."

"What brings you here, my child?"

She hesitated.

The priest waited.

She spoke again. "My family has been taken from me."

"Go on."

Kellie wet her lips. "First it was my sister-in-law. She carried her child to term when she had cancer. She was advised to do so. To kill her baby was a sin. She died instead."

The silence was long and serious. Finally the priest spoke again. "She was a brave woman. The child must be a comfort to you."

"He was, Father," Kellie said bitterly, "until he, too, was killed nearly two weeks ago. He and my brother were traveling through Wales. Their car went off a cliff."

"You've suffered a great deal. How can I help you?"

"By explaining to me why a young woman died to save her child only to have that child's life cut cruelly short."

"Perhaps God had a need for them."

Her voice cracked. "I needed them, too, Father."

"You are troubled. I hear your pain."

She swallowed the steel-wool feeling in her throat. "I don't know what I'm going to do without them."

He was well trained in the art of interpretation. "You've been away from your church for three years. Now you want assurance that God didn't take them from you because you turned your back on your religion."

"Yes."

"God doesn't exact revenge, my child. Nothing you did caused their deaths."

She rested her head against the wooden wall. Her hands shook. "Sometimes, I don't believe I can go on."

"God gives us only what we can manage."

"Does he ever make a mistake?"

"No." His reply was immediate, unequivocal. She bowed her head for his blessing. "In the name of the Father, the Son and the Holy Spirit. Come again and now go in peace." He lifted his head. "I will pray that you find solace in your religion. God will lead you."

Her meeting was over, the connection broken. She felt the same. Nothing had been accomplished. Why was she surprised? Her relationship with the Church had never been particularly beneficial. "Thank you, Father." She stepped out of the confessional box into the cool English night. There were twelve hours to go until morning. Somehow she would get through. She would go home and take a Xanax. She hadn't taken one in a while. Surely tonight deserved one. Until last week she had never spent a night in Oxford without Connor. Every day since she'd left Ireland she'd slept with the knowledge that Connor was here with her in the same city. Now she was alone.

The phone rang the minute she stepped through her door. Gillian was worried. "Where have you been?" she asked.

"I went for a walk." The subject of confession would generate too many questions.

Gillian sighed. "You sound odd. Is everything all right? Do you want me to come over?"

Kellie held the phone to her ear, picked up the

newspaper from the kitchen table and sat down. "What do you mean by odd?"

"Just odd, that's all. Has something happened?"

Kellie closed her eyes. Gillian was a wonderful friend, but she couldn't lean on her forever. "I'm fine, really."

"Call me tomorrow if you need me."

"I will, Gilly, and thanks."

Connor's house, closed up since the funeral, smelled musty and old. Like a sleepwalker, Kellie moved through the rooms, refusing to focus on anything that reminded her of the two who once lived there. She walked into the kitchen, filled the kettle, lit the stove pilot and turned up the flame. There wasn't much to speak of in the cupboards but loose tea. Tea would soothe her. She added a pinch of her favorite blend, Lady Anne, to her mug, sat down at the table and stared at the clock. Slowly, slowly, the minute hand moved forward. The kettle hissed. She poured the water and watched it turn a deep golden amber. The leaves swelled like tadpoles and settled at the bottom. She would have to drink it without milk.

Carrying the mug with her, she walked down the hall into Connor's study. The room was exactly as he left it, pencils sharpened, desk cleared, brandy snifter perched on the ledge. It was dark. Kellie pushed aside the heavy drapes and cracked open the window. Dust circled in the air above her head. She turned back to the desk, breathed deeply and opened the top drawer.

Pulling out the contents she sat down in the leather chair and began to sort through it.

Three hours later, she'd gone through the desk, the shelves and the chest of drawers. She would leave the computer for Mr. Griffith, if he ever came, but first she would delete Connor's personal files. The computer was incredibly fast with one of those narrow fancy monitors that took up half the space of the old ones. Clicking on the command that would take her into his accounts, she scrolled down to the end. She had decided to work backward beginning with his checking account deposits.

The amount on his last statement startled her. Kellie frowned. She scrolled up to the month before and the one before that. Every one was the same, the exact amount deposited on the first and the fifteenth. *The first and the fifteenth.* Was the deposit money from his paychecks? Could a police officer possibly earn such a salary? Dreadful thoughts, forbidden thoughts flickered through her mind. Could Connor have been involved in something illegal? Panicking, she scrolled up again and again. Every month was the same, the exact amount deposited on the first and the fifteenth. She scrolled still further back to the beginning of the year. Perhaps she should look through his paper files.

The doorbell rang.

Quickly she turned off the computer, pushed in the chair and walked to the door. John Griffith stood outside. She opened the door.

"I knocked but you didn't answer. I saw a car outside and assumed it was you."

"Hello, Mr. Griffith. You're very late. I was just about to leave."

His looked genuinely contrite. "I was held up. I'm terribly sorry to have inconvenienced you."

She attempted a friendly smile, hoping it looked real. "How long did you say you worked with my brother?"

"About six years or so."

"What exactly do you do?"

"I'm a forensics investigator."

She frowned. "Surely sorting through computer files isn't part of your job description."

"You would be surprised, Miss Delaney. We fill in where we can."

"I see." She stood for a minute, arms folded against her chest. "Well, then. I have a few things left to do." She stepped aside and gestured toward the study. "Help yourself."

"Thank you," he said and walked into the room behind her.

Kellie turned around. "Can I get you anything?"

"That's very kind of you, but it isn't necessary. Please, don't let me keep you."

"How long do you think you'll be?"

"About an hour or so if it isn't too much trouble for you to stay."

"No," she said, "no trouble at all." She walked away, through the house to the back door, down the steps of the porch, through the rosebushes to her destination, the side door of the garage. Connor's files were stacked neatly in a locked closet. Standing on a stepladder, Kellie felt around for the key on the top shelf. Then she unlocked the closet door. The files were dated. She pulled out the ones labeled July and August and began to sort through them. Her brother's pay stubs were there, reflecting the exact dollar amount of his deposits.

Kellie's hands shook. She reached for more boxes, the unlabeled ones. Pulling out a manila folder she opened up a sheaf of papers and began to read. Nothing there. She laid it aside and pulled out another one. Twenty minutes later, her face white, heart hammering, she examined the contents of the folder. Why would Connor have his picture on *two* passports and why was he using the names John Devereaux and Austin Groves? Why was he reporting to British Intelligence? What was the nature of the numbers on all his correspondence to them? She was having difficulty accepting the evidence and yet what other explanation could there be? Connor Delaney was no mere police criminologist. The signs were all there, large amounts of money, counterfeit identities, coded numbers, receipts for services rendered. Two current ones bore a single name. She latched on to the name, *Tom Whelan.*

Kellie replaced the files, all except the damning one, and locked the cabinet. She dusted herself off and followed the path around the back of the house to the carport where her car was parked. Looking around carefully to be sure she wasn't observed, she slipped the folder beneath the floor mat. She had no plan, but instinct told her to hold on to her evidence.

Back in Connor's bedroom, she opened his closet door. Her brother's smell filled her senses. She slammed the door shut again, drinking in great gulps of air. Rubbing her head, she paced the room, back and forth, back and forth, until the hammering of her heart eased. She couldn't do this. She simply wasn't ready. She would have Gillian clean out his closet and distribute the clothing to the Red Cross.

Reaching into her pocket, she pulled out a cleaning receipt she'd found in the top drawer of his desk. Connor's suit was still at the cleaners. She would pick it up today. The suit would be no more than a piece of dark wool, packaged in plastic, as sterile and impersonal as the great bolts of material on display in the tailor's window. It was a good suit. Connor had impeccable taste in clothing. Someone could use it.

Her stomach was beginning to complain. Kellie looked at her watch. She'd skipped both breakfast and lunch. There was still time to order a pub meal after she picked up the cleaning.

"Miss Delaney?" It was John Griffith. She hadn't heard his step in the hall. "I'm finished here. Thank you very much for your time."

"You're welcome. Do you have all you need?"

"I'm not sure yet. But I'll let you know."

"Do you have a card, Mr. Griffith?"

"A card?"

Kellie's eyes were a hard, ice-flecked gray. "Yes. A business card? In case I should need to reach your office."

He reached into his pocket and pulled out a pen

and a pad of paper. "I can give you a phone number."

Kellie took the number and looked at it. "Goodbye, Mr. Griffith."

Normally she loved autumn. Oxford, teeming with color, was best in autumn. Steam rose from fogged store windows, men and women wore colorful mufflers and drank hot spiced drinks. Delicious soup smells wafted out from restaurant kitchens. It was a season for eating comforting foods and wrapping oneself in wool. She did not love this particular autumn, however. Driving down the lovely, old familiar streets gave Kellie not even a hint pleasure. She wondered if she wouldn't be better to relocate, begin again somewhere where memories didn't assault her around every corner.

Sahid Pushnabi adjusted his turban, bowed and welcomed Kellie effusively. "It has been too long, Miss Delaney. How may I help you?"

Kellie pulled out the receipt. "My brother left his cleaning. Do you still have it?"

"Of course, Miss Delaney. I have called several times, but there is no answer at his home. I thought, perhaps, he was away on holiday."

Kellie swallowed. He hadn't heard. She thought everyone would have heard. "My brother and nephew were killed in an auto accident two weeks ago."

The Indian's face blanched and his hand flew to his lips. "I am so terribly sorry. Please forgive my rudeness."

Kellie shook her head. "How could you know?"

"If there is anything I can do—"

"Thank you. I'll just pay for the suit."

"No, no." He waved her money aside. "Please. It is little that I do."

In the end, she gave in. It was a small amount, really, not enough to argue over.

It was nearly time for tea before Kellie was home again. She turned on lights, adjusted curtains and lit the fire. It was a large flat, too large for one person, but she preferred living alone rather than sharing with a roommate, a reaction to a childhood where she never had a private moment. She would see about selling Connor's house, or should she? Someone, she couldn't remember who, had advised her to wait at least a year before making any permanent decisions.

She hung Connor's suit on the door and ripped away the plastic. It was a lovely piece. Expensive clothing had suited him well. She ran her hands over the sleeves of his jacket and heard the rustle of paper. Curious, she pulled out a small crumpled wad lodged in the pocket corner and unfolded it. A telephone number was scrawled in the center under the name, a name that was burned in the memory of her brain, *Tom Whelan.*

With shaking fingers, Kellie picked up the telephone and dialed the number.

It rang three times, the long double rings distinctive to Ireland.

A man answered. "Whelan Bed-and-Breakfast, Tom Whelan here." His voice was low-pitched, friendly.

"I want to book a room," Kellie said quickly. "Do you have any available?"

"When would you like it?"

When, when? Of course he would ask when. "Two weeks. I need a room in two weeks."

"That would be November. I'm wide-open then. No one in his right mind wants to come to Banburren in November."

"I do," said Kellie.

He had a pleasant laugh.

"Well, then, come away. What did you say your name was?"

"Delaney. Kellie Delaney."

"My daughter and I will expect you. You'll have the house to yourself."

"Thank you."

"Will that be all?"

"Yes," Kellie whispered and hung up the phone.

Thomas Whelan of Banburren. Thomas Whelan of Banburren. She said the name over and over. An idea began to form in her mind. The more she thought it through, the more credible it became.

Kellie wasn't a fool nor was she an idealist. Too much had been heaped on her in the course of a single day. She would sleep on the thought and look at it in the morning.

Exactly one week later, Kellie climbed the stairs of the Knightsbridge tube station and looked around. She had the address of Special Investigations, a division of British Intelligence with an office in the government buildings on the Thames. John Griffith had been only too happy to take her call.

London was a roiling mass of humanity on Friday. A fine rain had drizzled for hours and the city smelled of wet wool and exhaust. Umbrellas of the usual brown, navy and gray formed a somber roof over the footpaths. Storefronts with neon signs and the homey smell of fresh bread from the bakeries were the only brightness in the wet misery of the day.

Kellie snapped her umbrella shut, looked at the address on the massive door and compared it with the one on the piece of paper she pulled from her purse. A man came out of the building and held the door for her. She stepped inside. A guard sat at the desk. She gave her name. He checked the list and pointed her toward the lift.

John Griffith ushered her into a small office with glass windows. Kellie refused his offer of tea. Already she was uncomfortable. She had initiated this meeting because there was no alternative, but she had no desire to be here.

She glanced at Griffith, an average man of average height with regular features, brown hair, gray eyes, a man most would immediately forget. "Who are we waiting for?" she asked.

He smiled for the first time. "Cecil Marsh, our chief investigator, will be here momentarily. Are you sure I can't tempt you with a cup of tea?"

She needed a moment to collect herself. "Perhaps I will take a cup."

He left the office. Kellie settled back in her chair and breathed deeply, coaching herself for the interview to come. She needed help. She had no resources to find information on her own. Diplomacy was the key. She would need to be very, very careful in the questions she asked. They had agreed to see her. That was a good sign. It gave her hope.

Too soon Griffith returned with a plastic cup of milky tea. He apologized for the sweetness. Kellie finished half the cup before the man Griffith introduced as Cecil Marsh joined them.

Mr. Marsh was the opposite of nondescript. Black hair frosted with gray curled around his ears and a heavy mustache marked his upper lip. He was very tall and hunched with black eyes, a strong nose and crooked teeth. Kellie would not forget him if she saw him again.

He came right to the point. "What can I do for you, Miss Delaney?"

She'd already decided to presume her brother's affiliation. "My brother didn't normally discuss the details of his work with me, Mr. Marsh, but this last case was something of an exception." The lie she'd practiced came out smoothly.

He leaned forward. "Really?"

"Yes."

He stroked his mustache. "I assume you've come here for a reason."

"I want to know if his death had something to do with his investigation."

The two men glanced at each other. Marsh spoke again. "We have no evidence that would lead us to believe so."

She stood, praying her bluff would work. "I see. Thank you for your time."

"Please, Miss Delaney, sit down." Marsh hesitated. "We're in something of a bind. Connor was working on a lead. He was killed before he had time to deliver his report. Any information you have would be appreciated.''

He was killed. Kellie drained the last of her tea. It was difficult to swallow. She couldn't get past the words *he was killed.* Connor and Danny, innocent Danny, were killed, murdered. ''I could use the same consideration, Mr. Marsh.''

Again the two men looked at each other. Griffith shrugged and turned to gaze out the window. Marsh cleared his throat. ''The brake cables on your brother's car were cut.''

''How is that possible? He drove several hours before the crash. Surely he would have noticed that he had no brakes before climbing the mountain road.''

''We believe the brakes were partially cut before he started out that day. He stopped for petrol and a bite to eat at a convenience store. When he came out the brakes were gone.''

Kellie closed her eyes. Pain leaped to life in her chest, radiating outward until her entire back and stomach were on fire. ''Why?'' she whispered.

''We're not disclosing this to upset you further, Miss Delaney,'' Cecil Marsh assured her. ''We could use your help.''

''What kind of help?''

''Anything you can give us would be a start— names, locations, anything?''

''Will you find who killed my brother and his son?''

Cecil Marsh leaned back in his chair. Lines of weariness etched his cheeks. ''Honestly?'' He shook his head. "It's doubtful. These people are clever and the situation complicated. It isn't likely one person acted alone. The odds aren't good, Miss Delaney. They never are. I'm sorry. Can you help us at all?"

They wanted her help, these men who treated murder as blandly as they did the morning weather report. Rage loomed in her chest. Connor and Danny were dead, killed by assassins and it was merely *an unfortunate circumstance.* Kellie bit down on the inside of her cheek. Her eyes were blank, her words expressionless. She had a single name, a common name. It was all she would give them. "Tom Whelan," she said quietly. "My brother was communicating with a man named Tom Whelan."

John Griffith spoke for the first time. "There are thousands of Tom Whelans. Do you have a location?"

"No," she lied. "All I have is his name."

Marsh stood. "Thank you for your information, Miss Delaney. We'll let you know if anything develops." He had his arm under her elbow, leading her toward the door. "These things take time. It's best to get on with your life and let us do our business. Connor would have wanted that. He understood how things worked."

Kellie stood outside the door closed firmly shut against her. The interview was over. She had been swatted aside, an annoying fly in the path of a steamroller moving in the opposite direction.

There was nothing left to do but take matters into her own hands and go to Banburren, check into Tom Whelan's guest house and find out what she could.

Fortunately she had already booked her room. Two weeks had never seemed shorter. Connor's house would have to be listed and her flat sublet. There was no time to lose.

Three

He opened the door, took one look at the woman on the porch and his breathing altered. She stepped out of the shadows into the light and his heart resumed its natural rhythm. *She wasn't Claire.* The revelation came to him immediately, with the speed and surety of an epiphany.

Mustering the practiced skill acquired through years of renting rooms to boarders, Tom Whelan summoned a warm smile and reached for her bag. "Come in," he said easily. "You must be Kellie Delaney."

"Yes. Thank you for taking me on such short notice." Her voice was smoky, seductive, so like Claire's it shook him to the core.

Once again he recovered quickly. "It's no problem. There isn't much activity here in Banburren this time of year. Would you like a pot of tea?"

She smiled. "Yes, thank you. I'd like it very much. I've forgotten how hospitable the Irish are."

"You're not Irish?"

"Actually I am, from here in the Six Counties. But I've been away for a long time."

He led her into the kitchen where he filled a kettle with water and assembled the tea tray, all the while maintaining a steady flow of light conversation.

Tom cleared his throat. "I thought you'd be more comfortable if I made up the room overlooking the garden."

"Thank you." She sat down at the table and sipped her tea. "Do you have another job or does this take all your time?"

He was surprised at her bluntness, odd for an Irish woman. Claire was like that, quick to the point, not worrying about appearances. But Claire was a girl without education from a working-class family, with a bit of a chip on her shoulder. This woman was not. Still, there were similarities, enough to intrigue him. He sat down across from her. "I play a bit of music and I write poetry. Why do you ask?"

She ignored his question. "Poetry? Have I heard of you?"

"I don't think so." He grinned. "We're all poets here."

"We've a few where I come from as well."

"Ah, Seamus Heaney. I'll not be forgetting him." He changed the subject. "Where did you say you've been living?"

"I didn't."

He recognized a rebuff when he heard one. Apparently she was a woman who preferred asking the questions.

"That was rude," she said, surprising him with a lovely smile and more of her bluntness. "I live in Oxford."

Rude, perhaps some would call her so, but honest and straightforward she was as well. He liked that.

"On the phone you said you had a daughter."

If he narrowed his eyes and listened to her voice, she could almost be Claire. He caught himself. Not even seven years could change a woman so completely. "Aye. Her name is Heather," he said. "She's seven years old. Her grandmother is keeping her tonight."

"Where is her mother?"

Again, that shocking lack of formality. And yet it didn't offend him, not yet.

"She doesn't live with us," he said shortly. "And what is it that you do for a living, Kellie Delaney?"

"I'm a teacher."

"Isn't school in session?"

"Yes, it is. But I've taken a leave. I've had a—" she hesitated "—a loss."

"I see." He wouldn't probe, even though he imagined she would have had no difficulty doing so if the tables were turned. "Will you be here long?"

She fixed her eyes on his face. They were large and light gray, nearly colorless except for the odd dark flecks in the centers. Her hair was lovely, too—bright brown with strands of copper, so fine and wavy it sprang out with a life of its own from around the sculpted bones of her face.

"I'm not sure," she said. "Perhaps. Can you accommodate me?"

He smiled. "Stay as long as you like or as long as you can stand it. Banburren isn't Dublin. It isn't even Oxford. You might find yourself with too much time on your hands."

She ignored his comment and drank the last of her

tea. "If you don't mind, I'd like to rest for a bit. It's been a long drive."

He stood. "I'll take you up. The water runs hottest in the morning, just to let you know."

"Thank you."

He led her up the stairs and down a long hall. Dropping her bag inside the door of her room, he stepped back to allow her inside. "If you need anything else, let me know."

"I'll do that."

Tom hesitated. There was no polite way of asking. "Why did you choose Banburren?"

"I'd nowhere else to go," she said matter-of-factly.

He was more than a little intrigued. Her resemblance to Claire was truly remarkable. Perhaps they were related and the woman had come to find her roots. People were always looking up their lost Irish families. Deliberately, Tom suppressed all thoughts of his wife. He didn't want to think about her now, or ever. "Surely that isn't true," he said instead.

She shrugged. "It doesn't matter."

She stood behind the door and stared at him. Tom knew she wanted him to leave. He would never have believed another woman could have eyes like that, with the same shape, color and clarity. He opened his mouth but the words froze in his throat. Christ, years had passed. What was the matter with him?

"Is something wrong?" she asked.

Outside on the road, he heard the sound of a horn. In the warm, peat-scented kitchen the stew he'd started earlier in the day bubbled in its pot. Rain tapped against the windows misting the panes, co-

cooning them in a world of silence and memories and awkwardness. In the distance, the bells of Saint Isadora's tolled the hour. Seven o'clock and all of the night to get through.

"No," he said, mentally shaking himself. "I'm off to take the dog for a walk. Good night." Suddenly Tom was in a hurry to be away from her, but his feet wouldn't move. He didn't want this stranger in his house, this woman with his wife's voice taking up space, asking questions, prying into his life.

"Have a pleasant walk." She closed the door in his face.

It was a dismissal, subtle but firm, and he was more than pleased to take her up on it.

With renewed energy, Tom ran down the stairs, shrugged into his jacket and let himself out. The woman was odd. Perhaps she was hiding something. He recognized paranoia when he saw it. More than likely it was her upbringing. She was from the North and of the Catholic persuasion or she wouldn't have used the term *the Six Counties*. He would have known without her telling him. Her accent placed her, even if it was an educated one. He'd never heard anyone duplicate it successfully. One either was or wasn't from the North. If so, it couldn't be denied or escaped.

He shook his head. She was very like Claire.

Kellie waited at her window, watching until he disappeared around the corner with the dog. Then she opened the door and walked back down the stairs to explore. Walking through the house she ran the tips of her fingers across the polished wood, the runner on

the table, the buttery, half-smoked candles on the
mantel, the pictures framed in wood on the shelves.
There was only one subject in all of them, a little girl
with lovely eyes and fawn-colored hair, posing at various stages of her life. This must be Tom's daughter.
Kellie's heart skipped a beat. Would she ever be able
to look at a child and not think of Danny? She closed
her eyes and practiced the meditation ritual that had
seen her through the last few weeks. This time it
helped.

Kellie loved looking at photographs, but time was
slipping away. How long did it take to walk a dog,
ten minutes? An hour? Quickly, she walked down the
hall, peering into the various rooms. Most were bed-
rooms, starkly decorated, but clean and well maintained. She would find nothing here. Proceeding to
the end of the hall, Kellie found a small room with a
desk, a comfortable chair, a reading lamp, shelves
filled with books, filing cabinets and a computer.
Tom's study. A gold mine.

Kellie checked her watch. The computer would
have to wait until she was sure of how long he would
be gone. She opened the top drawer of the desk and
found nothing but office supplies. The next one was
empty except for a stack of white paper. The bottom
drawer looked more promising. Scraps of paper with
names and dates in no particular order. Kellie sorted
through a handful. Tom's handwriting, although leg-
ible enough made no sense to her. The words looked
like some sort of code.

The front door clicked. She heard steps on the
wood floor. Quickly she closed the drawer, switched

off the light and stepped back into the hall. She was outside the first guest room before he saw her.

His eyebrows rose. "Did you need something?" he asked.

"The house is lovely." Her voice sounded breathless, quivery. "I wanted to see the other rooms."

It seemed as if an eternity passed before he answered. "You've got the best one, but you're welcome to change if you like."

"My room is fine. Thank you." She went on the offensive. "You're back soon."

"I came for Lexi's leash. She runs after everything that moves when I take her across the bog."

"Do you have anything to read? I'm not sleepy after all."

He walked past her to the door of his study and flicked on the light. "Feel free to choose anything you like from here," he said, gesturing toward his well-stocked bookshelves.

It was too much to hope for, this carte blanche into his personal study. "Thank you," she managed to reply.

"Good night, Kellie."

She was tempted to take up where she left off, examining the contents of his bottom desk drawer, but she wasn't stupid. Selecting a book of Yeats's poems from the shelf, she turned off the light and left the room. If he came home again, he would find her in the sitting room reading his book.

Ten minutes later she hadn't yet turned a page. Her anxiety had returned in full force. It was always with her. At best it was an anxious fluttery feeling in her stomach. She could manage that. It was the gripping terror she couldn't face, the hideous screaming, the searing heat and melting flesh and then the emptiness and an ache so deep and bottomless and complete that it loosened her bones, caved in her chest and dry-sucked her heart. In the first few days after the funeral, the only help for it was a Xanax, two pills at once, washed down with one ounce of Irish Mist, straight up, no ice. Relief was immediate, followed by a twelve-hour stupor that left her weary and brain-dead and blissfully imagination-free. Thankfully, that part, the helpless desolation, so severe she needed drugs, was behind her. Now, it was manageable. Now she had a goal.

Tom Whelan didn't look like a murderer, but then what did one look like? Perhaps like this man—priestly, a clean-cut boy scout with fine, sharp features, dark hair that fell over his forehead and clear blue-green eyes. He was just above average height and quite thin, rather like Connor. Kellie knew the type. She came from a long line of chain-smoking, hard-drinking Irish men who consumed their food whole because their bodies demanded fuel, but took little pleasure in the process.

She bothered him. She could see it in the tense line of his upper lip and the set of his shoulders when he looked directly at her. She traced the final picture on the mantel, a small snapshot of a man, a little girl and a dog, a red-boned Irish setter with a sweet face and dark eyes. The child was two, maybe three.

The phone rang. She tensed and waited through three full double rings before she realized there was no answering machine. What if it was Tom? Quickly, she walked into the kitchen and picked up the receiver. Her stomach fluttered.

"Hello?"

A woman's voice spoke. "Who is this?"

"Who is this?" Kellie returned.

"I'm Susan Whelan, Tom's mother."

Kellie's cheeks flamed. "I'm sorry. I shouldn't have answered the phone. I'm a guest. My name is Kellie Delaney."

"Tom wouldn't mind," the woman said. "Is he around?"

"He's out for a walk."

"Isn't that a man for you? Shame on him. I raised him better than that, I did. Do you need anything, love? I can run over if you do. I've a hot stew bubbling on the stove and apple crisp in the oven."

Good lord, these people were friendly. "No, thank you, I've eaten."

"Where are you from, lass? You sound a bit different from those of us from the country."

She couldn't afford to like this woman. "Originally, from Belfast, but I've lived in England for quite some time."

"That's where it comes from, that crispness. I've a good ear. Tom gets it from me. That's why he's so clever at the pipes. Get him to play them for you. He's not at all bashful when it comes to his music."

"He isn't bashful at all."

"Really, now. I thought he was. How old are you, Kellie, lass?"

"Thirty-five," Kellie replied without thinking. Susan reminded her of her own mother. It never occurred to her to hold anything back.

"Thirty-five, you say, a mere babe in arms." She laughed. "Tell Tom that Heather's had her supper and she's nearly asleep. She'll be home bright and early in the morning."

"I'll do that."

"Don't be too hard on Tom. He's been alone now for seven years and isn't always the best company. What he needs is a good woman to take Claire's place although he wouldn't admit it. You've a lovely, clear voice. Are you married, Kellie?"

"No," Kellie stammered.

"Why not?"

"I'm not sure exactly. It never worked out."

"I'm sorry, love. It must be hard to be on your own when you're so young. Well, perhaps you won't be alone for long," said Susan. "I won't keep you any more tonight. Give Tom my message and tell him we'll be over in the morning. I've enjoyed our chat and I'll see you tomorrow."

Kellie replaced the receiver and leaned weakly against the wall. How could this be? She had no backup strategy, no alternative plan to accommodate goodness. Who was Tom Whelan? Surely not a man involved in a murderous plot. A man who was raising a seven-year-old daughter, a man who walked his dog and wrote poetry and answered to the likes of Susan Whelan couldn't possibly know anything about murder. And yet Connor had carried his number in his coat pocket. There was a connection somewhere, if only she could sort it out. More than ever she was grateful for her instincts to keep her plans to herself.

Crawling between the soft, clean sheets, Kellie pulled the comforter over her head. God, she missed Connor and Danny. The evenings were harder than anything. Gillian had buffered her at first but she had her own life. In a way maybe it hadn't been a good idea to wallow in the security of their friendship. Weeks later the ache was as fresh and raw as if it had happened yesterday. Kellie was unprepared for the magnitude of her pain. The overwhelming feelings of tenderness and delight she'd experienced every time she'd looked at her nephew, the glow that lit her from within whenever she thought of him, the miracle of his gurgling laugh, the softness of his cheeks, was gone from her forever.

A harsh, primitive sob rose in her throat. She was a coward. She didn't really want to do this. She wanted her life back, the pleasant easy days when Connor and Danny were alive and they'd lived in Oxford together. She wanted long walks amid falling leaves, bread and cheese by the river, tea and scones in the mornings and the indescribable joy of Danny shrieking with delight when she picked him up from the child care center. That life was over. Now she wanted answers, reasons for such a brutal tragedy. A start would be an explanation for Tom's phone number in her brother's suit pocket.

Pushing away the pain, blanking her mind, had become nearly physical. The grit of her teeth, the wrinkling of her forehead, the cold water on her temples, had become a nightly ritual. Eventually it worked and she came close to relaxing.

Her feeling was that her presence in Banburren was more than likely an error in judgment, that Connor's relationship with Tom Whelan, whatever it was, was a misguided shot in the dark. Still, she was here. Maybe, in this peaceful village close to the sea, she would find her answers and begin to heal.

She must have dreamed it, a sound from her youth, the sweet, aching notes of the uillean pipes, the sigh of the drones, the quick fingers on the notes. She recognized the tune, "A Brown-Haired Lass." Her father had favored the pipes. Only true musicians could play such an instrument. She hadn't heard them in years. She smiled and turned over. It was a lovely welcome to Ireland even if it was only her imagination.

Four

The child was beautiful in the fey, flame-lit way the ancient bards had immortalized in songs only the clever and very skilled could still play. At her feet sat a sweet-faced dog with a shiny red coat, the dog in the photograph. There was no sign of Susan Whelan. Kellie stifled her disappointment. She very much wanted to place a face with the voice on the phone last night.

Heather pulled away from her father and walked across the room to Kellie. The dog didn't move.

"Hello." Kellie held out her hand.

"Hello," the little girl replied politely. "Will you be with us for long?"

Kellie swallowed. Would children always be difficult for her? If so, her job was going to be a problem. "Not too long," she replied.

"Will you stay for the festival?"

"I'm not sure," said Kellie. "When is the festival?"

"Not for a few weeks," said Tom.

"I might be here that long."

"It's a wedding festival," Heather announced.

Kelly was intrigued. "What's that?"

Tom raised his eyebrows. "I thought everyone in Ireland knew about our wedding festival."

"I don't."

Tom explained. "Men and women from all over the world come to Banburren looking for a happy-ever-after ending."

"Do they find it?"

"I imagine some have. No one I know."

Heather's eyes shone. "Everyone makes puddings and we have a carnival."

Kellie laughed. It felt strange. How long had it been since she'd really laughed? "I can see where her priorities are."

Tom's eyes were on her face, narrowed, considering. "You're a teacher but you didn't say what level."

"Second grade," Kellie said. "I teach children Heather's age."

Heather slipped her hand inside Kellie's. "I hope you stay," she said honestly. "I like ladies. The washroom always smells lovely after they leave it."

Again, Kellie laughed. "I'll keep that in mind." She sat down on the couch. Reaching out, she drew the little girl to her. "What do you do when you're not in school?"

The child tilted her head. Her soft straight hair, the color of deerskin, swung across her cheek. How Kellie envied that hair, the straight lovely swing of it.

"I play with my friends or watch the telly. Sometimes Da and I walk Lexi. I like visiting my friends," she confided. "They all have mothers who make bread and jam sandwiches and they sweep the stairs and hang the sheets to dry.''

"Do they?''

Heather nodded. "Da does all that now. I don't know what he'd do if we had a mother.''

"He would do what fathers do, whatever that is.'' Kellie's memories of her father were restricted, most of them reduced to helping him to stagger home from various pubs.

Heather thought a moment. "They eat food, I think.''

Kellie chuckled. The little girl was lovely, warm and unspoiled. "What do you like to eat?''

"Puddings,'' she said promptly. "I like those the best. Da won't let me eat them first.'' The little girl brightened. "Do you have a little girl?''

"No,'' said Kellie. The darkness began to close in on her again.

Instinctively, with a sensitivity beyond her age, Heather seemed to understand Kellie's distress. She rested her hand on Kellie's knee. "I like you,'' she pronounced. She turned to her father. "I like her, Da. I want her to stay with us.''

Tom separated himself from the wall and walked toward them. "That was already decided, Heather, but it's grand that you approve. It makes everything much easier.'' He transferred his attention to Kellie. "I don't know how you're fixed for cash, but if you think you'll be here for a while, perhaps we could work something out.''

Kellie frowned. "I don't understand.''

"You said you weren't working. I'm dreadful in

the kitchen and right now I'm in the middle of something. There isn't much time for houseguests. I could use the help if you think you might be staying awhile."

"You said you weren't booked."

"Not now," said Tom. "But I've a pipe order and the wait for a set is long enough. If you wouldn't mind doing the meals and your own laundry, I could discount your rate."

He'd captured her interest. "A pipe order?"

"I make uillean pipes. My father did before me and his before him. We're one of the original families. There aren't many of us left."

"Do you play as well?"

"I'm fair at it."

"I'd like to hear you. My father played the pipes."

"I wouldn't mind striking up a tune or two if you're interested. What about my offer?"

"Is it a job you're offering?"

"In a manner of speaking. I can't pay you, of course."

She couldn't decide if his suggestion was a golden opportunity or a roadblock. She decided to go for it. "How about instead of a discount you make my meals complimentary?"

He thought a minute. "I can do that."

"What exactly would my duties be?"

"I haven't given it much thought," he said. "The idea just occurred to me."

"Why don't I look around and do whatever I think needs to be done?"

"All right as long as I can make a suggestion now and then."

Kellie nodded. "What about grocery shopping? Will you do that as well?"

"I don't mind giving up the shopping."

"And the cooking?"

"You can start tonight?"

A genuine smile lit her face. "You really don't like to cook, do you?"

He hedged the question. "I have a feeling you're a talent in the kitchen. Am I right?"

She looked directly at him, not at all intimidated. "I'm fair. Do you have any food preferences for this evening?"

"We have what it takes for shepherd's pie."

Heather cupped her hand over her mouth and leaned close to Kellie's ear. "It's Da's favorite."

Kellie waited a full minute before answering. *Shepherd's pie. Was there ever a week that her mother hadn't prepared it?* "I think I can manage that."

"It's settled then. I'll take Lexi for a run and then I'll work for a while in the study. Come along, Heather."

"I want to help Miss Delaney. May I, please?"

Tom hesitated, obviously torn between his protective instincts and his daughter's pleading.

Kellie stepped in. "I would love to have Heather help me. Perhaps you could walk Lexi after dinner?"

Tom relented. "I could do that." He reached down to stroke the dog. "You'll be all right until after dinner, won't you, girl?"

Kellie swallowed. It was now or never. If she didn't

take risks, she would end up with nothing to show for her time. All he could say was no. Breathing quickly, she dove in. "May I go with the two of you? I'd like to see some of the town and who better to show me than natives."

Tom's eyes narrowed, but his expression gave nothing away. "Banburren isn't much to look at, but you're welcome to come along."

"I was hoping to meet your mother. We spoke on the phone."

"I suppose we can stop by," Tom said slowly.

"Good." Kellie stood and took Heather's hand. "Shall we start dinner?"

Heather nodded and skipped alongside Kellie. In the kitchen, she pulled a chair out from the table, climbed on it and sat down on the edge of the counter. "I like cooking," she confided. "Da lets me stir the pots and mash praties. What I really like is to crack the eggs, but I'm not allowed."

"Why not?"

"Eggs are dear and I might waste one."

"I see." Kellie thought a minute. "Perhaps we can figure out a recipe where it doesn't matter if an egg or two is wasted."

Heather clapped her hands. "Today? May I crack one today?"

"You may."

"What will we make?"

"Your father's favorite."

"Da likes shepherd's pie before anything. Everyone knows that."

The child tilted her head thoughtfully. "This is

nice. It's like having a mum, but you're not like other mothers, are you?''

A cold fist closed around Kellie's heart. She wet her lips. ''Why do you say that?''

''Kathleen Mallory's mum is red-faced and she smokes cigarettes.''

''Is Kathleen your friend?''

''She's my best friend and so is Mollie Malone.''

''What is Mollie's mum like?''

Heather narrowed her eyes, deep in thought. ''She's nice but she doesn't say much,'' she pronounced at last. ''She gives us puddings and tea but she never speaks to us, not the way you do. She's not pretty either, not like you.''

Kellie's heart craved these children. ''Do your friends come to visit often? I could make a pudding and tea.''

Heather's cheeks glowed. ''May I?''

''Of course.''

''Shall I ask Da?''

''I'm sure he'll agree.''

Heather frowned. ''I don't usually have friends over.''

''Why not?''

''Da doesn't make puddings and he needs quiet to work. But I don't mind,'' the child said sunnily. ''May I crack an egg now?''

Kellie laughed and moved toward the refrigerator. ''You may. Shepherd's pie requires an egg and it doesn't matter in the least if the cracking isn't perfect.''

The sound, filtered through the hallway and around

several corners, was unmistakable and beautiful, the pipes. Kellie stopped, mesmerized. Another tune from her youth, "Isobel Mackay." "He's very good, isn't he?" she whispered.

"Da's one of the best," confided Heather. "Wait until he's warmed up."

The pie was delicious. Kellie noted with satisfaction the odd look on Tom's face after he'd tasted the first mouthful.

"Do you like it, Da?" Heather asked hopefully, her own food forgotten. "Miss Delaney and I made it together."

"I like it very much, love," her father answered slowly. "It's one of the best I've tasted."

"I cracked the egg myself."

"Did you now?"

Heather nodded. "Miss Delaney said it didn't matter if the cracking isn't perfect. But it was, wasn't it, Miss Delaney?"

Kellie nodded, her heart full. She was falling in love with a seven-year-old girl. "Absolutely perfect. Why don't you call me Kellie?"

Heather maneuvered her fork loaded with beef, mashed potatoes and vegetables into her mouth. "Tomorrow night we'll have a pudding. Kellie promised."

Tom stared. "Since when will you eat peas and carrots?"

"I made them myself," the child said. "It wouldn't be right if I didn't eat them."

"I see." Tom reached across the table and ruffled

his daughter's hair. "Perhaps you should make dinner every night."

Heather dimpled. "Perhaps I should. But what will Kellie do?"

"She can supervise," Tom said smoothly.

Kellie laughed. "We'll work something out, I'm sure. Meanwhile, if I have as many takers for doing the dishes, I'll be in heaven."

"I'll dry," Heather offered.

"Thank you, love. That would be wonderful." She looked at Tom. "And what will you do?"

He grinned and Kellie's throat closed. Could a man who smiled like that have something to hide?

"I'll check my e-mail," he said, "read and take a short nap, while you finish. How does that sound?"

Kellie smiled sweetly. "Self-absorbed."

He placed his hand over his heart. "You've a quick tongue, Kellie Delaney. Don't think twice about sparing my feelings."

"The idea never crossed my mind."

This time he laughed. "I'll wash and dry," he said. "I'd intended it all along. My thanks for the tasty meal."

Kellie folded her napkin and placed it beside her plate. "What shall you and I do, Heather, while your da cleans the kitchen?"

The child looked hopefully at her father. "We can watch the telly for a while."

"You have school tomorrow," Tom reminded her.

Kellie interrupted. "Shall we read together?"

Heather wrinkled her nose. "I don't like to read."

Kellie's eyebrows rose. "How can that possibly

be?'' She winked at the little girl. ''Everyone likes to read. It must be that you're not reading the right books.''

''I don't know about that.'' Heather looked doubtful.

''I'll tell you a story,'' Kellie suggested, ''a story that comes from a wonderful book. How does that sound?''

Heather brightened. ''I love stories.''

''Then it's settled.'' Heather stood and held out her hand. ''Come along.''

Heather slid off her chair and tucked her hand inside Kellie's. ''Sometimes Da tells me stories.''

''Does he now?''

Heather nodded. ''He knows lots of them.'' She looked up. ''Do you?''

''I'll try to measure up.''

Tom watched them disappear into the sitting room. Kellie Delaney was definitely not in the common way. On the one hand she appeared vulnerable, almost desperate, yet there was a sophistication about her that wasn't typical of Irish women from her class. He couldn't make her out. Not that twenty-four hours was enough time to give the matter any real thought. He frowned, filled the sink with soapy water and began cleaning the plates. Heather didn't normally warm up to people the way she had to Kellie. The woman had a way with children.

He finished drying the last of the silverware, hung the towel over the rack, turned down the lights and walked into the sitting room. It was empty. A small tick came to life in Tom's left cheek. He walked down the hallway toward Heather's bedroom and stopped in the doorway.

Heather was asleep; the comforter pulled over her and tucked in. Kellie had dozed off in the chair beside the bed and Lexi was on the floor at her feet, her head resting on her paws.

Gradually, so as not to wake them, Tom dimmed the lights and motioned to the dog. There would be no walk for Lexi tonight.

Lexi lifted her head and dropped it again. She was going nowhere. A knot formed in Tom's chest. Heather's experience with mothers was limited to her grandmother and the mothers of her friends. A young, attractive woman who promised dessert and told stories had suddenly dropped out of the sky into her lap. He didn't want his child to be hurt.

He made a decision. Gently, he shook Kellie awake. She blinked and would have spoken but he held his finger against his lips, motioning her to stand up. When she did, he tucked the blankets around his daughter.

"We'll have to postpone our walk," he said after he'd closed the door to Heather's room.

Kellie yawned. "I'm too tired anyway." She moved toward the stairs. "Good night, Tom," she said without turning around.

He was anxious and edgy, not in the mood for a run or a pint. Slowly, he walked into his study and opened his pipe case. She said she liked them. Still, he closed the door. Tucking the bag under his arm, he began to squeeze. The melody, slow and smooth, filled the room.

Five

Morning light, milky and pale, filtered through the kitchen window. Kellie sighed. Two weeks since she'd come and both of them gray. But then Ireland was always gray, not like England where even in winter the sun had a chance of piercing the cloud cover.

She cracked another egg into the bowl, added milk and whipped the mixture together. Butter sizzled in the frying pan. She poured in the eggs, set out bread to toast and lifted the streaky bacon from the grill. Coffee perked on the stove. Napkins folded like birds of paradise sat on top of the plates. Silverware gleamed. Lexi lay under the table, her eyes at half-mast.

A bubble of pleasure welled up in Kellie's chest. She stopped, motionless, and concentrated on holding it in, muscles tensing, eyes narrowing, keeping the feeling close for as long as it would stay. It happened seldom enough, this sense of pleasure, this cocoon of quiet joy, welling from the mundane routine of performing simple tasks. But at least it came. Not so long ago, Kellie believed she would never feel anything but pain again.

The toaster popped. Kellie pulled out the bread slices, golden and hot, slid them into the rack and poured the coffee. She didn't look up when Tom walked into the kitchen.

"What is it this morning?" he asked.

"Scrambled eggs with parsley and tomatoes."

He was silent and still for a long moment.

"Is something wrong?" she asked.

"Where did you learn to create culinary masterpieces for every meal?"

Kellie shook her head. "They're hardly that."

"Do you know you have the most subtle way of evading a direct question, which makes no sense because most of the time you're not subtle at all."

"I wouldn't call it evading."

"What would you call it?"

She leaned against the counter and sipped her coffee, welcoming the diverting burn of the hot liquid down her throat. "I would call it a sense of reserve," she said quietly, "a sense of personal space."

Tom hooked his leg over the chair and sat backwards facing her. "I might believe that if you weren't so inquisitive yourself. You want to know everything about me, but you won't disclose anything about yourself."

Kellie's cheeks burned. "Are you always so blunt?"

"No, you've the patent on bluntness. I'm rarely so, but then I'm not always up against such an immovable force."

"Why do you want to know about me?"

"You're living in my home. It's common courtesy to reveal something of your background. It makes one feel insecure to have a mystery woman in his midst.

I don't know if I'm allowing an escaped felon access to my daughter.''

She gave him the point. ''Fair enough,'' she said. ''What do you want do know?''

''For a start, how did you come to leave Belfast for Oxford? Why are you here in Banburren?''

''I earned my degree from Queen's and left for an employment opportunity in Oxford. It isn't unusual to move to England from Belfast.''

''For a Catholic it is.''

''I'm here because it's restful,'' she continued as if he hadn't interrupted her. ''Are you satisfied?''

''I should be.''

''But you're not.''

''No. What do you do all day?'' He hurried to finish. ''I'm just curious, that's all. What I mean is, why would a woman like you, an educated woman, be content doing a maid's work in a small town? What keeps your mind busy?''

Kellie's cheeks flamed. ''What kind of question is that? What do you think I do? I cook and shop and wash and clean. In case you haven't noticed, I've picked up just about everything there is to do which wasn't what I'd planned and it's worth a great deal more than the complimentary meals I'm receiving. Perhaps we need to renegotiate the terms of my employment, because I think I'm doing too much to be paying for my room.'' Her hand were on her hips. ''You've been very preoccupied, hardly coming out of that shed outside to breathe. Quite frankly I don't know what you did without me. I've gone to the library on occasion and I take a walk or two every day with *your* dog, but other than that I've my hands full. My *mind* and how I keep it busy isn't any of your business."

Tom stood motionless, stunned and properly redressed. She was right. The lion's share of work had fallen on her. She was so efficient, he'd relaxed, allowing her to pick up more and more of his responsibilities, even the phone calls and bookings. He'd stepped over the line and he knew it. Embarrassed, he opened his mouth to apologize, but even that was denied him.

Heather stood in the doorway. "I'm here," she announced.

Kellie sighed with relief. "Good morning, darling. Are you hungry?"

The little girl nodded, crossed the room and pulled out a chair. "I like your food. It's better than Da's."

"Traitor," muttered Tom.

Kellie laughed, her anger dissipated. She was a nurturer at heart and it was lovely being needed. She spooned eggs onto Heather's plate before reaching for Tom's.

Heather picked up her fork and looked at her father. He appeared deep in thought, staring at his plate.

"Kellie says breakfast is the most important meal," she announced.

"Perhaps she's right," replied Tom.

"Well?"

"Well what?"

"Why aren't you eating?"

Tom sighed. "I'm eating, I'm eating." He scooped

a healthy portion of eggs into his mouth. "Are you happy now?"

She smiled sunnily. "Yes."

Kellie sipped her juice. Between bites of bacon she spoke to Heather. "I'm going into town today to look at the shops. I've seen nothing at all except the Superquin, the butcher's and the bakery. Have you any other suggestions for me?"

Heather's forehead wrinkled and she looked at her father. "Da? Where should Kellie go?"

Tom considered the matter. "We can walk Heather to school together and you can look around a bit. There isn't much to see in Banburren beyond the harbor and the water. My family is having a dinner tonight. You're invited if you care to come. My mother particularly asked me to invite you."

It was a golden opportunity. It was also a dreadful violation of the heart of a family. Deception was difficult for her. She would not be comfortable conversing and sharing a meal with these people. Still, her motive for coming to Banburren hadn't changed. Perhaps she would learn something. So far, her quest had been relatively fruitless. She'd gone into his computer files, an easy enough task. He didn't even have his password secured. Not that she'd had long segments of time to go back into personal correspondence in his e-mail files, but she wasn't looking for anything that far back. It was frustrating. Her lack of progress after two weeks, and Tom Whelan, the man, hadn't helped matters. He was so pleasant, so accommodating and open. It was very hard to keep her reserve. Kellie liked him. She liked him very much.

* * *

It was odd at first, walking beside Tom with Heather between them, down narrow streets in a small town where everyone knew each other. People were too polite to stare or comment, but she felt their eyes on her back, speculative, wondering. Kellie felt as if she were back in the Falls only this time she was a stranger.

It was important that she do this, Kellie told herself. It was all for Connor and Danny and, she'd come to realize, herself.

Tom interrupted her thoughts. "You might take a look at Geary's Hardware. It's our claim to fame, a first-rate store with everything one could possibly need for home improvement."

"Your rooms could use some bookshelves," replied Kellie, "nothing complicated."

"Why do I need shelves?"

"People like a homey room and shelves filled with books."

He looked thoughtful. "I'd never thought of it."

"Think of it now. Don't you like books?"

"I do."

"Your guests will, too. Small things, like books and a basket of treats with some biscuits and bottled water, a teapot, things like that make a room memorable."

"You may be right." He waved his arm. "What do you think?"

"Of what?"

"The town."

Kellie glanced briefly around her. Curbs on one

side of the road were painted green, white and orange, Catholic colors. The Irish tricolor hung from upstairs windows. Tea shops were filled with men smoking down their breakfasts and reading the daily news. Mothers with prams walked uniformed children to school. There were more pubs than any other business establishment and most had customers at eight-thirty in the morning.

"It reminds me of home."

Heather tugged on her father's arm. "Where are we going? This is the turn."

Tom stopped and looked at the shops on the familiar corner. "I'm in a daze," he said to his daughter. "Lead the way."

Heather skipped ahead waving her lunch box and her pack. Knobby knees, scabbed from a tumble, peeped from beneath her plaid skirt. The red jacket matched her hair ribbon and the glow in her cheeks.

Kellie's breath caught. "She's a beautiful child."

"Aye." Tom's words formed a cloud in the cold air. "I'll give you no argument with that one." He glanced at the woman beside him. "She looks like her mother."

"She's her own person, unspoiled and enthusiastic and incredibly bright. You've done a wonderful job with her."

"Thank you."

"We're very formal with each other, aren't we?" she said after a minute.

"Did you expect something else?"

"Not really." Her hands curled in her pockets.

Somehow, she had to break through. "It was just an observation."

Heather was nearly a block ahead of them now.

"Tell me what it was like growing up in Belfast," he said.

It was the question she knew would come, the one everyone asked. "Very much like growing up anywhere else, I suspect. If a child isn't aware of anything different, it isn't strange. I had parents and brothers and sisters. We had our difficulties like anyone else. I left when I earned my degree." She looked at him. "What about you? How did you happen to stay in Banburren all of your life?"

"I didn't." His hands were in his pockets, his head bowed against the wind. "There was a time when I fancied myself the martyred revolutionary. That mistake earned me a stint in Long Kesh."

He was a felon, an ex-convict. Her stomach burned and she bit her tongue to hold back the obvious question. "How dreadful," she managed to say in a small, tight voice.

"It wasn't as bad as you might think. I was with men I knew, all political prisoners, all of us in for the same reason. We were treated fairly."

She hadn't thought he would tell her such a thing, so openly, without embarrassment. Again her doubts assailed her. Tom Whelan didn't appear to be the kind of man who harbored dark secrets. But he'd spent time in prison.

"Tell me about your loss."

"I beg your pardon."

"You told me you'd suffered a loss. Tell me about it."

Kellie tucked her hair behind her ears. Her hands hurt from the cold and the dull sick ache she dreaded rose in her stomach. She couldn't speak of Connor and Danny, not now, not yet. "I'd rather not. It's difficult for me."

He didn't press her.

Ahead of them, Heather turned into a massive gated entrance. Kellie raised her eyebrows. "You must be doing well for yourself."

Tom shrugged. "It's the only Catholic school and it's not so much more than the others that it makes a difference."

"What about the National School? I imagine most of Banburren attends that one."

He nodded. "I want more for Heather. She's very bright. Besides, there's none of the Catholic, Protestant garbage here. The focus is on learning, not hatred or politics."

They reached the gate where Heather waited. Kellie reached out to hug the little girl and kiss her cheek. "Have a grand day, love," she said.

Heather nodded, kissed her father and ran up the stairs, through the double oak doors and into the brick building.

"Well," Kellie said bracingly, "that's that." She looked at Tom. "Now, it's just the two of us."

He ignored her comment and pointed to a long, low building farther down the street. "Geary's Hardware is new. You'll find everything there." They faced each other. The street, wet and gray from recent rain, was empty, the mist shrouding them in silence. "Perhaps we could finish that conversation we started at breakfast."

She looked at him, *really looked at him,* black hair falling over his forehead, blue eyes narrowed, serious, intense, a man too weathered by life and tragedy to be truly handsome, but still quite attractive in his own way, a man whose angles and planes bespoke suffering and character. Who was the real Tom Whelan? A man who shared responsibility for two murders, an ex-felon, or a reformed man, sensitive enough to write poetry, play music and raise a small child?

Kellie swallowed. "Perhaps," she said softly.

The lines around his mouth deepened into a genuine smile.

With that, he turned and strode purposefully down the street, away from her. He didn't look back.

She watched him until he disappeared around the corner. There was more to Tom Whelan than met the eye. Something troubled him. He wasn't comfortable with women. She could feel his contempt mitigated slightly by a resistant curiosity. He wanted to trust her and yet trust didn't come easily to him. She didn't blame him. He was intelligent and there were many things she had left unexplained. Kellie understood his coldness tempered by brief bouts of compassionate remorse. He was like the agnostic who mumbles The Lord's Prayer, just in case God might really exist.

She felt strangely bereft standing there in the chill morning air. It was early by Irish standards. Nothing would be open except for small cafés and pubs. Indecision was an unaffordable weakness. She would find a café and nurse a pot of tea until the hardware opened.

Kellie stepped inside a small corner shop and walked to the counter. A young woman with a lovely face and a serious overbite smiled and approached her. "What can I get for you, miss?"

Before Kellie could answer, the woman's eyes widened. "Do I know you?"

"I don't think so," Kellie replied. "I've only just come for a holiday. I'm staying at Tom Whelan's lodging house."

"Of course," the woman said. "I see that now. For a minute I thought—" She smiled brightly. "What would you like?"

"Tea, please." The shop was empty and the woman looked ready to burst with what she had been about to say. "My name is Kellie Delaney. Would you like to share a pot with me?"

"Irene Donaldson here, and I'd love to."

When they were settled across from each other with a pot of steaming tea between them, Irene spoke up. "I thought you were Claire Whelan. The two of you could be sisters, but now I see that you're not that similar after all."

"What was she like?"

"Lovely to look at," Irene said promptly, "but she wasn't so lovely in other ways. She was very hard-headed so it was difficult to be her friend, even when Tom was in the Maze." Irene shook her head. "We prayed for her down there in that English prison. Her mam, bless her soul, lit a candle every day and bought Masses so she'd be treated right. When Mrs. Whelan brought back the little girl, there wasn't a dry eye in town. We never forgot it.''

Kellie's cheeks burned. ''Why was Tom in the Maze?''

''They were rounding everyone up in those days, anyone connected at all. I don't believe Tom Whelan was a saint, but he wasn't as bad as some of them.''

''Where is his wife?''

''She's in Maidenstone Prison in England.'' Irene's voice dropped and she spoke in a hushed whisper. ''She was sent up for the murder of an Englishman, a fancy lord. They gave her a life sentence. She hasn't seen her husband or daughter in seven years.''

''Why not? Prisons allow visitors.''

''I don't think she and Tom are married any more. He didn't approve of her activities. Tom came back from the Maze a changed man. All the spirit was beaten out of him, along with the hate. I don't think Tom Whelan could hate anyone again.''

Either that or he was a very good actor. Kellie changed the subject. ''What time does the hardware open?''

''Geary's always opens at half past nine,'' said Irene. ''He's regular as clockwork.'' She laughed. ''Unusual for an Irishman, but then the store is as well. You'll see when you go inside.'' She gathered their cups, brushed the sugar from the table and stood. ''Thanks for the chat but I'd better be getting back to work. I'll be starting the lunch stew in the back. There's no charge for the tea. Let me know if you need anything else.''

"I will. Thank you for the tea and the conversation."

"My pleasure."

Alone again, Kellie stared out of the window. Slowly, Banburren came alive. Trucks stopped in front of shops and unloaded their wares, completely oblivious to the traffic backing up behind them. Peat smoke drifted from chimneys, gray against a grayer sky. Women brandishing umbrellas and men in wool caps nodded, called out and stopped each other on the streets. Meaty smells wafted from pubs offering luncheon specials. Diligent clerks washed windows, set out menus written in chalk and swept porches clean.

Kellie was enchanted with the normalcy of a small Irish village readying itself for a normal day. *It was so safe, so sane.*

"I'll be off now," she called out to Irene.

The woman popped her head over the swinging door. "Don't be a stranger," she said.

Kellie smiled. "Thank you for the welcome, Irene. It means a great deal to me."

Irene blushed. "Go along now. I've work to do."

Geary's Hardware was like nothing Kellie had ever seen in Ireland. More warehouse than store, it was an organizational miracle arranged thematically, with garden supplies on one end and raw lumber on the other and rows and rows in between.

An older man with a blue apron approached. "May I help you, miss?"

Kellie tilted her head so the hair swung across her cheek. "I'm looking for bookshelves and a desk."

"This way." He motioned for her to follow.

She walked a few paces behind.

"Here we are." He pointed to an aisle filled with a myriad of bookshelves. "When you're done choosing, let me know and I'll show you the desks."

"Thank you."

He frowned. "You're not local, are you?"

Kellie shook her head. "No. I'm staying at Tom Whelan's."

"I didn't think you'd been here before. I'm a newcomer myself. The Mrs. and I moved here five years ago. We came to visit and decided to stay." He extended his hand. "I'm Cormac O'Donnell."

Kellie repressed a laugh. Only in Ireland was one considered a newcomer after five years. She took his hand. "Kellie Delaney."

"Call out when you're ready."

"Thank you. I will."

Methodically, Kellie ruled out the most expensive woods as well as those needing complete assembly. She didn't know the exact moment she became aware of the woman standing at the end of the aisle staring at her. She wouldn't have noticed her at all, except that she stood completely, unselfconsciously still, all her attention focused on Kellie.

Intrigued, Kellie turned to look at her. She was a small, slim woman, dark hair peppered with gray, tight skin and beautiful bone structure. She looked familiar. Did she know her? "Hello," she said.

"You must be Kellie."

"Yes. How did you know?"

"Tom described you. I'm Susan Whelan."

She was Tom's mother.

"I'm sorry I haven't met you before this. Every time I've come, you're out. Are you settling in all right?"

"Yes, thank you." Kellie smiled. "I was hoping to meet you."

"And I you. Tom has said lovely things about you."

"About me?" Kellie was incredulous. "Surely you're mistaken."

"Not at all. It isn't every day that an attractive, unmarried woman moves into Banburren and sets up housekeeping with my son."

Kellie reddened. "It isn't like that at all."

"I'm joking with you, love. Seriously, how are you doing?"

"Everyone's been wonderful to me, especially Tom."

"What do you think of Heather?"

"She's priceless. The two of you have done a wonderful job raising her. Tom is a natural father."

Susan raised an eyebrow. "Has he told you about the child's mother?"

"No. I understand she left the family."

"In a manner of speaking. Claire wields enormous influence even when she's not around. Remind me to tell you about her when you have a spare afternoon. You should know your competition."

"Mrs. Whelan, Tom offered me a job, that's all," Kellie protested, uncomfortable with the direction of the woman's thoughts. She very much wanted to tap Susan's brain, but without the obvious implication.

Susan's blue-green eyes sparkled. "You've only just arrived, lass. Our wedding festival's coming up. Stranger things have happened."

"I won't be here that long."

"Will you be here tonight?"

"Yes," said Kellie, "of course."

"Then I'll expect you for dinner. We're all looking forward to it."

"*All?* What does that mean? Who else will be there?"

"Why the whole family, love. Tom hasn't expressed interest in a woman since Claire was sent away."

"We wouldn't suit, Mrs. Whelan. We disagree on everything."

Susan smiled her blinding smile and changed the subject. "Geary's has wonderful bulbs. It's time to plant if you want them for spring. I'll look forward to seeing you tonight."

The woman's energy was all around her. Kellie felt electrified, empowered. "I won't be here for spring," she whispered to the space where Susan had been.

Six

Kellie was slow to shower, to shampoo and dry her hair, slower than usual to dress and apply the small amount of makeup she wore. Outside her closed bedroom door, she could hear Heather and Tom conversing, his voice low and measured, Heather's higher, vibrant, eager. It was past time. They were waiting for her. Her fingers were thick and clumsy, unable to fit the buttons into the holes of her jumper. She couldn't make them move faster.

With shaking hands, she brushed her hair away from her face and stared into the mirror. What had she been thinking? A family party. Tom's family, together under one roof, all of them looking at her, asking questions, matchmaking, asking about her life, where she was from, why she was here. She shuddered. The thought made her physically ill.

"Kellie." Heather's voice was outside the door, impatient, excited over the idea of a party.

Kellie cleared her throat. "I'm nearly ready, Heather. Give me another minute."

She heard the child's steps on the floorboards, walking away. Wetting her lips, Kellie smoothed her hair one last time, picked a piece of lint from the front of her skirt and stood. It was only a dinner. It would be over in a few hours. The first time meeting people was always the hardest. Her anxiety would ease with a glass of wine and a bit of food. Tom and Heather would be with her. Susan had invited her. No one suspected she was there under false pretenses.

She walked into the sitting room. "Hello," she said, "I'm ready."

Tom's head was bent over Heather's. At the sound of her voice they looked up. Heather clapped her hands. "Da said you wouldn't want to go."

Kellie's smile didn't waver. "He did, did he?"

Heather nodded.

"Why wouldn't I want to go?"

Tom shrugged, unwilling or unable to defend his words. "It hardly matters now." He picked up his pipe case, walked to the door and held it open. "Shall we?"

Kellie took Heather's hand in her own. They both wore gloves. Even though she couldn't feel the child's skin beneath the wool, the contact gave her courage. "I haven't been to a party in a very long time," she confessed. "My nerves are a bit punchy."

"Gran's parties are jolly," said Heather. "Perhaps she'll have pie."

"Will everyone come?" Kellie asked casually.

"Everyone who's still here," replied Tom, "and everyone who loves a session. My sisters will show, and their husbands." He hesitated. "I assume you heard what happened to my brothers, Martin and James. This town thrives on gossip."

"Yes. A terrible tragedy. I'm so sorry."

"Aye. It was, but they knew what was coming.

Anyone who refuses to listen and continues to travel in dangerous circles is walking the edge.''

Kellie looked thoughtful.

"Is anything wrong?" he asked.

"No, nothing at all."

Susan's house was rich with smells of roasting meat, fresh bread and cinnamon. From the porch, Kellie could hear laughter and conversation. Her hands were blocks of ice and her smile felt garish and unnatural, as if someone had pasted it across her face. She wanted nothing more than to run in the opposite direction, as far from Banburren as it was possible to run.

"You're nervous," Tom said, surprised. "They're just people. Rather pleasant ones if I do say so."

"I've never been comfortable in crowds," she whispered back.

They stepped through the door. All at once the room was silent. Even the children playing a board game on the floor near the fire stopped their conversation in midsentence. All eyes focused on Kellie and then, as if the gathering had received some silent communication, they turned away and began to talk once again. Her cheeks burned. They were insufferably rude. Even Heather had defected, in search of her grandmother in the kitchen. If this was what passed for manners in the Whelan family, she was better out of it. A surge of adrenaline rushed through her veins. She lifted her chin. If need be, she would wait here all night until someone spoke to her.

Tom's hand slipped beneath her elbow. Gently, he

maneuvered her into a small group seated near the fireplace. "Kate, Tim, say hello to Kellie," he said.

Kate, a black-haired, green-eyed beauty smiled warmly and held out her hand. "Welcome, Kellie. It's lovely to have you."

Some of the tension left Kellie's shoulders. "Thank you. It's wonderful to be here."

"Kate is from Dublin," Tom offered. "She teaches at Heather's school."

A slim blond with cool blue eyes spoke up. "I'm Maggie, Tom's sister."

"Hello, Maggie," Kellie said politely.

"Tom has never brought home a woman before."

"He's not bringing one home now, at least not in the context to which you're referring," she replied quickly.

They stared at her in astonishment.

She blushed at her rudeness, took a deep breath and resolved that nothing else tonight would rouse her temper.

"What is it that you do, Kellie?" the lovely Kate asked.

"I'm a teacher, on leave."

"What are you doing in Banburren?" It was Maggie again. "Were you sacked?"

"For Christ sake, Maggie, give over." Tom shook his head. "Where have your manners gone?"

"No," said Kellie. "I wasn't sacked. My reasons for leaving were personal, but you can rest assured your children are safe with me. I didn't molest anyone or anything like that. I intend to return to my position and will definitely be welcomed with open arms."

She wanted to strangle the woman. Instead she turned her back to her. "What level do you teach, Kate?"

"Sixth," replied Kate. "I love it. It's what keeps me here in Banburren, that and the Whelans. They're my family now. I've no one left in Dublin."

"It's a lovely school. It must be wonderful to teach there."

"Yes." Kate nodded. "We've no problem."

"Problem?"

"You know. The Catholic-Protestant thing."

"I'm glad to hear it. If only everyone could forget."

"We can all raise a glass to that sentiment," said a sandy-haired man who stood beside Maggie. "We never got over James and Martin dying the way they did. It took the rebel spirit out of us. Now we're staid old men and women." He wrapped his arms around Maggie. "Aren't we, love?"

"Speak for yourself," said Maggie. "I'll not admit to being old."

He winked at Kellie. "Why, then, all that pulling at your eyes and patting the soft spot under your chin every morning?"

"I do no such things, Danny Sheehan." His wife slapped his arm playfully. "Shame on you for spying on me."

"Now, love, you wouldn't be denying me a good laugh, would you?"

"What will Kellie think of us, you with your mouth flapping and me vain as a queen."

"She'll think we have a sense of humor."

Kellie laughed. She was beginning to relax. "I'll check and see if Susan needs help in the kitchen."

Conscious of eyes watching her back, Kellie walked down the hallway and stood at the entrance to a well-lit kitchen. Susan stood at the sink, speaking to Heather. Kellie stepped back into the hallway before they could see her and breathed deeply. She placed both hands on the wall, bracing herself. She didn't particularly want to isolate herself in the kitchen with Tom's mother but the room filled with curious people was too much.

It was Heather who saw her first. "Kellie, look at the cake Gran made. She said I can ice it as soon as it cools."

Kellie walked into the room, leaned over the cake and sniffed appreciatively. "It's lovely and it will be even more lovely when it's iced." She touched the little girl's bright hair.

Heather skipped across the floor. She stopped at the door. "I'm going to play with Sam and Willie. Call me when the cake's cool."

Susan wiped her hands on a towel. "I'll call you the very minute it's ready." She smiled. "Did you need something, Kellie?"

"I wondered if you could use some help. It's a big crowd you're feeding."

The woman's eyes were bright and probing. "I'm accustomed to it but I imagine it's hard on you to meet them like this, all at once."

"A bit."

Susan opened her mouth to speak, changed her mind and then changed it again. "I invited them all tonight because I wanted you to be done with it, to recognize everyone if you see them on the street. They're naturally curious and protective of Tom. Tonight will be awkward for you but then it will be over. Do you understand what I'm saying, Kellie?''

These people were impossible. She smiled politely. ''Thank you for caring, but you've misunderstood. Tom and I are acquaintances,'' she reminded the woman. ''That's all. There's nothing more between us.''

''Perhaps that's all there is for you, but I can tell you he hasn't asked me to cook a meal for a woman since he married Claire. What do you think that means?''

Kellie felt as if her skin was peeled back and every nerve exposed. *Be calm,* she told herself. *Honesty is always best. Be honest whenever you can.* ''I know that for some reason you think Tom needs a wife. Perhaps he does, but it won't be me. I grew up in a community like Banburren and it simply isn't going to happen. I can't live here. I don't belong. Do you see that?''

Susan was silent for a long time. Finally she spoke. ''You're a far better woman than the one who left him seven years ago. I can see it and apparently Tom does as well, to his credit.'' She smiled brilliantly. ''Heather tells me you cook. How are you at peeling praties?''

Dinner was surprisingly pleasant. Kellie was seated between Maggie, who'd obviously called a truce, and the warm and lovely Kate. Eileen, another sister completely caught up in her infant son, sat across the table beside her husband, a large man who had the thick hands of a farmer. Mary Catherine, the youngest of the Whelans and the first to graduate from university, kept the entire family entertained with tales of her new job as a chemist in nearby Ballybofey. Tom was at the other end of the table near his mother and the children. Somewhere between the soup and the lamb, Kellie began to enjoy herself. The conversation was lively and the people far more decent and warm-hearted than she'd expected under the circumstances.

"Tom tells us you've a degree in literature," said Kate after the plates were cleared away and the two of them had moved back to the sitting room. "Perhaps, if you'll be staying awhile, you'd be interested in helping out at the library while you're here. The librarian is a friend of mine and I've heard they need someone. The position doesn't pay well but it's something."

Kellie looked across the table at Tom. He must have told them he was working her too hard. "It sounds lovely. Shall I call your friend?"

"I'll tell her I've spoken with you. That way she'll expect you."

"Thank you, Kate." Kellie was humbled and ashamed. She hadn't expected such complete acceptance so soon. These people were lovely, too lovely to lie to.

"You're welcome. I remember what it felt like after I'd left Dublin. If it hadn't been for Maggie and Eileen I don't know how I would have managed. Banburren is a lovely place but it's a small town. Even though I had James, there wasn't a great deal to do until I took a job. Now, with James gone, I'm even more grateful.''

"What made you stay on?"

Kate tilted her head and the shining mass of black hair swung across her cheek. "I don't know, really. I had to finish the term and then I was offered another contract and I took it. One year turned into the next and here I am.''

"You're very young and very attractive. No one like you stays in Banburren.''

"You're here.''

"But I've no intention of staying.''

Kate smiled. Her teeth were good, even and straight and very white. She was breathtaking. The question popped, unbidden, into Kellie's mind. What would a woman like Kate, a woman who could have anyone, want with James Whelan, an IRA man from Banburren? She shook the thought away. There was no explaining love.

It was the session that made the evening. They were a musical family. Maggie's husband played the fiddle, Mary Catherine the whistle, and even Eileen was persuaded to hand her baby to her husband while she took up the bodhran. And of course there was Tom on the pipes. The music was sweet and slow and haunting, raucous and inspiring, soaring and swooning and rousing, breaking down inhibitions, lifting their spirits, drawing them together in a way that words could never do. When the last notes died away, Kellie was flushed and content and satisfied in a way she hadn't been since she was a girl on her own at Queen's.

It was after eleven when the family, sated and filled with pudding and spirits, called an end to the evening. The Whelans, a small community in themselves, content in their togetherness and their culture, gathered their coats and their children, kissed each other goodbye and went their separate ways.

Susan stood at the door, her trim figure framed in golden lamplight. "Goodbye," she called out. "Hurry home or you'll catch your death. It's a cold one."

Kellie buried her nose in the fleece of her collar and stuffed her hands into her pockets. It *was* cold, a damp, bone-chilling cold that whistled in on the wind from countries far to the north. She'd forgotten that cold could be like this, a cold that froze lips and noses and caused the back of her teeth to ache. A hot bath would warm her, but in Ireland hot water was in short supply.

Tom walked beside her with Heather in the middle. The two of them chatted back and forth with the ease of people comfortable with one another and the occasional silences that permeate a long acquaintance. Kellie recalled the feeling, wondered if she would ever know it again, shrugged off a twinge of self-pity and concentrated on ignoring the cold. She shivered. The streets of Banburren were empty at this time of night. It wasn't so much an ominous feeling, more a lonely one as if the dark shops and quiet streets had been abandoned by their inhabitants.

Tom had left the lamp on in the hallway and the

small peat fire had taken the chill from the room. He kissed Heather good-night, reminded her to brush her teeth and watched her climb the stairs to her room.

Kellie went immediately to the hearth, stripped off her gloves and held her hands over the flame. The shivering that had once been controllable and confined to her jaws and teeth spread throughout her body. The cold was painful.

Tom came up behind her. "Are you all right?"

She nodded and rubbed her arms.

He took both of her hands in her own. "You're freezing."

Again, she nodded.

"Kellie, you're ill," he said gently. "Come with me. I'll get you to bed immediately."

Unresisting, she allowed him to lead her into the bedroom where he removed her coat and shoes and tucked her snugly beneath the down comforter. Then he rummaged through her chest of drawers, pulling out and tossing aside articles of clothing until a small white pile had formed on the floor. Frowning, he sat back on his heels.

"What's the matter?" Her teeth chattered.

"Where do you keep your pajamas?"

"I don't wear them."

"Why not?"

"I'm out of the habit. Usually the duvet is warm enough."

"Tonight, in your condition, it won't be."

"I have flannels for exercising. They're hanging in the closet."

She watched him push the hangers aside until he found a pair of gray leggings and a flannel shirt.

''These will do,'' he said, tossing them to her.

Unwilling to lose an ounce of the warmth, she stared at them over the edge of the duvet.

''Brace yourself,'' he said. ''It will only take a minute and you'll be much warmer.''

She nodded and reached for the clothes. Under cover of the heavy comforter, she removed her skirt and jumper, dropped them on the floor beside the bed and tugged on the leggings and shirt.

Tom picked up the discarded clothes, hung them in the closet and walked toward the door. ''I'll fix you a hot drink and bring in an electric grate. If you're ill it won't help much but if it's just the cold you'll be fine in the morning.''

''Thank you,'' she replied.

He was back with extra pillows and a cup filled with a fiery liquid that tasted of lemons, honey and alcohol. Kellie's head swam and the burning sensation that seared its way past her lungs gave way to a delicious numbness. Cool pillows were slipped under her head and once again the duvet was tucked tightly around her shoulders. She was no longer cold, only tired, very tired, and only too grateful to allow Tom to minister to her needs.

Her last thought was that the Whelans were lovely people, especially the warmhearted Kate. It would be too much to expect that she would find a friend in Banburren. Friendship, however, real friendship, required full disclosure and that wasn't possible. She couldn't confide in anyone. Still, someone to pass

ideas with or to stop in occasionally and share a pot
of tea with would be wonderful. Perhaps that, at least,
could be achieved. "Your music is lovely, Tom," she
whispered before drifting off to sleep. "I liked it very
much."

Seven

She looked down the nearly empty street. He'd caught her alone, outside the bakery. It was early. She'd biked into town to pick up a loaf of fresh bread for breakfast, preferring the early hours when fewer people walked the streets.

At first it seemed like nothing, the hand on her arm, a polite moving her out of the way. But when she turned to smile, her blood ran cold. He was a large man with a nose spread across his face, heavy-lidded dark eyes and a wary, closed look about him.

"Hello, Kellie," he said softly.

She nodded. "Hello." The word came out without air, her voice unrecognizable to her own ears.

"Shall we walk a bit?"

It wasn't a question at all. She knew that, just as she knew who he was. Everyone who'd grown up in Andersonstown recognized the type—thick, beefy, tattooed men with cropped hair, thick necks, a single hoop earring piercing their left earlobes, black leather jackets and blue denims with a bulging pocket, men no one argued with or asked questions of.

"Please," she whispered.

"I'm not going to hurt you."

She swallowed and nodded.

"McGarrety's gone to quite a bit of trouble to find you."

Dennis McGarrety, brigade leader of Belfast's Irish Republican Army, an assassin. "Oh?" Instinct told her to say something.

"He would like to ask you some questions."

She waited.

Kellie opened her mouth to explain and then closed it again. Perhaps she should see McGarrety. She had questions of her own, but not here in the middle of Banburren. "Not now," she said firmly.

"When?"

"Tomorrow, at nine o'clock Mass."

"That's a crowded one."

"Eight o'clock then."

He nodded and walked away.

Tom sat at the kitchen table reading the newspaper. He looked up when she walked in. "Good morning. You're out early. Are you feeling better?"

"Much better." She held up the bread. "It's better when it's just fresh."

"So it is." He regarded her steadily.

Uncomfortable, Kellie babbled about nothing. "I thought I'd work on the computer today if you'll be out, and if you don't mind," she added. "Of course if you need it I can find something else to do. Perhaps they need help at the library today. Never mind. It doesn't matter. Whatever you like." She sounded ridiculous.

He continued to stare at her, saying nothing. Something close to amusement flickered in his eyes.

Deliberately, Kellie closed her teeth around her tongue, setting the sharp edges around the most sensitive part. She would say nothing more until he spoke.

Tom folded the paper, sugared his tea and drank half of it down. "You're welcome to the computer. I've a pipe order to work on."

"Do you have many at one time?"

"Usually no more than three. It isn't fair to hold someone up if he's interested in playing. It takes some time to get one out. Although—" He stopped.

"What?"

"I've accepted a deposit for an order, quite a large one, from a fellow in England, but I can't reach the man. If he's changed his mind, I should return the money."

"How can you return the money if you can't reach him?"

"Therein lies the problem."

"Is his name a common one?"

"As a matter of fact it is. Austin, I believe he said. Austin Groves."

Kellie froze. Surely she couldn't have heard correctly. Austin Groves was the name on one of Connor's passports. Her mind wasn't working. That was it. The encounter with McGarrety's man had muddled her brain. She would wait for the drumming to stop and then she would ask again. It was impossible, an incredible coincidence. Austin Groves was an ordinary enough name. It couldn't be Connor. He didn't play the uillean pipes. He was fairly proficient on the oboe, but the pipes, no. And yet Connor had communicated with Tom Whelan.

"I'll wake Heather," he said after a bit.

"Wait." She bit her lip. "I know—" She stopped. "I knew an Austin Groves, but he may not be the same one. What does he look like?"

Tom shook his head. "I've never met him."

"Where does he live?"

"Somewhere in the south of England, I think, although he sounded Irish. Apparently his sister loves the pipes. They're very close. He wanted to please her by taking them up. I take it he's already a bit of a musician."

Kellie could no longer feel her fingers. "Are you saying that your only association with Austin Groves was to make him a set of pipes?" Her voice sounded high and shrill.

Tom frowned. "Aye. What is this all about, Kellie? You're white as bone."

"I'm not sure yet," she whispered. "I have to think."

He sighed and stood. "You'll let me know when you've sorted it out?"

She nodded and automatically began pulling out the pans she needed for breakfast.

The library was the loveliest building in Banburren. Wooden shelves, thick with books, were spaced far enough apart for two people to peruse opposite sides. A reading room with deep chairs, warm lighting and long windows faced the hills. A librarian sat behind a desk advertising both circulation and research, and smiled benevolently at visitors. Now she smiled at Kellie. "May I help you, love?"

"I'm Kellie Delaney and I'm looking for Mrs. Jamison. Kate Whelan said she might need some help."

The woman beamed. "I'm Barbara Jamison. It was lovely of her to think of me. Do you have a Leaving Certificate?"

"Yes." Instinct told her not to mention her university degree. She would do that after she'd settled in, after she had a chance to look at the computer.

"On Wednesdays and Fridays the schoolchildren come and check out books for pleasure and various projects. It does get a bit much for me with all of them wanting something at the same time. Are you available on Wednesday and Friday mornings?"

"I am. When would you like me to be here?"

"If you come at half past nine on the first day, I'll have time to show you what to do before it gets crowded. After that you can come at ten."

"Thank you. I'll be here."

The woman frowned. "We haven't discussed wages."

Kellie interrupted her. "It doesn't matter."

"I'm afraid we can't offer much above the minimum."

She was desperate for a computer. "The minimum will be fine. Do you have a computer with access to the Web?"

"We certainly do."

"Would you mind terribly if I used it from time to time, after my workday is over, of course."

"Not at all."

"May I use it now?"

"Absolutely, love. It's in the room with the glass window." She pointed to an office space surrounded by clear glass. "I'm afraid I can't be of much help to you except to point in the right direction. I'm an old dinosaur when it comes to computers. I've neither the avocation nor the interest."

"I'll manage. Thank you."

Kellie sat down in the chair and pressed the power button on the computer. She waited for the computer to boot. The monitor leaped to life. Plenty of memory and RAM. Good. She moved the mouse to the Internet icon and clicked. Fortunately, the password was automatically stored. She could open the files on her own. It wouldn't be a good idea for Mrs. Jamison to view the Web site she was researching.

The green Sinn Fein logo rolled onto the screen. The menu followed. Bypassing the introductory page, she clicked on the Recent News bullet. The Nationalist newspaper masthead, *Anphoblacht,* replaced Sinn Fein. Articles were highlighted in red. She scrolled down stopping occasionally to click on those that might be relevant. None of them were. Perhaps Recent News wasn't the place to look. She entered a random year, 1995, and quickly scanned the list. Nothing there. She entered another year. Still nothing. This time she typed in a year much earlier, 1989. Her heart pounded as the screen filled with text and pictures. She'd found what she was looking for. Tom and Claire Whelan were definitely not saints. Perhaps she hadn't made a mistake after all. But what did it mean? It was all too much of a coincidence. If she was here because Connor had ordered a set of Irish pipes— Settling herself in, she began to read.

Two hours later she let herself into the house she shared with Tom and Heather. Quickly she glanced in the hall mirror. She looked all right, paler than usual, but still herself. A fire burned steadily in the hearth. Tom was home.

"Hello," she called out tentatively.

"Hello," he answered from the room that served as his study. "I thought you would be longer."

She stood in the doorway. "I thought you were out for the day."

"I changed my mind."

"I spoke with Mrs. Jamison. She needs someone a few mornings a week. I'd like to help her."

Casually, he cleared the computer screen. "Do it."

"It doesn't pay well."

"Nothing here pays well. Since when has that stopped anyone?"

She shrugged and turned away.

"Kellie."

She turned back.

"I didn't mean to be dismissive."

She tilted her head. What did she have to lose? "*Dismissive* isn't the right word. *Sarcastic* would be a better one."

He looked at her for a full minute. "I'm sorry," he said at last. "It wasn't my intent."

"We rub each other the wrong way, don't we?"

He thought a minute. "Now that you mention it, I suppose so. I wonder why."

She shrugged. *Damn her telltale Irish skin.* The last

thing she wanted was for him to know it bothered her. ''It happens sometimes,'' she said airily, and left the room.

He watched her go, already regretting his lie. He knew exactly why. She reminded him of Claire. Claire, his wife, who made his heart thump at the mere thought of her walking through the door. But he wasn't about to tell that to this woman despite her lovely voice and her quick smile and her sweet ways. It was past time to face the facts. Claire was gone and there was no going back. But even after seven years the loss of her was like a rawness on a wound that wouldn't scab over.

There had never been a moment when he hadn't loved Claire Donovan. She was part of his youth, those innocent days when he believed goodness and proper behavior were all it took for life to be fair, long before he knew how the world cut a piece out of a man, knocked him to his knees, humbled him in the eyes of those he most wanted to impress. Claire had been one of those. At first.

Even as a child she was lovely with her front teeth missing and a spray of freckles across her nose and cheeks. He did everything to be near her. His first job had been washing dishes at Fahey's Pub. He remembered the epiphany that hit him when he was elbow deep in bubbles, his mind on Claire and the evening before. *I'm going to marry Claire Donovan and live with her for the rest of my life.* He remembered the surge of warmth in his chest, the hope in his heart, the sheer joy of believing that a woman, the right woman, was all a man needed. He was fifteen years old, in love for the first time with a girl so beautiful his head swam. And the best of it was she wanted him. *Claire Donovan with her sparkling eyes and lovely smile wanted no one else but him.*

When had that changed? Tom knew the answer to that one. It had dawned on him one day after months had passed without either touching the other. Why hadn't he brought it up? Kissing and caressing and the wonderful silky slide into sex were the glue that cemented relationships. It carried a couple through the difficult times when each wondered what they had done, why they were together in the first place. Why hadn't he brought it up? Because he hadn't wanted it, either. Because Claire, the rabid revolutionary, no longer appealed to him. After his sojourn in Long Kesh, the entire nightmare of life on the run no longer appealed to him. Nights spent with an ear for a door crashing open. Wet palms every time a member of the RUC walked past. Always on the move, no roots, no spot to settle in, not a single moment of rest. And then the wasted, lonely years in prison. It hit him solidly one morning, after he had been shuffled out into a frosty dawn with others like himself, that this could be his life. He wanted none of it. After that he'd become a model prisoner, unobtrusive, obedient, submissive. The prisons were crowded. His sentence had been reduced by half. He'd come home bursting with gratitude for another chance, this time getting it right.

But Claire had seen things differently. During his prison years, she'd become more heavily involved than ever. She'd told him what she'd done, the missions in which she'd participated. The pride in her voice terrified him. He talked of leaving Banburren, moving to the Republic, beginning again. She wouldn't hear of it. They became strangers sharing a house, she coming and going, he adjusting to life outside prison walls. He would have left her. But the miracle of her pregnancy stopped him. Surely, he'd thought, a child would turn her around. He was mistaken. Claire had disappeared for nearly a week before he learned where she was. Indicted for the murder of Lord Mountjoy, she was transported to Maidenstone, the women's prison, where she awaited trial. Tom hired a lawyer but Claire would have none of it. She wasn't a criminal, she'd told him. She was a soldier, a member of a guerilla army who did not recognize the jurisdiction of the British government or its servants.

Tom would never forget that morning when the barrister walked back into the room where he waited. The man had shaken his head and returned the check for services rendered. "She won't speak to me," he'd told him.

Then Tom had seen her. He'd pleaded, threatened, painted a graphic picture of days and nights in a British prison. But Claire was adamant. She would take nothing from him. He washed his hands of her after that, hardened his heart against her and the child she carried. Self-preservation, he called it, when his conscience smote him. She was an adult and she'd refused him. What else could he do?

When Claire's labor began, the matron called him. Gently, she explained that Claire would not see him, but that the child would have to be removed. In the end it was his mother who brought the tiny scrap that was Heather back to him. Without a word, she'd handed him his daughter. That was seven years ago. Not once in that entire time had he heard from Claire, nor she from him. He'd heard *of* her, of course. She was something of a celebrity in Banburren, a town that harbored Nationalist sympathizers. Information filtered down even to those who had little use for it.

His mouth turned up in a brief, humorless smile. No one who had ever really known his wife would believe that this woman who cooked and cleaned and smiled and devoured books as if they were religion could possibly remind him of Claire. But why had she come and, more importantly, why was she staying? He'd been working at the answers to his questions for some time without success. Tom no longer had the connections he once had. He preferred it that way. All his instincts told him that Claire's look-alike was troubled. Not that it was any of his business, but she had come to him and he had a curious streak.

Perhaps he was going about this the wrong way. Perhaps he should exercise a bit of the charm that had won Claire, if that was still possible. Perhaps this woman would respond to a different kind of attention, the kind every woman wanted. The very idea of subterfuge was repugnant to him. Gone were the days when he had to manufacture emotion. He was Tom Whelan himself. He'd paid a dreadful price but he was alive and walking free in the town of his birth. Many had less. Still, it wouldn't hurt to be kind to the lass. She had her own demons to vanquish and if he was completely truthful, he rather enjoyed having her around. She was a grand cook. The house was warmer somehow, cozier. Heather was happier, settled, more childlike, less precocious. Tom couldn't put his finger on it but he noticed the difference. So had his mother.

Susan Whelan wasn't one to stamp her mark of approval on just anyone. Tom was surprised when she befriended Kellie. "Take the woman out for a bit of supper," she'd told him. "She's worn out with fixing meals and cleaning house for you and Heather. I'll keep the child with me tonight if you like."

He'd never considered it. The thought frightened him. An evening alone with a woman, maintaining casual conversation, living a lie. "I don't think so, Mam," he'd said quickly. "This is just temporary after all. She'll be leaving eventually. Better not get involved."

Susan had shrugged her shoulders. "Stranger things have happened, Tom. Don't be trying to live in the future. Look at what you have today and see if it's such a bad thing."

He wondered if he'd gone mad, if he was the only one who could see the obvious. Did his mother believe he could replace Claire, *his* Claire? Susan Whelan was a shrewd woman. Either she was turning a blind eye or something else was up her sleeve. The years had mellowed Tom. He no longer lived on the edge of his nerves. Neither did his mother concern him. There was no need to analyze his mother. She had his best interests at heart.

* * *

Kellie dipped her finger into the font of holy water and crossed herself. Eight o'clock Mass was poorly attended. Ireland was a country whose population slept late, a result of daily rain and dark skies until nine in the morning for most of the year.

She genuflected, crossed herself again, rose, slipped into the pew and pulled out the knee rest. She knelt again. Perhaps the man she was meeting would allow her to stay for the entire service. Oddly enough, her research verified that terrorists were religious. Religion was the issue along which boundaries were drawn, Catholics the persecuted, Protestants the persecutors.

Out of habit, she bowed her head and closed her eyes. She was no longer sure how she felt about her religion. She believed in God. That was an absolute. Centuries of Catholicism were too heavily ingrained for her to believe otherwise. But she wasn't quite sure about a benevolent God, one who considered her prayers. More likely His grand design was unfolding without influence of the lonely mortals He created.

Kellie much preferred addressing her requests to the mother of Christ, Mary, a mortal, mother of a son too early taken from her. Kellie found comfort in reporting to a woman, a woman like herself whose pain was universal.

She opened her eyes and slid back in the pew. Someone slid in behind her. She felt the give as he knelt, his breath against her neck. She tensed, waiting. A hand touched her shoulder. Words breathed in a gravelly whisper brushed against her ear. Her heart pounded. Her breathing was labored, ragged and harsh in the dim silence of the church. *What was he saying?* Her mind refused to register. Kellie closed her eyes again and concentrated.

"Dennis McGarrety wants you to leave Banburren. It's dangerous for you here. Do you understand? *You must leave Banburren.*" The words took root in her brain. She was clear now. She knew what he wanted of her. Slowly, she nodded. She felt him leave, felt the absence in the space behind her.

Waves of relief flooded her body leaving her limp, exhausted. She would go home and sleep. Thinking could wait. She would think later.

A door behind the altar opened. The priest emerged and the congregation, such as it was, rose. She tensed, waiting. "The Lord be with you," the priest droned. The ancient soothing response of the Catholic ritual rose to her lips. "And also with you."

The house she shared with Tom and Heather was set back on a green knoll that would serve as a garden in spring. The house was lovely, nestled between two oaks, painted white with a dark roof and red door, a streak of life in the muted colors surrounding it.

Her hand closed around the doorknob. Drawing a deep breath she turned it and stepped inside. "Hello," she called out tentatively.

No answer. Thank God, she was alone. Quickly she moved through the sitting room and down the hall to her bedroom. She closed the door behind her and leaned against the wall until the fluttering in her stomach normalized. She was exhausted. Her lack of sleep and the mind-numbing message delivered by the harbinger of a man she had been taught to respect and fear for as long as she could remember had taken its toll. She could no longer think. Dropping her handbag, she stepped out of her shoes, pulled the covers back and climbed into bed. She would sleep now and think later.

Tom shook the rain from his hair, wiped his feet on the mat and opened the door. The house was quiet. He frowned. No tantalizing aromas from the kitchen, no hum from the computer, no roar of the vacuum, not even her step on the floorboards. Where was she?

In the kitchen he turned on the burner under the kettle. He read portions of the paper while the water heated, his mind only half-aware of the words he read.

Fortified with a mug of tea, he stoked the fire in the sitting room and walked down the hall. The door to her room was solidly shut. She was home, the forbidding door a message as powerful as if she'd hung a Do Not Disturb sign above her head. So much for his new resolve. She was obviously not of like mind. He wondered if she was ill. Should he inquire? The door would not be locked. There were no locks in Banburren.

Deciding against disturbing her, he turned back toward the study and pressed the power button on the computer. He was a coward. The truth was she disturbed him. Her presence and her energy stirred his emotions, pulling him into the world again, forcing him into feelings he would just as soon have left alone. Would he ever be comfortable again? There had been some degree of comfort these past few years, but no real pleasure. With the exception of a few fleeting moments with Heather, true pleasure had eluded him. There was something about this woman, something that pulled at him. He couldn't describe it, he who was usually proficient with words. Tom knew that she felt it, too. She was stretched to the limit. It was only a matter of time before she snapped.

Eight

Kellie walked into the kitchen and glanced at the stove. Soup bubbled on the burner. Tom and Heather sat at the table, their attention focused on an open book. "Can I help?" she offered.

Tom looked up and smiled. She looked relaxed, her eyes wide and free of makeup, her hair wild and sleep-tousled. He motioned toward the stove. "I thought I'd give you a rest."

"It smells wonderful."

Heather closed her book. "Can we stop now, Da? I don't need to finish this until Thursday." She reached under the table and patted the dog. "May I take Lexi for a walk?"

Tom grinned. "Run along but don't be all night about it. Dinner is almost ready."

Tom waited until Heather left the room. It was awkward between them without the child. He stood and leaned against the counter, arms folded against his chest. "You've slept the day away," he said. "Are you ill?"

Kellie shook her head and sat down at the table. "Just tired. I haven't been sleeping well." She looked around the kitchen and repeated her initial request. "Can I help you with anything?"

He shook his head. "I'll manage for a change. Do something you'd like to do. We'll eat in about twenty minutes."

Their eyes met and the words burst from her mouth. "I don't mind doing my part, Tom. You've been quite generous with me." She bit her lip. The question of the pipes and Connor and Tom, who they were and how it was all connected was like a weight she couldn't shift. She didn't know where to begin. "May I ask you a question?" she blurted out.

"Of course."

"How do you live?"

"I thought we'd cleared that one up," he said. "I play a bit of music now and then and I'm paid for my poems. It isn't much but we don't require much. There's no mortgage on the house."

"What about making uillean pipes?"

"The pipes take an enormous amount of concentration. I can't take many orders at a time. Fortunately, I'm one of a few in Ireland who makes them. Pipes are expensive. One can make a living."

"I see." She avoided his eyes, looking at a spot directly above his head. "I know what you were," she said finally. "I looked you up on the computer in the library."

"So, that's what this is all about." He knew his own computer had been tapped as well. He'd known it from the beginning. He hadn't even bothered to change his password. Kellie Delaney was looking for something. Whatever it was, she was more than welcome. He didn't have it and he wasn't hiding anything. In fact, he knew more about her from the sites she pulled up. "My past isn't a secret. Everyone in Banburren knows. I don't talk about it much but I never intended to hide it."

"Are you through with it?"

"Yes."

Minutes passed.

"Is there anything else?" he asked gently.

"No, not for now." She sounded defeated, tired.

He cursed under his breath, crossed the room and rested his hands on her shoulders. The words came, sincere and low, from deep within him. "This is killing both of us. I wish you would trust me."

She stiffened and pulled away. "I wish I could," she whispered, and walked out of the room.

He dropped his hands and let her go. Whatever she hid was consuming her. He felt it. She wasn't a woman given to deception. He could see the haunted desperation in her eyes. She'd lost weight. The lies would eat at her from the inside out until she couldn't hold them in anymore. All he had to do was wait. Somehow the thought didn't cheer him. He heard the lock on the bathroom door click into place. He was a fool. Only a fool would feel the sting of conscience in a situation like his. She was the one with the burden. Why should he feel stirrings of guilt?

He returned to his meal, turned down the flame, tasted the soup and added more salt. Logic told him to ask her to leave. But that wasn't what he wanted. She was a puzzle he was curious to piece together. Besides, he'd never before run from a challenge and he didn't think this woman was the place to start.

* * *

Kellie leaned her head back against the tile wall and closed her eyes. The hot spray bathed her throat and chest. Trust. What did it mean, really? He had asked her to trust him. Had she ever trusted anyone with anything so important as her life? Some did, every day. The man she'd met in the church. Did he have a wife? What did she know of his chosen profession? What of Ireland's heroes, Hugh O'Neil, Daniel O'Connoll, Wolfe Tone, Eamon De Valera, Michael Collins? Did their women trust them? Did they trust their wives with secrets? Doubtful. Ireland was a patriarchal country. Women counted for very little, even today.

Tom Whelan was a mystery. A man who wrote poetry, a musician, a loving father, on the surface a gentle decent man with pain in his eyes, a sharp wit and a quiet strength. This was his face, the face he showed the world. Was it also the face of a man who'd completely changed his stripes? Possibly. Quite possibly. But what did she know? How did a woman gauge a man practiced in the craft of murder and deception even if those events took place years ago? Did it really matter in the end? Did one ever recover from the decisions one makes in the beginning?

She toweled herself dry, pulled on her clothes and looked into the mirror. What would her mother think if she saw her now, a woman with lines around eyes that took up too much of her face and hair plastered to her skull? Her mother who wore her prejudices for all to see, who stereotyped all nationalities with fierce impartiality, who condemned her oldest daughter for the immorality of marrying an Italian. The boys she left alone. Far be it for a mere woman to criticize the men in her family. What would she think of Tom and of her need to know him as he really was? The answer popped unbidden into Kellie's mind. She would hold up her hands and glare. *A man's ways are not ours, lass. Let him be, for God's sake. Mind your own business and do your duty.*

Kellie stifled a laugh. Perhaps it would be best if she didn't ask advice from her mother. She combed out her hair. Feathery curls were already drying around her face. How long had it been since she'd dressed up? Impulsively, she pulled out her makeup bag, sat on the floor in front of the long mirror and dumped out its contents, picking over the shadows and blushes she'd been given what seemed a lifetime ago and never used.

Lining up her selections, she applied them carefully, foundation first, then powder and blush along the cheekbones. Pale taupe across the eyelid, cream over the brow and a line of deep navy along the bottom ridge of the eye. The mascara tube separated with a pop. Gently, she worked it into her lashes, lengthening, thickening, separating. Only her lips were left. She chose a shiny berry color to fill in both the top and bottom. She was finished, a painted woman, done up for what purpose? To allure, perhaps, or else simply to be more interesting than she was before.

Staring critically at her reflection, she decided she looked nothing like herself.

"Kellie?" Heather knocked on the door. "I have to use the toilet."

Kellie kept her eyes on the mirror. She reached up and unlocked the door. "Come in."

Heather opened the door, took a cursory look at Kellie and looked again. Her thumb edged towards her mouth. "What are you doing?"

"I've taken a shower and now I'm dressing for dinner."

"You look different."

"I'm wearing makeup. Do you like it?"

The thumb was wedged tightly in her mouth now. She spoke around it. "I don't think so."

Kellie turned her head to the left and then the right. "Why not?"

"You look different."

Something in the child's voice caught her attention. Heather was troubled. Reaching out, Kellie took her hand and drew the little girl into her lap. "Different isn't always bad, is it, love?" she asked gently.

Heather shrugged, fighting back tears.

Kellie kissed the top of her head. "Shall I wash my face? Would that make you feel better?"

Again the child shrugged.

"I know what we'll do. We'll both be different."

"How?"

"We'll both wear makeup."

Despite herself, Heather looked intrigued. "Will you put it on me?"

"If you like."

Heather thought a minute and then nodded.

Keeping the little girl in her lap, Kellie nodded at the assortment of colors and pointed out the specifics. "This is color for your eyelids," she explained, "and this is for cheeks and this for lips. Which ones would you like to wear?''

Interested at last, Heather picked over the vials. ''I want these,'' she said at last, and held them up.

Kellie smiled and selected a small sample compact and a brush. ''Let's start with this one.''

Ten minutes later a glowing Heather, clutching Kellie's hand, stood in front of the dinner table. ''Look at me, Da,'' she ordered.

Tom turned around. ''Good lord.'' The words leaped from his mouth. His eyes met Kellie's. He recovered quickly. ''Don't you look lovely, the both of you, all dressed up and ready to go out.''

Heather beamed. ''Kellie did it. She was wearing makeup and she said I could, too.''

''Did she now?''

''We were in a mood,'' explained Kellie.

His eyes were very bright. ''Will you be expecting an evening on the town?''

''May we?'' Heather breathed.

Tom thought a minute. This was Banburren after all. Not much was open after eight o'clock in the evening except for the pubs and that was out of the question. ''Where would you like to go, love?''

''We could go to Mrs. Reilly's café and order a pudding.''

Tom considered her suggestion. ''What do you think, Kellie? Shall we order a pudding at the café?''

''What a lovely idea.''

Heather clapped her hands and Tom laughed. Kellie stared at him. It occurred to her that she rarely saw him laugh. He looked younger, more vulnerable. His eyes were very blue above the blue of his shirt.

''Shall we eat?'' he asked.

Heather took her usual place. Kellie followed while Tom ladled out the soup, a delicious cabbage and onion variety.

His hands were large, capable, the nails short and clipped. Masculine hands. Awareness flooded through her as if she had awakened from a long and dreamless sleep. Her senses were sharper, cleaner, the details of the kitchen, the sounds and smells, the child and the man who sat across the table from her were clearly defined for the first time. She noticed his wrists, the bony strength of them, the way he turned up his shirtsleeves below the elbow, the faint shadow of hair growth on his chin, the way his eyes, an ice-flecked blue, direct, intelligent and light-filled, rested on her face when she spoke to him.

Horrified at the path her thoughts had taken, she looked down at her plate. What was the matter with her? Her appetite had disappeared. She left the soup and crumbled the bread on her plate. How much longer could she manage this? How had she ever believed it was possible? She had her answer although it wasn't the one she'd come for. Tom Whelan was no more a murderer than she was. It was time to go home. Why then, did the thought of leaving turn her stomach inside out?

The small café was cozy with flowered cloths on the tables, linen napkins and windows steamy with heat. A peat fire smoldered in the corner hearth and copper pans hung from the ceilings. Mrs. Reilly beamed as she ladled out lumberjack portions of her apple tart and cream. "Isn't it a lovely thing to have an outing on a weeknight?" Birdlike, she cocked her head. "Is there an occasion?"

"Heather wanted a pudding," Tom offered.

"The darling. Do you like the tart, love?"

Heather nodded, too busy delving into the sweet to answer.

"And how are you settling into our town, Miss Delaney?"

Kellie swallowed a bit of apple before answering. "It's a lovely town."

It took no more than that. "It is, isn't it? I've never been away, not in sixty-two years. Not for me the bright lights of Dublin or Galway. My husband wanted to leave when he retired. He's a Ballybofey man. But I said to him, 'There's nothing in Ballybofey that you can't find in Banburren.' So we stayed and we're happier for it. I'm sure Tom feels that way, too, don't you, Tom?"

Kellie smiled, hoping she appeared interested.

Tom spoke up. "We don't want to be keeping you, Alice. I'm sure you're nearly ready to close up. Perhaps a pot of tea would do with our sweets."

Mrs. Reilly's face lit. "The very thing. I'm sorry I didn't think of it myself."

"She's very friendly," Kellie observed when the woman had disappeared into the kitchen.

"Alice Reilly was always a gossip," Tom replied. "She's lonely since her husband passed on. We all bear with it."

Kellie nodded. Her dilemma was very much on her mind. Distracted, she pushed her dessert to the edges of her plate.

"I'll be driving into Galway tomorrow to visit Kenny's Bookstore," Tom announced. "Would you care to come with me?"

At first Kellie didn't realize he was talking to her. He repeated the question.

Surprised, she looked up. "Who will pick Heather up after school?"

"My mother. She'll stay with her until we come home. I'll turn on the answer machine to take any bookings."

Tomorrow. Tomorrow. Why not? Recklessly, she agreed. The idea of a day driving through the green-and-gold bogland of Ireland appealed to her.

Morning dawned clear and cold with no sign of rain. A milky sun filtered through silver-and-pink clouds. Breakfast was simple, oats and brown toast, tea and cocoa, a special treat for Heather.

Tom walked his daughter to school, returning home just as Kellie had finished the last of the dishes. She lifted her coat from the peg and pulled on her gloves. She felt light and free, a brief glimmering of what she'd known before.

He took the direct route out of town, through the roundabout, circling the one-way street around the square. Soon they were traveling at a comfortable speed down the two-lane road leading to Galway, Ireland's cultural capital.

Kellie had always loved Galway. Her father, a devout Nationalist, had thrilled her with stories of the violent, renegade clans that populated the west of Ireland, a land of bogs and misty mountains and cairn stones with wild, pagan markings where Irish dynastic lines were true Celt, untainted by English or Scots blood. She'd listened, wide-eyed and silent as he called up the fierce O'Flahertys, the O'Malleys and Granuille, their pirate queen, who exacted tribute from Elizabeth herself. Today, Galway's charm lay in narrow, medieval streets, lichen-aged buildings, smoky pubs, cozy teahouses, traditional music that began at ten and continued throughout the night and plays written, directed and played out by Ireland's most talented playwrights. Kellie had never attended its world-renowned film festival or women's writing conference, but she'd heard of them and it was enough to be in a city that fostered such an appreciation of the arts.

Kellie stared in amazement at the bookstore. This was not the Kenny's of her memory. Once a dark, musty world of lost books and twisting stairways, Kenny's Bookstore was now a famous landmark. Large windows let in the light. Books were categorized according to subject. Shelves were widely spaced for browsing and Irish art filled the walls of all three stories. Cups and saucers with the makings for tea sat out on a low table and overstuffed chairs filled the corners of the store.

Tom spoke close to her ear. "Don't let the trappings fool you. Kenny's is still the finest bookstore in all of Ireland. Everything you need will be here."

And it was so. Normally, Kellie would have lost

herself in the neoclassic section where Irish writers wrote of Ireland, evoking images of peat smoke and peat bogs, the smell of rain on the wind and wet wool and growing things, of too thin children with light, clear eyes, no shoes and bowed legs, of rich green soil and lively music, of stories that lasted for days and men who'd lived on the dole for so long they no longer cared to work. Theirs was a language rich in words of emotion tightly repressed, a storied world of women who shook hands and men who drank and swore and replayed wars in which they took no part. The Ireland of Yeats and Synge, Stephenson and Wilde was not the Ireland of Behan and Heany, Flannagan and Kilpatrick. Those who earned degrees from Trinity were not the same as those who were prevented from applying because of their religion and their heritage, men who drank themselves free of worry every night and staggered home to cold-water flats. Those were the writers whose words burned Kellie's soul. What did William Butler Yeats know of physical suffering, he with his housekeeper and valet and butler to ease life's discomforts?

Casually, she wandered among the shelves, back and forth, glancing occasionally at Tom. When she was sure he was absorbed, she moved purposely to the back of the store. The history and politics section was tucked away in an alcove by itself, the books categorized by centuries. Her fingers trailed across the spines, disregarding the rising, the revolution, the early years of the troubles. A title caught her eye. She stopped, pulled the book and flipped through it to the slick photos in the center. Faces of Sinn Fein, the Nationalist party jumped out at her, men and women who'd changed the course of Irish history, Gerry Adams, Martin McGinnis, Siobhan O'Flannery. They were well-known political faces. What of the others, she wondered? Where were they? She reached for another book, turned the pages and placed it back on the shelf. She pulled out another and still another. Completely engrossed, she didn't notice the passing time.

"Are you looking for something in particular?"

Startled, she dropped her book. "No," she stammered, reaching for it. "I just wanted some information."

"May I?" Tom held out his hand.

She hesitated, reluctant to have him see her choice. There was no reasonable explanation for refusing him. She handed over the book.

He glanced at it briefly and returned it to her. "What is it that you're looking for?"

An idea rooted in her brain. Why not? she thought. The truth was always easiest. "I've been living in England for a long time. I want to know what's happened since I left, from an Irish perspective. I want to know what the world thinks of Ireland."

"Why?"

"I'm curious. Everything's changed. People accept one another. Why now and not five years ago? What's the difference?"

"You won't find that in these books."

"Where will I find it?"

"Most likely in the economics and computer sections."

"I don't understand."

He took her hand, pulled her forward and tucked it under his arm. "Let's go for a cup of tea and I'll explain it to you. Then you can come back and choose your reading material."

He chose a restaurant that served considerably more than tea. It was noon and Kellie was hungry. They ordered rare beef, boiled potatoes and a pale ale that left her warm and slightly dizzy. Over tea, he brought up the subject of politics.

"For the first time Ireland is competitive. The European Union has helped us dramatically. We're exporting computers, offering jobs, educating our population. Men and women are working. Many expatriates are returning. The church has lost its influence. Large families are anachronistic. Everyone has a television. We've been pulled into the modern era. Gunfights and pipe bombs no longer have their appeal when opportunity exists for all."

"What about in the Six Counties?"

"Our universities are filled with Catholics. Educated people think differently about blowing up neighborhoods, although I don't know if we'll ever really be friendly with one another."

"What about you, Tom? Have you truly put it all behind you?"

"God, yes. It was a miserable existence, not knowing where it was safe to sleep at night, living from one day to the next. That's no way to live."

He spoke to her as if telling a story, as if she had no part in those early days. She wondered if he realized it.

His next words shattered the rosy glow of the ale. "Tell me what you're doing here in Banburren. I think I deserve to know."

The blood drained from her face. She felt weak, vulnerable, unable to move her hands or lips. She knew the words she was supposed to say. She'd practiced them often for just such a moment. But they wouldn't come. She hadn't the energy to formulate another lie. "I can't," she managed. At least that was the truth.

"That argument is old."

She shook her head. "I'm sorry."

"Is this about Claire, my wife?"

"No."

"What then?"

Again she shook her head.

Her hands were on the table. He took them in his and leaned forward. "It's possible that I can help you. I can't be sure. But unless you trust me, nothing is possible. Do you understand?"

"Yes."

"Will you think about it?"

"Yes."

"Is Kellie Delaney your real name?"

"Yes."

"Has someone sent you?"

"Not exactly."

"What does that mean?"

"Nothing. It means nothing." She threw up her hands. "I don't know what I mean. The reason I came no longer exists. I should go home."

"Is there something pressing waiting for you at home?"

"My job."

"You said you'd taken a leave."

"Yes."

His voice was soft, his words revealing. "Can you stay a bit longer?"

"Why would you want me to do that?"

"I'd like to know you better."

Her eyes met his briefly. Then she looked away. How ironic life was to bring Tom Whelan to her in such a way. All of her childhood friends were married with children, their days filled with normal decisions like what to eat or which bill to pay or should Liam go to school despite his runny nose. Why wasn't it the same with her? Had she been born with fairy debt, that her life should run along a different track than most? What did one say to a man whose life one entered with a lie? *By the way, I came to implicate you in the murders of my brother and nephew. Do you mind?* Such a confession merited a response, and most likely it would be a vindictive one and rightly so. She sighed. "That isn't a good idea."

His eyes were level and very blue as they flicked across her face. "No," he said. "I suppose not."

Nine

They cut the day short. Their drive home was silent, tension filled, all thoughts of Kenny's or any other Galway novelty forgotten. She would tell him nothing more. Tom knew despair when he saw it. He knew she lived it along with frustration and anger, nearly every conscious moment. Kellie Delaney was a strong woman, intelligent and composed. She'd taken risks coming here, giving up her job, searching through his computer files. Yet she was compassionate and warm, as well. Quite simply, he was taken with her. At first it was because of her resemblance to Claire. Now, it was for herself. He wanted to know her, all of her. He wanted to know if it was even possible. Her reticence was making it very difficult.

They argued for nearly an hour with no results. She was afraid. He tried another approach. "Am I in danger?"

Her nostrils flared sharply. "No." She hesitated. "I don't think so. Perhaps."

"Would you tell me if I was?"

"Yes."

"Why should I believe you?"

"Because you have no alternative," she snapped.

"Please," she leaned her head against the window. "Don't badger me. I can't take any more."

He said nothing further until they left the M6, twenty kilometers from Banburren.

"Tell me about your schooling."

She looked skeptical.

"Surely that's a harmless question?"

"I suppose so," she said slowly. "Why do you want to know?"

He shrugged. "Curiosity and to make conversation."

"My degree is in Irish literature. I graduated from Queen's. You already know that. There's nothing more."

"And now I've got you scrubbing toilets."

She laughed and he felt some of her darkness lift.

He was thinking out loud. "You don't seem to be a woman who acts on impulse. In fact, I've never known a woman to think as much as you do."

"That's a very sexist comment."

"This is Ireland, Kellie. We've come a long way but we're not there yet. Actually my comment was intended as a compliment."

"Thank you."

"What will you do when this is over?"

She looked at him. "What do you mean? Are you throwing me out?"

"That's a ridiculous question."

"Why do you say that?"

"Because you should know by now that I would never hurt you. Besides—"

"What?"

He grinned. "You're a marvelous cook."

She looked incredulous. "You're an odd man, Tom Whelan, to find amusement in a situation like this one."

"Humor can make all the difference when things seem too difficult."

She stared out the window.

He changed the subject. "Your resemblance to my wife is remarkable."

"Is she still your wife?"

"In name only."

"I'd like to see a photo."

"There are more differences between you than similarities."

"Such as?"

"Small things. The way you carry yourself. The texture of your hair is thicker, wavier. Your voice is different. Claire has a fair singing voice although she thinks it's better than it is. She's mastered the high notes, but her range is poor. You, on the other hand, can't sing at all and you're clearly right-handed. Claire has no preference. She's ambidextrous. Although she nearly always uses her right hand, she can write and work as well with her left. I don't think I've seen anyone as right dominant as you are. You're hopeless with your left hand."

She stared at him. "Good lord," she whispered. "Do you notice everything?"

He laughed. "Not everything. I'm just particularly observant when it comes to you."

Her throat went dry. She had to ask even though

she both dreaded and craved his answer. "Why is that?"

"I think the answer is obvious."

"I'd like to hear it anyway."

If that wasn't an invitation, he was an idiot. A spatter of rain blurred the windshield. Visibility was nonexistent. Tom pulled over to the side of the road. He turned to look at her, blue eyes intense. "I'm attracted to you, Kellie. I haven't felt this way since I fell in love with Claire. I want to know you better and I'm wearing myself out trying to find a way to interest you." He laughed. "Christ. I haven't even kissed you and I'm declaring myself."

"That can be remedied," she said softly.

Not taking his eyes from her face, he drew her toward him. Gently he touched the bones of her face, her chin, her cheeks, her lips and then he bent his head and found her mouth.

"My God," he said when he could breathe again.

"Yes."

He leaned toward her again.

She stopped him, her finger against his lips. "May I ask you a question?"

"Go on."

"Do you have enemies?"

He thought a minute. "Other than my wife, no."

"Tell me about her."

"We didn't part on the best of terms and we haven't been in touch for more than seven years. I know she's still in prison, or at least she was. That's all I know."

"Do you still love her?"

"No," he said woodenly, all his previous warmth wiped away with the monosyllable.

"I'm sorry," she whispered. "I had to know."

"We're nearly home," he said ignoring her apology and turning back to the wheel. "My mother will have Heather. Don't worry about a meal. I'll fend for myself."

The next morning Tom walked into the bakery at the corner of High Street and Carlisle. The yeast smell was strong and irresistible and the temptation of hot bread on a cold morning too great to pass up. His sister-in-law stood near the counter paying for her purchase.

"Hello, Kate."

She turned, a smile lighting her face. "Tom. What brings you out so early on a Saturday morning?"

"Sun and appetite. And you?"

"The same. I always intend to sleep in on the weekends but I never do." She motioned toward an empty table. "Will you share a pot of tea with me?"

He hesitated, saw the hurt spring into her eyes and changed his mind. "Of course. Sit down. I'll order the tea."

"How is Kellie?" she asked when they were seated opposite one another.

"Well, thank you. She enjoys working at the library. Thank you for that."

"They're lucky to have her."

"I'm lucky to have her. She's worth far more than free meals and lodging."

"What about you, Tom? It's been quite some time since I've seen you. How have you been?"

He sipped his tea. Kate was his sister-in-law, James's widow. She was incredibly attractive, warm and companionable. He was fond of her and even though she'd married his brother and settled in Banburren permanently, she was from the Republic, a world apart, and he had the Northerners' natural reticence toward those he hadn't grown up with. He'd flirted with her on occasion, when she invited it, and meant nothing by it. But she had taken it to heart and he'd been sorry for it later. It left him with an uncomfortable feeling in her presence and, ever since, he had discouraged confidences between them. "I'm doing well," he said evasively, and turned the subject. "How are you faring, Kate?"

She smiled brightly. "School never changes. I'm looking forward to my holiday. I'm thinking of traveling a bit this time, maybe to France or Italy."

"Now, there's a plan."

She sugared her tea. He noticed her hands. The skin was smooth, the nails tapered, well cared for.

"Do you have any desire to leave Banburren, Tom?"

"It has crossed my mind."

"Why did you never leave? Surely, anywhere would have been better than this town after Claire—" She left the rest of the sentence unsaid.

"Heather needed her family and I needed a place to live. Ex-prisoners aren't always well received." He was uncomfortable with the intimate nature of the conversation. Damn it, why did the woman always come back to this? "Are you feeling trapped, Kate? Are you thinking of leaving Banburren?"

Her laugh was brittle. She looked over his shoulder and then down at her cup, everywhere but at him. "There really is nothing for me here. At times I think I'm wasting my life."

"That depends on your expectations. Your profession is an important one."

"I'd like to marry again," she confessed. "I want children of my own."

"I understand."

"What about you, Tom? Will you divorce? I thought—" She stopped.

He looked at her, steadily, forcing her to meet his gaze. "It took a great many words for you to say that, Kate."

"Yes, it did. Forgive me, but there was a time when I thought that maybe you and I—"

"You were mistaken. If I've given you any reason to believe otherwise, I apologize."

Her eyes were very bright. "Don't be ridiculous. You've nothing to apologize for." She stood, leaving her tea. "Say hello to Kellie for me."

He nodded. "I will."

Tom paid the bill and left the shop. He was late. Kellie and Heather would be having breakfast. He wondered if they had waited for him. Probably not. Heather was always ravenous in the morning and Kellie had no expectations, nor did she make any demands where he was concerned. He could be gone a week and she wouldn't ask him where he'd been. Tom didn't know whether to be grateful or annoyed.

There was a time when independence had meant everything to him. With maturity had come wisdom. Freedom often meant a man had nothing to lose. There was comfort in a home and a woman's concern. He wondered if he would ever be worthy enough to warrant such a gift.

She was in the sitting room reading the paper, her stockinged feet close to the fire. She looked up when he came in and smiled, yesterday forgotten, a woman who didn't carry grudges. He liked that. He liked everything about her.

"Heather is still asleep," she said softly. "I thought I'd wait for her before making breakfast."

He relaxed. Breakfast with his family was not to be denied him after all. He sat down across from her and reached for a section of the paper. He wanted to share his morning and yet he felt vestiges of guilt. He had, in a small way, led Kate on. Even though his marriage was a sham it disturbed him, not because of Claire, oddly enough, but because of what he had now, a skeleton of a life with his child and with Kellie. He didn't want to upset it. "I saw Kate at the bakery," he volunteered. "She said to say hello."

"How is she?"

"Well enough. She's making noises about leaving Banburren again."

Kellie set aside the paper. "In the beginning I thought we might be friends. But it didn't work out."

Tom felt the warmth rise in his face. "Why not?"

"I'm not sure. My fault, most likely."

He felt a surge of anger. "Why do you say that?"

She looked surprised. "What?"

"Why do you always take the blame for everything? Perhaps it's she who is at fault."

She stared at him without apology, eyes huge and clear and guileless. How could a woman with eyes like that harbor a secret?

"I didn't think to place blame anywhere, Tom. There's none attached when people don't suit one another. I've never been one for female friendships, except once."

"Tell me about her." Tom was intrigued at this voluntary admission of another life.

Kellie shrugged. "She was bright and lovely and fantastically loyal. She took me in when I needed a friend."

"An Englishwoman?"

"Yes."

"Where is she now?"

"In England."

"I'm sorry. I was prying again."

"Don't be. I wouldn't have told you at all except that you're thinking poor Kate is snubbing me."

He laughed. "I stand corrected."

She took a deep steadying breath. "I came here because the two people I loved most in the world were killed in an auto accident."

He nodded, afraid to speak for fear of dispelling her mood.

"They were murdered."

Again the brief, inadequate words. "I'm sorry."

She nodded and looked at her hands.

"Was the killer found?"

"No."

Her admission, bald, understated, smote him. *Who was this woman?* "Would you rather have not loved them?"

She looked up, arrested. "What an odd question. No one has ever asked me that before. They say it was God's will, but no one ever says would it have been easier if I'd loved them less." She thought a minute. "Do you think it would have been?"

She'd lost him. "Easier, do you mean?"

She nodded.

"Perhaps, but losing someone isn't all that the grief is about. It's about patterns as well, rising together in the morning, tea and biscuits after dinner, the safe comfort of another person who cares if you come through the door at night. That's part of the loss, as well. So, despite what they say, loving someone more or less may have very little to do with how easy it is."

"I'm not sure I understand you."

He stood and reached for the poker, stirring the embers of the fire. They burst into flame, a surge of warmth in the morning chill. "I'll give you an example. A woman, a mother of forty years, loves her son. She lives in Dublin, he in Ardara with his family. For some reason, his life is cruelly cut short. She mourns him dreadfully but her routine doesn't change. She lunches with the ladies once a week, gardens in the morning, Mass at nine. Her life, except for holidays, is the same. Now, take the mother of a child Heather's age. She wakes her seven-year-old every morning, walks him to school, reads to him at night, looks across the table and sees his face at every meal. Without him her life is irrevocably changed. Both mothers love their children, but who suffers more?''

Kellie's cheeks whitened. ''You're very good at painting pictures.''

''Too good, from the look of you. I'm sorry if I disturbed you.''

She stood, her hands shaking. ''I'll start breakfast. Why don't you check on Heather? She's slept a long time.''

He watched her leave the room, a thoughtful expression on his face. Small chinks in the armor of her reserve were coming loose. Pain, unresolved and suppressed, was rising to the surface. He realized now that she'd been in shock when she arrived, but the numbness was disappearing. Soon, very soon, it would all come to a head. He wondered if she would be ready when it happened.

Heather slept soundly, her cheek buried in her pillow, her breath even and sweet. Tom sat down on the bed and touched his daughter's arm. ''Wake up, love. It's late.'' The child didn't move. He frowned. She was unusually flushed. He felt her forehead. It was clammy and hot. Her pulse fluttered beneath his fingers. Again he tried to wake her, his voice urgent, peremptory. ''Heather, it's time to get up.''

Still no response. Kellie appeared in the doorway. She took one look at Tom and another at Heather. Then she ran down the hallway to the telephone.

Tom heard the ring-ringing of the medical van and saw two men he often shared a pint with at Feeney's

Pub enter his daughter's room. He stepped aside while one checked her vital signs and the other asked the necessary questions. Kellie answered automatically.

"Heart rate and breathing are normal," announced the medic.

Relief flooded through him releasing his tongue and the muscles in his arms and legs. "What's the matter with her?" he managed.

"She's out of danger, lad," said the medic, "but she needs a hospital. My guess is that her blood supply was cut momentarily."

"Is she in a coma?"

"Aye."

"Will she come out of it?"

The two men looked at each other. "I don't know," said one. "Better get her to a hospital and a doctor."

Somehow Kellie's hand was in his. "Go with her in the lorry," she said softly. "I'll call your mother and follow you in the car."

The doctor was sympathetic but practical. The Banburren medical facility was a small one with no provisions for intensive care. Heather would have to be airlifted to Belfast. Tom watched the ground disappear beneath him as the chopper rose into the air. Filled with tubes, Heather lay pale and still beside him. A nurse kept a careful watch on her vital signs. The noise eliminated all possibility of conversation. The diagnosis wasn't yet conclusive but all signs pointed to a swelling on the brain. Heather would need surgery.

When he thought too deeply of the consequences, a horrifying blackness threatened to consume him, wiping away reason and rational thought. How could this happen to his healthy, beloved child?

The Royal Victoria in Belfast hummed with activity. Nurses in starched uniforms patrolled the sterile floors. Doctors perused charts, orderlies administered medicines and pushed wheelchairs. Disinfectant and efficiency prevailed. Tom was immediately reassured. Surely, this was a place where his child would recover.

Heather's physician was a young woman with cropped hair, smooth skin and a soothing smile. She confirmed the original diagnosis. "She has a swelling on the brain, possibly from some sort of trauma, perhaps a fall. It's large enough to put pressure on the artery which temporarily cut off her blood supply. She needs surgery to drain the swelling and relieve the pressure. We'll need blood for the surgery, Mr Whelan. We prefer that you or the child's mother donate. Is that possible?"

Tom looked surprised. "Of course. Why wouldn't it be?"

"If you're HIV positive or if you've had hepatitis, we can't use you," she explained, keeping her tone ever professional, "or if your blood is of a different type."

"I haven't had either of those but I don't know if Heather's blood type is the same as mine."

She smiled. "We'll find out. The lab is down the hall. I'll show you the way."

* * *

Two hours later, after he'd forced himself to eat several biscuits and down a large glass of juice, the doctor found him in the waiting room. This time her smile was regretful. "We don't have a match, Mr. Whelan. Your daughter's blood type is B positive and you're an A negative. We don't have enough B positive blood in storage to attempt the surgery. Where is the child's mother?"

The child's mother. Good God. He knew less than nothing about genetics. "Is B positive an unusual blood type?"

"Most people are O positive. About twenty percent of the population has blood type B, however those that do cannot receive blood from any other type. We have stored units, of course, not to worry, but it works best if we receive donated blood from family members."

He cleared his throat. "I see."

"When will your wife be arriving?"

His wife. When would his wife be arriving? The young doctor looked pleasant enough, friendly, just the right amount of personal mixed with professional. She was obviously Protestant, from East Belfast. What would she say when he told her his wife was a Nationalist sympathizer, a terrorist, a murderer, serving time in Maidenstone for the murder of a British lord? Would her smile disappear? Would her pleasant manners and her resolve to administer the Hippocratic oath to all patients despite their religious persuasion change? Would Heather suffer?

Over the woman's shoulder he saw the double

doors of the hospital open. Kellie walked in and Tom made an instant decision.

"She's here now," said Tom. "Perhaps she has the same blood type."

"There is no perhaps, Mr. Whelan. One of you must have it. A child has one parent's blood type or the other's. There are no exceptions."

Kellie walked up in time to hear the doctor's comment. "Has what?"

"Your husband doesn't have the same blood type as your daughter, Mrs. Whelan. We're hoping you can donate several units for Heather's surgery."

Kellie didn't blink an eye. "What type do you need?"

"B positive."

She drew a deep breath and nodded. "That's me. What shall I do?"

Tom released his breath. Luck was with him.

The young doctor smiled at her. "Don't go anywhere. I'll see if I can get something set up right away. Have you ever given blood before?"

Kellie shook her head.

"It's quite simple." She smiled brightly. "We're preparing her for surgery now. You'll be able to see her one more time before the procedure. If you need anything, check with the nurses' station."

Tom watched her walk away. His hands balled in his pockets. "I shouldn't be doing this to you. I didn't even ask."

"Did you think I would refuse a few pints of blood?"

He ran his hand through his hair. "I don't know

what I thought. I didn't want the doctor to know about Claire.''

"What difference does that make?''

"I just don't think it would help Heather's cause to have anyone know her mother for what she is.''

"What is she, Tom?'' Kellie asked softly.

He opened his mouth to answer and then closed it again. "I don't know,'' he said. "We never talked in the end. Suddenly she was gone and it was over.''

"Do you want to know?''

He thought a minute and when he spoke his answer was honest and painful. "I don't know that, either.''

Ten

She looked no more than asleep, her cheeks porcelain and slightly pink beneath their spattering of freckles. Her small chest rose and fell with each steady breath. It was a peaceful scene except for the occasional bleating of the monitor, the tubes that fed her thin body and the knowledge that she wasn't asleep at all, but rather in the throes of a coma that could sap the memory from her brain and the strength from her limbs.

Tom sat by her bed, his eyes fixed on her face, his mind someplace outside himself. Kellie did not attempt to interrupt his thoughts with small talk. No one knew where a parent's mind was at a time like this, except the other parent and that wasn't possible. Tom was alone in this.

Involuntarily, she reached out to grip his hand. "I've heard that it helps to talk to her," she said.

He nodded and said nothing.

Still holding his hand, Kellie sat down on the side of the bed. She wasn't Heather's mother or Tom's wife but she'd fallen in love with the little girl and it wouldn't hurt to try. "Hello, love," she said in the soft, sweet tones she'd used with Danny. "You've had an operation to remove pressure in your brain.

The doctor says everything went well. She expects you to rest now. But, soon, you'll need to wake up and tell us how you're feeling. We miss you, love. Your da is here. Can you see him?" Kellie took one of Heather's hands. "If you can see him, squeeze my hand." Nothing. "He's quite worried about you, you know," she continued. "I, on the other hand, know how strong you are." Tears formed in the corners of Kellie's eyes. She blinked them back and looked around, searching for more words. "The room they've put you in is lovely, blue and white with animals painted around the ceiling and cartoon pictures on the walls. When you open your eyes you'll see them. I'm sure they'll cheer you up."

Tom's jaw was very tight and his grip on her hand crippling. Men didn't cry, especially Irish men, and not in front of women. They found solace with friends in the pubs and with God in the confessional, but never with their women.

Gently, Kellie extricated her hand from Tom's, rummaged through the large bag she carried and pulled out a book. "I visited the library, Heather. I found the book we were reading. Would you like to continue with it? Squeeze my hand, darling. Let me know you can hear me." Nothing.

Undaunted, Kellie opened the book. "Why don't you find the cafeteria and eat something," she said to Tom. "I'll be here when you get back."

He shook his head. "Not yet. I can't bear to leave her yet."

Kellie began to read, punctuating the beloved sentences of the C. S. Lewis book with the expression that Heather loved.

Beside her, some of the tension left Tom's face. She read for a long time, stopping for sips of water at chapter breaks. Tom's eyes had glazed over long ago. Heather lay still as death.

The young female doctor stepped into the room. She picked up the chart hanging at the foot of the bed. Then she felt the child's pulse. She smiled warmly at Kellie. "She's doing fine. The surgery went well. Don't worry. Children are resilient."

"When will she wake?"

"Give her some time. The anesthesia is still in effect. We'll know more in a few hours."

Susan Whelan tiptoed into the room, took one look at the child on the bed and another at her son's face. This was not to be. She shook him. "Tom."

Startled, he jerked awake. "Mam, thank God you're here."

"The doctor said the surgery was successful."

Kellie walked into the room with two cups of hot tea. Her eyes lit up. "Thank goodness. I didn't know you were coming."

"And where else would I be I'd like to know with my granddaughter in the hospital and everyone at all sixes and sevens. How is she?"

"The same," Tom said dully. "She's still unconscious."

"That's to be expected," Susan said practically. She reached for the tea. "I'll take one of the those and sit with the child while you two get some rest. Have you booked a room?''

Kellie shook her head. ''Not yet.''

Susan adjusted Heather's blanket, tucking it around her chin. ''There are some lovely places on the Stranmillis Road. You'll find one to cheer you up.''

''I'm staying here,'' said Tom.

''They won't give you a bed,'' said his mother. ''You won't be any help to Heather unless you're thinking clearly.''

''I'll look into it,'' Kellie said quickly.

''Meanwhile you need food,'' said Susan. ''Off with you, now.'' She tugged at her son's arm. ''Things will look better on a full stomach.''

Tom ignored her. Kellie knelt down beside him. ''Your mother is here to help, Tom. She'll call us if there's any change. Please, come with me.''

He looked at her, unseeing at first, and then his expression changed and he stood. ''Thank you, Mam,'' he said to his mother. ''You're right. I'm not thinking clearly.''

Susan nodded. ''Call as soon as you're settled in.''

Belfast was home. Kellie had walked these streets for most of her childhood, not the trendy, upscale Stranmillis neighborhood with its quaint tourist shops, its tea and coffee houses and touristy eateries, but her old haunts bordered by the Ormeau Road, the Protestant Shankill and the Catholic Falls, working-class streets with graffiti on the walls and giant-size murals depicting the oppression of the last thirty years. Still, she knew Stranmillis. Anyone who'd been educated at Queen's knew it. It was an area that catered to students.

She pulled into the Lisburn Road and turned east on Eglantine. The guest house she had in mind, a charming brick structure set back on a long green lawn, had recently been renovated. One of the rooms was available. She booked it with a credit card.

Tom fell asleep immediately. Kellie frowned. How long had it been since he'd eaten? Ignoring her own rumbling stomach, she pulled aside the duvet on her own bed and crawled in. Perhaps she could persuade him to eat something after they'd both had a nap.

Her nightmare was a recurring one. The small blond child and the large man, the luxurious automobile and the mountain road narrowing into a series of twisting turns, the car picking up speed, the gathering momentum, the squealing of tires and, finally, the dreadful careening of the car off the road, down the mountain onto cliffs jagged and slick with ocean spray.

She jerked into consciousness with a scream in her throat. Tom sat on the side of her bed, his eyes warm with pity, his hand holding down one of her arms. She stared at him, muscles tensed, eyes wide, horror filled.

"Easy," he said softly, "easy now. It's over. It's all over. You're all right."

She nodded. Slowly her body relaxed.

He released her arm and whistled under his breath. "We're a pair, aren't we?"

She laughed raggedly. Embarrassed and exposed

she turned her head to the wall, bracing herself for the questions she was sure would follow.

Surprisingly, they didn't. "I could eat something," he said. "How about you?"

She thought a minute, gauged the level of her hunger and nodded again. "Where shall we go?"

He checked his watch. They had slept less than an hour when her screams woke him. "There's a restaurant near the city centre on the Donegall Road. It's called The Merry Monk. The last time I was there the food was decent. Shall we try it?"

Kellie sat up and swung her legs over the side of the bed. "Yes. Give me a minute."

"Take your time. I'll call and check on Heather."

The restaurant was dim with white tablecloths, ivory candles and a respectable wine list, the kind of establishment Kellie could not afford in her student days at Queen's. Grateful for the full-length coat that covered her casual sweater and slacks, she waited for the maître d' to leave before slipping it off and hanging it over the back of her chair. Tom did not seem concerned that they were underdressed.

"I recommend the fish," he said.

"Fish sounds perfect." She looked at him curiously. "Do you come here often?"

"I've been here several times, but I'm not a regular customer if that's what you mean. I don't come into town often enough."

"I wouldn't have thought—"

"What?"

She shook her head. "Never mind."

His eyes glinted in the candlelight. "Let me guess. You wouldn't have thought that a blue collar lad from Banburren would know anything about fine dining."

The red tide washing over her face was answer enough.

"I could say the same about you. Catholic girls from the Six Counties are more likely to wait tables than to dine in establishments like these."

"That's a dreadful comment," she admonished him.

"Is it true?"

She hated to give him the hand even if he was right but her innate sense of honesty prevailed. "Yes, unfortunately."

"From where in Belfast do you hail?" he asked casually.

She saw no point in keeping it from him. "From Andersonstown. How did you know?"

He shrugged, lifted his glass and swallowed a healthy portion of Guinness. "No hesitation at street corners. No looking at signposts. You know the lay of the land, so to speak."

Not for the first time did she wonder what she was up against. "I told you my undergraduate degree is from Queen's."

"So, where do the nightmares come from?"

She kept her expression neutral, a woman in white wool with hair the color of toast. "From my head," she said simply.

He changed the subject. "You're very good with children. Were you married, Kellie?"

Carefully, she lifted her wineglass to her lips and sipped. "No. Why don't we talk about you?"

The glint came back into his eyes. "My life is an open book. What can you possibly want to know that you don't already?"

She hedged. What she wanted to know was unspeakably rude. "Have you always wanted to be a musician?"

"God, no. It's enough for me to kick around with a few of those who have a bit of talent, fill in with the pipes when they need me and go home when the music is done. I'm not one for wanting to stay up half the night to tour the countryside."

The server arrived and Tom ordered the white fish for both of them.

She waited until they were alone. "What about your writing?"

He drained his glass. "What about it?"

"Are you published?"

"Aye, but not enough to pay the bills."

"Does your pipe making pay the bills?"

"Didn't your mum ever tell you that's a rude question to ask a man?"

"Yes, but I assumed we were beyond that."

"All right then," he said agreeably, "the pipes pay the bills to the tune of about five thousand pounds each."

"You make twenty-five thousand pounds on the pipes alone?"

"I do. With that, a gig now and then and my poetry, I'm a fairly good catch. Maybe you want to get married."

"The last time I checked you were already married."

Tom grinned. "I forgot about that."

She laughed back at him. "A minor roadblock."

As they enjoyed a moment of comfortable silence Kellie decided not to mention the files she'd come upon, files stored in the hard drive of Tom's computer. The verses were deceptively complicated, serious, throat-catching, filled with everyday images, hazy pubs, smoky mists settling over the peat bogs, the smells of wet wool and bus exhaust, the grind of milk trucks on gravel roads, sheepdogs barking at their flocks, the sounds and sights and smells of Ireland. Tom Whelan had a voice, the voice of his world, subtle and unique, that tenuous quality that could be learned but never taught. She wondered if he knew how talented he was. How ironic to be in the presence of innate talent, she who'd been taught along with minds gifted enough to be admitted into the hallowed halls of the finest universities in England. No, she wouldn't mention the verse. Every instinct she'd grown up with shouted *invasion of privacy*. She was ashamed of her deception, ashamed of the role she played. More than anything she wanted to confide in him, to make him her ally, to enlist him in the conspiracy to find out why Connor was targeted. It was more and more apparent that she couldn't manage alone. In all this time she'd found nothing, more than likely because there was nothing to be found.

The wine was excellent, the fish thick and flaky, perfectly prepared by a chef who knew his food. Ireland was no longer a land of mushy vegetables and overcooked meat. Kellie, who thought she wouldn't be able to manage more than a few bites, worked her way through her plate quickly. She noted that Tom had done the same. "We were hungrier than we thought."

He wadded up his napkin and dropped it on his plate. Once again, Kellie noticed his hands, wide, capable, neat hands. Perhaps it helped him to play his pipes.

"You love her, don't you?" he said abruptly.

The question was blunt, unexpected. She had no time to construct a safe answer. "Yes," she said simply. "Who wouldn't love a child like Heather?"

"Do you want children, Kellie?"

She shrugged. The question had never been more painful.

"If that's a no, why not?"

The beep of his mobile phone interrupted them. Tom answered. Kellie waited, a tense anxious knot filling her stomach.

His face changed, every emotion raw and exposed. It was too much to watch. She looked down at her plate.

"Thank God." He laughed. "We'll be right there. Thank you." He pocketed the phone. "She's awake. Mam said the doctor had been in again and Heather is responding." He reached across the table and clasped both of her hands. "She's going to make it, Kellie. She's all right." His voice cracked.

Tears clouded her vision. She blinked and they rolled down her cheeks. She would have spoken but her throat was closed, the words crowded, locked inside her. Shaking her head, she pulled her hands away, folded the napkin and pressed it against her face.

Tom stood, pulled out his wallet and left several large bills on the table. "Shall we go?" he asked.

Kellie nodded. Head down, she preceded him out of the restaurant and turned toward the car park.

"She's sleeping," Tom said conversationally, his hand under her arm. "She won't know we're there, but we'll see her."

He opened the passenger door for her, closed it and climbed into the driver's seat.

"Where is your mother staying?" she asked.

"Near the Ormeau Road with her sister." He pulled out into the flow of traffic.

The car park of the Royal Victoria Hospital was filled. "You go in," Kellie said. "I'll find a spot and join you. If not, I'll wait at the front entrance."

His eyebrows rose. "You're not coming in?"

"If I can manage it," she said gently. "Go now. Spend some time with your daughter."

He looked at her. Then he smiled. "I won't be long."

"Take your time."

She found a spot near the back of the car park away from the light. Turning off the engine, she leaned back against the headrest and closed her eyes. Tom Whelan was a complicated man, thoughtful and reserved, obviously intelligent, even attractive in the lean, ropy, sharp-checked way of Irish men who were all planes and angles and ice-flecked blue eyes that took up the color of the sea around them.

At first she'd disregarded the core of him, her mind on what she was to do. But the frozen part of her had thawed and her natural curiosity had eventually prevailed. He was different, unpretentious, not motivated by material possessions. It was difficult to reconcile the man she knew with the reports in the news clippings. She wanted to ask him who the real Tom Whelan was and what had lured him to the dark side of the law, in his youth. She wanted to ask him if Austin Groves was nothing more than a man who'd ordered a set of pipes. But something held her back, something she couldn't quite put her finger on.

And there was more. In the asking she would have to reveal parts of herself. Self-disclosure was the price one paid for another's revelations. It would mean she was finished here. If she was sure of anything, it was that she wasn't ready to leave Banburren. And there was Heather to consider.

Heather. Her feelings for the little girl defied description. They were frightening feelings, even dangerous ones, for a woman who'd given her heart away once already. Kellie knew she should pull back, protect herself from the inevitable hurt. And yet, it was impossible not to love such a child, a baby still, but with pockets of wisdom that made one believe in *old souls* and lives lived more than once.

The passenger door opened. Startled, she sat motionless while a man in a dark jacket climbed in beside her. "Dennis wants to see you."

She wet her lips. "When?"

"Tonight at ten. I'll pick you up outside your room."

Kellie nodded.

"Don't make me go in after you."

"No," she said, after he had climbed out of the car and disappeared into the night.

It seemed no more than a minute later when Tom knocked on the window. She opened the door. "How is she?"

"Sleeping soundly." His eyes moved over her face. "You're tired. I'll drive."

Kellie climbed out of the car without arguing and sat down in the passenger seat. "When will she come home?" she asked.

"Possibly the day after tomorrow." He rubbed his day-old beard. "I haven't felt this gamy since Long Kesh."

He spoke of his prison time easily, as if he were comfortable with it. "Were you on the hunger strikes?" she asked.

He grinned and her stomach tightened. "The strikes were in the eighties, Kellie. I'm not old enough for that."

"How old are you?"

He appeared to consider her question. "What if we work something out?"

Instantly she was on the alert. "How do you mean?"

"For every question I answer, you'll answer one for me."

"No." Her response was instant, automatic.

"Why not? What do you have to lose? If you don't feel like answering, you don't have to ask the next question."

Surely she could turn this to her advantage. "All right, then, you go first."

"What's your middle name?"

She smiled. He was warming her up, starting out with the harmless questions. "Maureen."

He nodded. "Your turn."

"Where is your poetry published?"

"In obscure journals that no one reads."

"Where specifically?"

"Not fair. Only one question at a time. It's my turn again." He waited this time before forming the words. "Who was it that passed away?"

Because she was ready for it, it wasn't as bad as she'd expected it to be. She drew a deep breath. "They didn't *pass away,* Tom. My brother and nephew were murdered, nearly four months ago."

He frowned. "I didn't realize it was so recent. Why—"

"It's my turn," she said. The words came out unexpectedly from somewhere deep inside of her. "When did you know you were no longer in love with Claire?"

He was silent for a long time.

"You don't have to answer if you don't want to," she reminded him. "Those are your rules."

"It has nothing to do with what I want. I just can't remember. I don't think it happened all at once. It was gradual. I cared less and less until there was nothing left."

"I see."

They were nearly at the Stranmillis Guest House. He looked sideways at her. "Do you?"

"Is that your question?"

"No. I'd like to know if your coming to Banburren had to do with your brother's death."

"It did."

She saw his hands tighten on the wheel.

She looked away. Outside the guest house was a parked car, inconspicuous in its make and model, but the man seated inside was recognizable enough. Kellie's heart pounded. It was only nine o'clock. Would he stop her here in front of Tom, or would he wait until she was alone? There was no point in avoiding him. Sooner or later he would find a way.

Eleven

She was nervous. He could see it in her refusal to meet his eyes and in the shaky, breathless tone of her voice. He thought back to when her mood had changed but couldn't pinpoint a moment. He knew she'd been comfortable in the restaurant but the hours before, when his mind was filled with Heather, when the terror of not knowing whether his child would live or die had consumed him completely, were a blur.

His child. His and Claire's. Tom was ready to examine his feelings for his wife. At the time, when his daughter's life hung suspended, his rage was at a peak. Now? He turned the question over in his mind, thought of the person Heather was and decided that anger wasn't the emotion he should be feeling. Without Claire he wouldn't have Heather. Without her he wouldn't have had the pleasure of raising a child, the shared conversation and meals, walking her to school, buying her clothes, looking over her schoolwork or sharing a run with Lexi on country roads. He'd been given the privilege of experiencing everything that made a child a person, everything that Claire would never have. Claire was to be pitied. The rest of it— what he should do with a marriage that had long since run its course, he didn't know yet. Perhaps that would come later. He was sure of only one thing. It was long past time for him to face Claire again.

Meanwhile, there was Kellie and the worry in her eyes. Somewhere, in the last weeks, his feelings for her had grown. Where they were going he wasn't sure, but on the important issues he was clear. She loved his child and she had deep reserves of compassion. In her recent past she had suffered a life-altering trauma. The circumstances of her subsequent actions intrigued him to the extent that he spent a considerable portion of his morning hours thinking about the various possibilities for her flight from Oxford to Banburren.

He emptied his pockets on the nightstand, keeping her in his peripheral vision. They had never been confined to one room before. She seemed at odds, unable to settle in. He was feeling awkward himself. "Perhaps you'd like to go out for a magazine or a book?" he suggested.

She jumped at the escape. "I would. I'm not ready to sleep yet, not after the nap."

He handed her the keys. "Take these, in case you need the car."

"I think I'll walk. The shops are still open and we're close enough. I could use the exercise."

Tom headed for the bathroom, relieved and at the same time disappointed that she was leaving. There was something about sharing a loo with a woman. It was deeply personal, the running of water, damp towels hung over the heater, jars and bottles, womanly things cluttering the basin, the flushing of a toilet, intimacies the two of them did not share.

It occurred to him for the first time that he would not have minded sharing such things, that after seven years of independence he felt the stirrings of need for a woman in his life. The part of him that he'd rigidly suppressed after consciously pushing Claire out of his heart and mind, the sexual flame that, at an earlier time, had been all he could think about when he had a beautiful young wife had, once again, in the presence of this new woman, slowly risen to the surface. Quite simply, he wanted her. Whoever she was and whatever she wanted from him he would be willing to put aside for an hour's pleasure, for that sweet slide into liquid heat, the satisfaction of pleasure given and gained, the momentary sensation, however fleeting, of belonging.

He leaned over the sink, stared at himself in the mirror and grimaced. He was not yet forty and he looked haggard as hell. Even at his best he had no right to a woman like Kellie, educated and lovely. Under normal circumstances they would never have met. Until Kate had married James, he had never even known a woman who'd gone beyond secondary school and there were few enough of those. The direction of his thoughts was absurd. He would be better served the sooner she left. And yet the very idea of it shook him. What was happening to him?

Head bent against the cold, Kellie walked briskly down the empty street, grateful that her escape was so easily accomplished. The car was gone but she had no doubt, now that she was alone, that her contact would find her.

Sure enough, a car she would not have recognized again pulled up beside her. The door opened. "Get in," the driver ordered.

Kellie climbed in, adjusted the seat belt and stared straight ahead, saying nothing. Oddly enough she wasn't afraid for her life. It was easy enough to murder a person. If someone wanted her gone, she would be.

He drove quickly, competently, negotiating the jumble of one-way streets that was Belfast, crossing the Ormeau Road into the west side of the city. He turned down the Kashmir Road and stopped at a large gray structure set apart. A light glowed in the window. For the first time since his original command, the man spoke. "This won't be long." Kellie followed him into a shabby sitting room. He took a position near the door.

A fire burned in the grate and a man approaching his middle years, blond and balding, smiled thinly and held out his hand.

Dennis McGarrety looked very much the same. She touched his fingers just long enough and then pulled her hand away. "Hello. It's been a very long time, Mr. McGarrety."

"So, you do remember?"

"Of course." She looked around. "Things don't change much here, do they?"

His smile hardened. "Not all of us have the benefit of a fancy English education."

"Mine came from right here in Belfast. You know that, I'm sure."

"How is your mother, Kellie?"

"I haven't spoken to my mother in some time. I would have thought you knew that as well."

"She would want to see you."

"What do you want with me? I left this place behind."

He waved her to a chair with a floral print and high back. "Sit down. What do you take in your tea?"

Kellie sat. "Milk, please."

He handed her a mug of milky tea. "If you'd left this behind, as you say, you wouldn't be here. We have no interest in making you uncomfortable."

"Why am I here?"

McGarrety sat down and leaned forward. "We have certain loyalties, contracts that are necessary to keep."

"Is Tom Whelan one of those contracts?"

"Tom left us long ago. We are interested in him for only one reason."

"I don't understand."

"We haven't brought you here to understand," he said, a subtle reminder of who was in charge. "We ask the questions and if it is in our best interests to share information with you we will."

Kellie heard the incredible words. Her mind leaped to the obvious conclusion and it terrified her. For the first time, the vulnerability of her position was glaringly evident. She wet her lips. "What do you want?"

"Go home, Kellie. Forget Tom Whelan and whatever it is that has brought you here."

"You know perfectly well what brought me. Connor and his son are dead. I want to know why."

"Do you really imagine you can find out on your own?"

"I don't know," she replied honestly. "But I'm not giving up yet."

"Not even if you endanger Tom Whelan and his child?"

She frowned. "What do you mean?"

"Connor represented British Intelligence. Whelan spent his life resisting British occupation of his country."

"That was long ago."

"There are those with long memories. Go home, Kellie. Go back to England."

Her throat was raw, on fire. She swallowed. Her mind reeled. She felt sick to her stomach. Everything was intensified; the nerve endings beneath her skin, the clock ticking on the wall, the moisture beading on the bridge of her nose, the pulsing blood in her throat. Dennis McGarrety was, at one time, the brigade leader of the Belfast Irish Republican Army, an organization so tightly run and so incestuous it was nearly impossible to infiltrate. Her father and brothers had trusted him, lived their lives by his dictums. It had destroyed them. Was Connor one of their victims? There was no other way but to ask. "Did you have my brother killed?"

He stared at her, a man aging too quickly, a man who would never retire quietly by the sea with his wife and his books and his grandchildren beside him. His end was foretold in destiny. "I know something about you, Kellie Delaney," he said softly. "You're from a Nationalist family and you have our sympathies. You know that believing in something strongly requires personal sacrifice. Countries do not gain their independence if men and women will not risk everything they have. Connor gave his life for his country. He knew the risks. Content yourself with that.''

"Are you saying my brother cooperated with you?" She was aghast. Connor Delaney an IRA sympathizer? "I don't believe it.''

"Connor Delaney was not IRA. He was removed because he stood in the way of a man who will change the course of history in Northern Ireland.''

Her eyes were wide, horror filled. "Tell me why you killed him.''

McGarrety didn't answer. His silence condemned him. Kellie's hands clenched.

One more question. She needed just one more question answered and then she would ask no more. "Was Tom Whelan involved in Connor's death?''

"No," said McGarrety. "Go home before it's too late.''

Kellie's hands shook. She laced her fingers together. "Heather Whelan is ill. She needs me. I need more time.''

"Every day you stay endangers Tom Whelan and his daughter that much more. Don't lose sight of that.''

Tom was sleeping when she returned. Breathing a silent *thank you*, she tiptoed across the floor into the bathroom and closed the door. She didn't have the energy to lie, not tonight. Shedding her clothes, she pulled on a nightgown, splashed water on her face and brushed her teeth. Then she turned off the light and felt her way to the unoccupied single bed. Gratefully, she crawled beneath the covers and closed her eyes.

Two hours later she was still awake. Visions of her childhood faded in and out of her consciousness, her mother hanging the washing on lines attached to rusted supports; her brothers kicking a sorry-looking ball on a patch of insignificant grass, a park by the standards of West Belfast; vacant-eyed women wrapped in blankets smoking on the stairs; buildings with knocked-out windows; streets with broken pavement; the sick acrid smell of tear gas, pipe bombs and fear, always the fear that one's sleep would be interrupted by men breaking down the door and tearing apart the house.

There were other memories as well, all the more confusing because they weren't entirely negative. Her mother turning off the telly to help her study, waiting dinner because a bus was late, counting coppers from the jar to pay for music lessons, denying herself meat so that her children might have enough. Kellie felt the sting of remorse. Mary Delaney was a product of time and place. She couldn't help her circumstances. Somehow, before she left the city, she would find a way to see her mother.

Tom's voice pierced the darkness. "Kellie, are you awake?"

She considered feigning sleep and decided against it. "Yes."

"Why?"

"It's been a difficult day." She shifted to her side. "What about you?"

He was silent for a long time. Just when she thought he'd drifted off, he spoke. "That, too, but there's something else there as well."

"What is it?"

"Something I haven't felt in a long time."

She said nothing, waiting, knowing somehow what was coming, as if all the time in between had been a slow dance, complicated in its execution, but every step plotted and choreographed to this inevitable moment. She heard the rustle of the bedcovers as he left his bed, heard the whisper of his feet on the carpeted floor, felt the mattress give as he sat down beside her, saw his eyes in the dark move over her face. His hand cupped her cheek and she closed her eyes. Did she want this? Yes, she decided. She'd always wanted it, from the moment she began to live again.

What was it about the comfort of a man's hands on a woman's bare skin, of his mouth on the curve of her throat and the dip of her waist, the long, slow primal climb of desire from an idea in the back of her mind to the pit of her stomach, spreading until her entire body opened, stretched, pleaded for the feel of hard muscle, warm skin and the slick, turgid length of him between her thighs, separating the folds of skin, entering the most intimate part of her? In the end it always came to this.

Her arms separated and wrapped around him, urging him closer. Her hands slid down the leanness of his hips, cupping his backside, pulling him deep inside. She found his rhythm, matched his movements, felt the perspiration on his forehead, the curve of his back.

She wanted to see him, to see his face, to pierce the darkness. "Look at me," she said. "Look at my face. Who are you making love to?"

Bracing himself on his arms, he looked down at her. "To you, Kellie. To Kellie Delaney of Andersonstown." He moved faster, his thrusts deeper, harder.

She had to ask, to be sure. "Is it me that you want?"

He froze, arms outstretched, hair falling across his forehead, eyes narrowed, intense.

She waited, heart in her mouth.

"You're all I've ever wanted."

"You don't know me."

"I know you," he said fiercely. "Make no mistake about that."

Her hands tightened on his shoulders. "Don't stop," she pleaded. "Please, don't stop."

A small, triumphant sound left his throat. Lowering himself, he stretched out on top of the slender softness of her, giving what he'd thought was no longer possible for him.

He woke late the following morning, pleasantly sore and sated. She was gone. He kicked aside the sheets and walked into the bathroom. Her toothbrush and toiletries were still on the shelf along with a note. He read it and relaxed. She'd gone to pick up a few things she couldn't find in Banburren. He pulled aside the window curtain; saw the car parked on the street. She couldn't have gone far.

Tom turned on the tap in the shower, tested the water and stepped into the stall. Twenty minutes later she still hadn't returned. He felt the familiar burn in his stomach signaling the beginning of panic. Where was she? What was she thinking? He had no regrets. He wouldn't take back the night, not even if it meant they'd crossed a divide, not even if they could no longer continue as they had.

Tom didn't know what he felt for this mystery woman who'd invaded his life. It wasn't love. Not yet. He was fairly sure of that. He didn't love quickly or easily and he was long past the time when desire and love are one and the same. He knew enough to know that love required honesty, trust and the possibility of commitment. All three were missing in the relationship that he and Kellie shared. He intended to remedy that immediately.

He could wait no longer. It was time to see Heather. He would leave the car for Kellie and take the bus to the hospital.

Heather was sitting up in bed chatting with her grandmother when he arrived. Careful not to disturb the tubes, he hugged her gently.

"Where's Kellie?" she asked immediately.

Tom settled back against the pillows. "She'll be along. She had to run a few errands."

Satisfied with his explanation, Heather leaned into him. "I want to go home, Da," she whimpered. "My arm hurts."

He looked down at the small hand. The skin around

the tiny catheter was red and angry looking. "Have they noticed this?" He held up her hand for his mother to see.

Susan frowned. "I don't think so."

Tom pushed the red button near the bed. Several minutes later a nurse appeared.

He pointed to the welt on Heather's hand. "What's this?"

The nurse frowned. "Poor little love. She's probably knocked it against something in her sleep."

"When can she have this taken out?"

"When the doctor feels that she's out of danger. Most likely another day or so. Would you like me to ask her?"

"Thank you. I would. Meanwhile, she's in pain. Can you do something?"

"I'll check and see if that's possible. She's very young for pain medication."

"She's young to be here at all."

"I'll see what I can do."

Susan squeezed her son's arm. "There's no point in biting her head off, Tom. Heather will get better care if you're sympathetic."

Tom grimaced. "You're right. I'm not myself."

Heather was nodding off. Susan lowered her voice. "What errands could Kellie have in Belfast?"

"Her mam is here. Kellie grew up in Belfast."

Susan's eyes narrowed. She reached across the bed and took her son's hands in her own. "Listen to me, Tom, and listen well. You've been given a second chance. Don't throw away a blessing when God hands you one."

Tom stared at his mother. "She won't talk to me, Mam. I know nothing about her."

"I know you, Tom. You're still thinking of Claire. But you haven't lost anything there. This one is a gift. Take care of her."

"Have you considered *why* Kellie might be here?"

"I've thought many things. I know she's troubled. That's plain to see. Make her trust you, Tom. She's a good woman. I know it in my heart."

Twelve

Kellie stared out the window of bus number thirty-two. Time rolled back. Barbed wire curled around the new brick fence separating the Catholic Falls from the Protestant Shankill. The old row houses were gone now, replaced by identical brick dwellings on tidy streets. Tricycles and prams, rusted swing sets and tin cans, paper bags, pieces of raw wood and used brick littered the small treeless yards. Clotheslines stretched across every available space flouting sheets, table linens and nappies. Women, old before their time, accompanied schoolchildren with light eyes and pale skin, dressed in the plaid skirts and gray trousers that proclaimed their heritage, their religion and, above all, their politics. This was the Falls, a small enclave of Catholic life in the Protestant world of Ulster.

Not much had changed in fifteen years despite the Peace Accord and new civil rights for Catholics. Poverty didn't discriminate, not here in the blue-collar neighborhoods of her youth. The same jumble of streets, graffiti-covered walls, murals with portraits of martyrs and masked men imploring those who looked upon them to remember that Northern Ireland was an occupied country and the British were the enemy.

The bus stopped at the corner of the Springfield Road and Divas Street. The old bookstore was still there, flanked by the library and a shop specializing in religious icons. Kellie stepped off the platform and made her way down to where the Falls Road began. She hadn't called to say she was coming. She still wasn't sure that she would actually go through with it.

Her steps slowed as the familiar streets brought her closer and closer to her past. The small house the Delaney children had once called home sat close to the footpath. The door was painted red, a new bright touch. Even though the day was gray and drizzly, the windows were open, a habit Mary Delaney had cultivated to accommodate the male smokers in her family.

Tentatively, Kellie knocked on the door. Long seconds passed. She was very aware of her heart racing in her chest. Footsteps sounded behind the door. It opened and she stared into her mother's face.

Mrs. Delaney's eyes widened. Her mouth opened as if she would speak. She closed it without saying anything.

"Hello, Mam." Kellie could barely form the words.

"Hello, yourself." She held the door half open, her body barring the entrance.

"May I come in?"

Slowly, Mary moved aside. Kellie walked through the door and looked around. The dim light revealed that nothing had changed. The sagging couch was the same one where Kellie had curled up to learn her letters. The tea table and china closet were in the same spot on opposite sides of each other. Even the pictures on the mantel were the same. The only change was the television. It was a recent model, smaller and lighter than Kellie remembered. Just now it blared loudly announcing the contestants of a popular quiz show.

Her mother wiped her hands on her apron and turned it off. She waved Kellie to the couch. "Sit down."

Kellie sat. "How have you been?" she began.

"Just grand. And you?"

Kellie nodded. "I'm well enough, considering."

"How are you gettin' on without Connor and the boy?"

"I'm managing." Kellie's eyes were bright and dry.

Mrs. Delaney sat down across from her in a hard-backed chair. "Aye," she said softly. "No one should lose a child, especially not the good ones. It hasn't been easy to sleep at night. You haven't called in months. It isn't like you. I was beginnin' to worry."

The hard tight knot in Kellie's stomach began to dissolve. "Why didn't you come to Lizzie's funeral?"

"Connor didn't call me until the night before. I tried to call but no one answered. I can't talk into those machines."

"Would you have come?"

Her mother's gray eyes clouded. She wiped away a tear with the corner of her apron. "Aye," she whispered. "For that I would have come."

Kellie could no longer control the hurt. Her hands came up to cover her face. Tears fell through the spaces between her fingers. "I'm in trouble, Mam. Terrible trouble."

She felt the couch beside her give and heard her mother's words. "Tell me."

In a halting voice, Kellie began by describing her first meeting with Cecil Marsh and John Griffith. A smattering of sunlight filtered through the blinds as she continued, leaving nothing out, nothing except the events of the night before. She wasn't sure yet how to describe her feelings for Tom Whelan. She would wait a bit, put last night in the think-about-it-later portion of her brain until she was better able to sort it out.

Her mother's face had frozen into an expressionless horror. "Are you sayin' that Connor and Danny were murdered and you're tryin' to figure it out all by yourself?"

Kellie nodded. "I don't know what I'm doing anymore."

"These people don't play games, lass. You're in danger."

"I know."

"Why can't you just go home?"

"It's Tom's little girl. She's very ill. I can't just leave them. Besides, there's more. I want to know why Connor and Danny were killed. It isn't enough to know who did it." She looked helplessly at her mother. "I don't even know why it's so important to me. Maybe I'm being foolish. That's why I came home, Mam. I need your advice."

Mary's eyebrows rose. "Since when have you listened to me?" she muttered.

"I'm listening now," Kellie said softly.

Mary stood. "Come into the kitchen. I'll make a pot of tea."

Despite herself, Kellie smiled. Was there any darkness that couldn't be erased by a pot of her mother's tea? Kellie recognized the offering for what it was. A peace offering. She was back in the fold.

"You're in quite a spot, Kellie Delaney," her mother said when they were seated at the small table in the kitchen, the teapot between them.

Kellie nodded. The brew was strong and sweet and comforting.

"Tell me about Tom Whelan."

Color flooded Kellie's cheeks. "I believe he's a good man although he wasn't always."

"Show me a man who claims to be always good and I'll show you a liar," Mary said wryly.

"He loves his daughter very much and he's been kind to me."

"Why do you think he's tolerated you at all?"

"Curiosity. He wants to know why I'm staying in Banburren."

"Tell him," Mary suggested.

Kellie frowned. The idea had occurred to her. "I don't know."

"Why not? Two heads are better than one. If he's a good man he'll help you."

"What if by telling him, I'm putting him in danger?"

"I would say it's a bit late for that. You won't be

playing games with the likes of Dennis McGarrety for very long, love. Something must be done and done quickly. Tom Whelan is your best chance, perhaps the only one.''

''McGarrety had Connor and Danny killed.''

''Did he tell you that?''

''Not in so many words, but by implication.'' She looked at her mother. ''What do you think?''

Mary's face softened. She reached across the space separating them and squeezed her daughter's hand. ''I never did like the idea of Connor workin' for Scotland Yard. I wouldn't rule it out that McGarrety had it in for him.''

When it was time to leave, Mary didn't ask when she would see her daughter again and Kellie made no promises.

It was early afternoon when the bus dropped her on the Stranmillis Road. She let herself into the bed-and-breakfast, climbed the stairs and opened the door to the room she shared with Tom. The curtains were drawn against the feeble light. Kellie stretched out on the bed and closed her eyes.

Sleep evaded her. She tossed and turned and finally sat up. It occurred to her that Tom didn't know where she was. She looked at the clock. Half past two. He would be at the hospital with Heather. She wanted to be there, too, and wondered if Tom wanted her there or if she was encroaching where she didn't belong.

The thought of seeing him at the hospital with Susan and Heather didn't feel right. Still, he should know where she was. Kellie picked up the phone and punched in the number to the hospital.

Tom's first reaction was relief, his second, anger. "Don't do that again," he said fiercely.

Surprised by his vehemence, she apologized.

"Do you have any idea what I've been through?" he demanded.

"I'm sorry," she said again. "I didn't think."

"Where have you been?"

She nearly told him when she remembered that the room wasn't secure. "I'll tell you in a bit."

"Are you coming to the hospital?"

"Do you want me there?"

"Lord, yes."

There was no doubting his sincerity. "I'll be right there."

"I left the car for you."

"I'll shower first. Give me an hour."

"We'll be waiting."

She stepped into the shower smiling. He wanted her. *They* wanted her. She felt different, lighter, sharper, not quite happy. Happiness was too much of a step with everything else on her mind, but she was somewhere on the border of satisfied.

Kellie liked living with Tom and Heather. It was almost like being married. She liked the rituals, the regular meals, the sharing of dishes, of work space, the occasional conversations, the presence of another filling the empty space in a room.

Last night she'd slept her first dreamless, uninterrupted sleep in months. Kellie admitted that she was attracted to Tom Whelan, dangerously so. The line of courtesy they'd created had been crossed. The question now was could she trust him? What would happen to the two of them once he knew everything?

Trust was a learned response, Kellie decided, something entirely subjective depending on one's experience. It was against human nature to trust beyond the blood circle. Survival instincts dating from eons ago when man first walked upright precluded the very idea of leaving oneself open to danger, physical or otherwise. For Kellie, born into an unfriendly world where men and women watched their backs, trust did not come easily. Her decision to confide in Tom would not be a simple one to make.

She crossed the Malone Road, taking the back streets to the hospital.

Heather's doctor flagged her down in the car park. "How are you today, Mrs. Whelan?"

She'd forgotten Tom's fabrication. "Please, call me Kellie. I'm grand, thank you."

"Your daughter is progressing nicely. I'll be signing the release order tomorrow. Can you bear us for one more night?"

Kellie smiled warmly. She liked this unpretentious, frank-speaking young woman and she was embarrassed about the deception. "You've been lovely. Whatever is best for Heather will be fine."

"All the tests have come back and they look good. Don't coddle her," the doctor warned. "She'll be out of school for another two weeks or so, and she'll need more rest than usual but otherwise she should do what she normally does. Exercise is particularly important."

Kellie nodded. "I'll remember that."

"I've already spoken to your husband. I believe he's with Heather now."

"I'll go up and see them."

Tom stood when she walked into the room. The brief brushing of his lips across her own was new. It startled her. To cover her confusion, she avoided his eyes and went directly to Heather. "How are you, darling?"

The child's smile was strained. "I want to go home."

"You shall, but not until tomorrow. Is that soon enough for you?"

"I want to go now."

Kellie sat down on the bed. Careful to avoid the IV attached to the little girl's hand, she drew Heather gently into her arms. "I know, love. But you've had a serious operation and you need to be completely fixed before we can take you home."

"When will I stop hurting?"

"Every day it will get a bit better," Kellie promised, "and in about two weeks you won't even remember the hurt at all. Then you can go back to school and be with your friends."

Heather thought a minute, her face grave. "Everyone will be very surprised when I tell them what happened to me."

"Without a doubt, you'll be the talk of the school."

Heather held up her hand. "May I bring my hospital bracelet and show it?"

"You may."

She leaned back against the pillow. "I'll stay until tomorrow."

"Good girl."

The nurse arrived with a wheelchair. "This won't take long," she promised, "but you'll have to leave for now. I'll be taking Heather to the laboratory for a bit, just to check things out before her release."

"How long?" Tom asked.

"About an hour."

"We'll be back." He took Kellie's arm and walked with her down the hall and into the lobby.

"Have you had lunch?" she asked.

"No."

"Neither have I. There's a pub nearby that has reasonable food. We could eat now and skip dinner later."

They walked side by side down the wide street. "How well do you know East Belfast?" Tom asked.

"I grew up in the Falls, but I know the east as well because of Queen's."

He whistled under his breath. "A girl from West Belfast who went to Queen's University. Have you always been out of the ordinary?"

Kellie considered the question. "Yes," she said, after a bit, "although I would have called myself odd. The connotation is different."

"I see what you mean. I imagine it was difficult for you to have aspirations to an education."

"My mother encouraged me and the nuns helped."

"How many of you were there?"

"Seven. I'm in the middle. I don't see them regularly."

Tom's eyebrows lifted. "Why is that?"

"I'm not sure, really. We drifted apart when I went to university."

"Belfast isn't large enough to drift apart."

She took a deep breath, feeling like an exposed onion whose layers have been peeled away. "It was after I left for England."

"How long were you there?"

"Four years."

He nodded. "How old are you, Kellie?"

She laughed. After all they'd shared, the basics were still unknowns. "Thirty-five."

"You look younger. I would have said ten years younger."

"I think there's a window where not much changes. It will catch up with me, I imagine."

His lips twitched. "Undoubtedly."

The pub was dim, upscale, with cozy candlelit booths arranged for privacy. Stained-glass windows filtered in amber, rose and golden light. A fire burned in the hearth and the long wooden bar gleamed with polish and care.

Several tables were occupied by young people, obviously students, and at the bar solitary men sat nursing their pints.

Tom slid into the booth beside her. "Very nice. Was this one of your old haunts?"

Kellie shook her head. "I found this yesterday. Fifteen years ago when I was in school this place didn't exist. Belfast, as you probably know, was a war zone."

He did know. He remembered it all too well—the bombed-out ruins that once were buildings, burning lorries, limbs strewn amidst the rubble, British soldiers on every corner, tanks patrolling the streets, sullen youths perpetually unemployed loitering aimlessly and eager for trouble. At thirty-five Kellie had been a mere two years behind him. Where had she been, he wondered, during those difficult days? When had she made the leap that took her away from it all and what had brought her back? "I want to thank you for being here for Heather and me," he said.

A flag of red colored her cheeks. "If you're referring to last night, I wouldn't exactly call it an act of compassion."

"What would you call it?"

She looked directly at him, eyes wide and clear and silvery gray. "Lust," she said softly and smiled. "You're very attractive and it's been a long time for me. I miss having someone touch me."

He stared at her, stunned. Then he threw back his head and laughed. Several heads turned in their direction. "Good lord," he said, "I can't believe you said that. It's so completely out of character."

She reached for the menu. "Not really. There's quite a bit you don't know about me."

"That I believe."

Again her words surprised him. "I think I'm going to tell you everything."

His stomach clenched. Afraid to breathe, afraid that his slightest move would make her change her mind, he waited.

Thirteen

"First, I'd like a glass of white wine, the steamed mussels and a salad. If we order now, we won't be disturbed." She spoke clearly, calmly, her voice filled with purpose. It was a new side of her, a woman sure of herself, with a cool, intent resolve.

"I'll be right back," he said. Pushing his chair away from the table, he stood, walked to the bar and ordered. It gave him a moment to think, to clarify his questions, the important ones that must be asked in case she changed her mind before he'd learned what he needed to know.

But when he was seated across from her again, their food untouched, there was no need for him to say anything at all. Once she began talking everything became terrifyingly clear.

Her words were deliberate, cold, pitched so that only he could hear. "My twin brother, Connor, worked for British Intelligence. We were very close. His wife died shortly after their only child was born. I went to Oxford for the funeral and ended up staying. Connor really needed me. I had no idea that my brother was anything more than a criminologist. I wondered how he could live so well, but I didn't really give it much thought. He'd planned a vacation in

Wales with his son. Shortly after they left, a police officer told me there had been an auto accident, no survivors.'' Her voice caught, choking the words.

Tom watched her leave him and go somewhere else in her mind, a survival instinct she must have learned to separate herself from the pain of her memory. He knew it well.

''He was taking Danny to the coast for a holiday when the brakes failed.''

Tom realized this was the point where he should have expressed sympathy but somehow he knew she couldn't bear it. ''Were they cut?'' he asked instead.

''Yes.''

''Then what?''

''A man named John Griffith came to see me. He said Connor was working on something and he needed access to his home computer. I wasn't comfortable but I allowed him in the house.'' She grimaced. ''It's absurd, really. As if those people need permission to enter a house. Maybe it was easier than sneaking around. That's when I found Connor's passports in the garage as well as some very revealing correspondence.'' She looked directly at him. ''Your name was on two receipts.''

''My name?'' Tom's eyebrows rose.

Kellie nodded. ''At first I didn't know what to do. I hid everything in my car. Then I picked up his suit at the cleaners. On a piece of paper in his coat pocket was a phone number.''

''Let me guess. It was mine.''

Again she nodded. ''I visited Connor's office. John Griffith was there with another man, Cecil Marsh. I implied that I knew more than I did. That's when they went a step further and told me his death was intentional, that the brakes were cut. I told them about the receipts. Basically, they told me they had bigger fish to fry than to focus on Connor's murder investigation." Her eyes were wide and very bright. "Their disregard infuriated me. That's when I came here."

The unasked question hung between them, so obvious it was almost physical. Finally, he asked it. "Did you think it was me?"

"At first, yes, especially when I learned about the life you once led."

"What changed your mind?"

"Two things." She sipped her wine. Her hands shook. "Living with you, watching you with Heather and Lexi, listening to your music. I don't believe you would do such a thing."

"Thank you for that."

"My intuition was confirmed when I was approached by Dennis McGarrety."

He laughed shortly. "Is he still around? I haven't heard anything from Dennis in a long time. The IRA is nearly an anachronism. But you already know that."

"How would I know such a thing?"

"By reading the newspapers and visiting your family in Belfast. Paramilitaries no longer have the support of the community. The population is intent on peace. Without community support the IRA can't exist." Even to his own ears his voice sounded harsh.

The desolation in her voice chilled him. "Why did my brother have your number in his pocket?"

Tom pushed his food away. "I don't know. I've never heard of Connor Delaney."

"You do know Austin Groves?"

The name sounded familiar. He thought a minute and remembered. "The man who ordered the pipes."

"Yes."

"Austin Groves is your brother?"

"That was the name on one of his passports."

Tom frowned, trying to recreate his telephone conversations with the man. Was there something he'd missed? Finally, he shook his head. "We spoke of nothing except specifics about his instrument. He was the man with a sister who loved the pipes. Are you that sister?"

"Yes."

"I'm sorry, Kellie."

Her eyes shone with hope. "That's it? You had no association other than a pipe order?"

He hated to wipe the light from her eyes. It was rare enough. "There's more, Kellie. Surely you can see that. It's all too coincidental. Your brother wanted something from me and he made contact through the pipe order. It would be a mistake to believe otherwise."

"Dennis McGarrety had him killed."

Tom's eyes narrowed. "Did he tell you that?"

She swallowed and lifted her water glass to her lips. Her hand shook.

"Not exactly. He told me to go home, that you were in danger. He said Connor gave his life for a man who would change the direction of Northern Ireland."

He leaned forward. "We've got to sort this out, Kellie. It's clear that your brother was on to something and that it involved me. Otherwise you wouldn't have been approached or threatened by McGarrety."

"What shall we do?"

"There are still a few out there who will talk to me."

She relaxed. She'd been right to trust him. They were in this together. Her heart lifted. For the first time in months she allowed herself to hope. Kellie picked up her fork. His next question shattered her fragile security.

"When this is over will you go back to Oxford?"

Her mind went blank. *When this is over.* She hadn't thought about it, never once considered it. "I don't know, really," she said. "I don't think so." The idea was not appealing. She didn't want to go back to the same streets, the same city where Connor and Danny were part of her life. The memories crowded in on her. She didn't trust herself to speak.

Tom's voice reached out to her, flooding her senses like warm oil on chapped hands. "You don't have to think about it now. We'll worry about it when the time comes."

She nodded and pushed the mussels around on her plate with her fork.

He reached out and gripped her hand. "We'll sort this out, Kellie. I promise you we will."

She looked at him, her eyes bright. "But what will be left when it's over?"

"No one can predict the future, but that's true for

anyone. We'll take what comes and see what happens.''

''Do we have a choice?''

''No.'' He grinned, and suddenly everything seemed possible.

Heather was very weak. Caring for her consumed Kellie's time to such a degree that her own plight was pushed to the back of her mind. The entire household revolved around the little girl's comfort. Even Lexi sensed that all was not as it should be. She lay beside Heather's bed, motionless, her head resting on her paws, her eyes alert.

Tirelessly, Kellie created confectionery delights in the kitchen, read stories endlessly and played board games until her mind froze with the monotony of it. When she could take no more she changed places with Tom, grabbed Lexi's leash and walked down lovely country lanes where green hills covered with gorse rose before her. She'd forgotten how lovely Ireland could be when the days lengthened and the weather turned from bone-chilling to brisk, when lads rode bicycles and pitched coins into the rivers, when mist lay like gray smoke over the land, when priests played hurling in the streets and flocks of sheep crowded the main roads, slowing traffic to a crawl. Banburren, a community with a Nationalist population, seemed very far away from the hostile environment Kellie remembered from her childhood.

The walks stimulated her, the cold and the hills stretching her body and sharpening her mind. It was then that she considered her predicament, racking her brain to reach some solution. Nothing came to her.

Schoolchildren lingered on the streets and shops were as crowded as they would ever be in Banburren. Lovely Kate, Tom's sister-in-law, waved to her from the market. Keeping a firm hold on Lexi's leash, Kellie crossed the street and met her at the entrance.

"How lovely to run into you," Kate said. "Do you have time for tea?"

Touched by the rare invitation, Kellie nodded. Kate was always friendly but she'd never extended herself in Kellie's direction. "I'd love it if you don't mind Lexi."

"Of course not. You can tie her up by the door. Everyone knows Lexi. I'll just leave my purchases in the car and we can walk together."

"How is Heather?" Kate asked when they were seated at a small table.

"Much better. She'll be back at school next Monday."

"That's grand. Poor little love." She shrugged out of her coat and looked around. "What I wouldn't give for a cup of *Bewley's*."

"You'll have to go back to Dublin for that."

Kate sighed. "It's tempting."

Kellie sipped her tea. "Why don't you go back? Banburren is lovely, but wouldn't Dublin offer you more?"

Kate's eyes, very green and fringed with thick black lashes, narrowed. "In terms of culture and entertainment, I suppose that's true. However, teachers aren't paid all that well. It's less expensive to live here. Besides, the Whelans are here and they're all the family I have anymore." She smiled brightly. "How is the job at the library coming along?"

"It isn't. Not since Heather's illness."

"Where is she now?"

"At home, with Tom."

Kate hesitated.

"What is it?" Kellie asked.

"Never mind. It's nothing."

Kellie didn't know her well enough to continue to persuade her.

"Oh, all right." Kate shook her head and the dark curls spilled over her shoulders. "I wonder how you're managing with Tom. After all, it's been seven years since he's lived with a woman. Has it been difficult for you?"

Kellie considered the young woman seated across from her taking in the glossy dark hair, the perfect features, the clear skin and the color coming and going in her cheeks. She really was lovely. It was possible that she was merely curious, but there was something else, too. An odd emotion, rusty and long-buried rose within her. "Not difficult," she said carefully, "but cautious."

"Are you—" she hesitated "—involved?"

Kellie stared at her.

"We all thought you were," Kate said quickly.

"All?"

"Maggie and everyone."

"I see."

"Don't be upset. It isn't that we're talking behind your back."

"Of course not." Kellie smiled sweetly.

"Tom surprised us, that's all, falling for you so quickly."

Kellie picked up a spoon and stirred her tea. "Who was most surprised?"

"I couldn't say, really," Kate stammered. "My goodness, you do ask the most peculiar questions."

The anger simmering in Kellie's chest leaped to life. "I have one that's even more peculiar."

"What is it?"

"Did you have aspirations in that direction, Kate?"

"No," she said, a bit too sharply. The red deepened in her cheeks.

Kellie continued to smile. "I'm relieved to hear that."

A voice called out, interrupting them. "Hello, you, two. What a lovely surprise."

Susan Whelan waved from the door.

"Susan!" Kate jumped up and pulled out another chair. "Please, join us."

The older woman shook her head, took one look at Kate's face and another at Kellie's and changed her mind. "I wouldn't object to a cup of strong tea," she said and sat down.

Kellie had passed the point of diplomacy. "We were just discussing how my coming to Banburren was a shock to everyone, especially since Tom was a confirmed bachelor."

"Nonsense," said Susan. "I don't remember anyone saying anything like that."

Kate hurried to explain herself. "It's just that we thought Tom had sworn off women after Claire."

Susan looked astonished. "Why Kate Whelan. Who would think such a thing?"

"Maggie, for one," said Kate, now on the defensive.

Susan chuckled. "Maggie and Claire were close friends. I imagine it's difficult for her to accept that Tom may have moved on and left Claire behind."

"Tom said it, too."

A cold, sharp pain settled in Kellie's stomach.

Susan looked at Kate for a long moment before she turned to Kellie. "I imagine Tom has changed his mind since then. What do you think, Kellie, love?"

Kellie wet her lips. "I really can't speak for Tom."

"Of course you can. You're quite close. Besides," Susan reached over and squeezed Kellie's hand, "the man's in love. Anyone with eyes can see that."

Kate looked at her watch. "Well, now that we have that settled, it's time for me to be going. It's been lovely, Kellie. We'll do it again. Goodbye, Susan." She left without looking back.

"My goodness," said Susan when they were alone. "That was a surprise."

Kellie nodded.

Susan drank her tea. "It's for the best. Now she's properly rousted. I was wondering how to do it gently, but perhaps she needed a more direct approach."

Kellie laughed. "Why doesn't that make me feel better?"

Susan's keen eyes pinned her. "You've no need to be jealous, lass. If he wanted her, it would have happened long ago."

Her stomach twisted. "I'm not jealous."

"Of course not." Susan's voice brimmed with amusement.

"It would be ridiculous to be jealous. We're beyond that."

"No one is beyond that. There's nothing wrong with not wanting anyone fawning over your man. It's only natural."

"He's not—"

"Don't say it, Kellie," Susan warned her. "It will make it so."

"That's superstitious and ridiculous."

"You're a lovely woman. My granddaughter is content and my son has another chance for happiness. That's all that matters."

"What if—?"

"Don't borrow trouble. Take the days as they come. Let Tom help you. It's time you trusted someone."

Kellie begged a bowl of water for Lexi before turning down the road that led to the long way home. She needed to run, to feel the ground swallowed up beneath her, the burn in the back of her throat, the cramp in her calves. She craved the physical test of endurance, the numbing anesthetic of exercise to mitigate her conversation with Kate. *Jealous.* The word itself had a dreadful ring. Was she jealous? If so, what did it mean?

Heather was sleeping when Kellie finally arrived home. Tom was in the sitting room cleaning out the fireplace. The room was cool and dim. An odd resentment rose in Kellie's throat.

"You're home," he said, sitting back on his heels. "I was beginning to worry about you."

"In Banburren?"

He frowned, wiped his hands free of ash and stood. "You know what I mean." He waited for her reply. She said nothing. "Where were you, Kellie?"

"I met Kate and your mother in town. We stopped for tea and then Lexi and I went for a run."

"My mother and Kate were together?" He looked surprised.

"No. Susan came later. It was a coincidence."

Tom's eyes flicked over her, his gaze measuring, assessing. "Is something wrong?" he asked at last.

"Nothing." She sat down on the couch and began to unlace her hiking shoes. She didn't want to tell him, not just yet. A part of her wanted him to worry, to share the insecurity carving a hole in the pit of her stomach. The other part, the mature reasonable part, wanted to clear up the problem and settle into the normal, comfortable routine that had become her life with Tom and Heather.

He sat across from her and picked up the newspaper. She stood and walked into the kitchen. Turning up the flame under the kettle, she opened the refrigerator. His step sounded in the hall, passing the kitchen, continuing into his study. Such casual unconcern inflamed her even more. Pulling out the vegetables she'd planned for lunch, she opened the cupboard and pushed aside a stack of pans, searching for the soup pot. The clatter was loud and satisfying.

Lexi, sprawled out under the table, moaned in protest. She imagined Tom walking into the kitchen, imagined him asking, again, if anything was wrong, demanding to know why she was upset. This time she would tell him.

She waited. No Tom. Disappointed and more than a little annoyed, she pulled out a platter from the cupboard above her head, knocking over several glasses in the process. Two of them tumbled out, shattering on the tile counter. She picked up a large shard. Blood seeped from her middle finger. Tears sprang to her eyes.

She heard him walk down the hall and into the kitchen. "Let me look at that," he said from behind her.

Kellie shook her head. "It's nothing."

He reached for a paper towel, turned her around and examined her finger. Then he pressed the towel against the cut. "I imagine you'll survive," he teased.

She nodded. He lifted her chin and his voice changed. "You're crying. Surely it isn't that bad."

Her lip trembled.

"Kellie," his voice was low, intimate. "Tell me what's bothering you."

"Why, so you can run over and discuss it with Kate?"

"What are you talking about?"

She bit her lip. Even to her own ears she sounded childish, petulant. Still, she'd gone this far. "She said you didn't want Claire to come back, that you had sworn off women for good."

"That's right," he admitted. "Why should that bother you?"

Tears poured down her cheeks as the irrational words spilled from her mouth. "You're talking about me, about us," she amended, "with another woman."

"That was a long time ago, Kellie, long before you came," he said patiently. "We were discussing Claire, not you. I haven't had a personal conversation with Kate in nearly two years."

She hiccupped and wiped her eyes with the back of her hand. "Why not?"

"Because it isn't appropriate. She's my sister-in-law, my brother's wife. Because I have no interest in leading her on or making her believe there can ever be anything between us."

"Is she in love with you?"

"Of course not. Our relationship doesn't extend beyond family gatherings or accidental meetings in town. She's never even been here."

"I don't think she would see it that way."

"Then she's a fool." He brushed her cheek with his hand. "Don't be an idiot, Kellie. If I had any intentions toward Kate it would have happened long ago."

Susan had said the same thing. Kellie was embarrassed. What was he thinking?

"You're jealous." His voice was soft, filled with wonder.

She nodded. "I'm sorry."

Gently, reverently, he traced the bones of her face with his fingers. "I'm not." Lowering his head, he kissed her. She leaned into him, opening, responding, kissing him back until he pulled away, his eyes narrowed, his breath short. "God help you if you don't mean this," he said.

Sliding her arms around his neck, she pulled him toward her once again.

Fourteen

Susan Whelan reached down into the cool earth, positioned the seed, covered it with soil and moved to the next row in her garden. She was so intent on her task that she didn't see her only living son open the gate and make his way to where she worked.

His voice, rich and pure and easy on the ear, interrupted her. "Hello, Mam."

"Tom." She looked up and squinted. "You startled me. Whatever are you doing here this time of morning?"

"I wanted to catch you alone."

"I'm always alone."

Tom laughed. "You're never alone."

Susan pressed her hand against her back and stood. "Age is difficult, Tom. Don't ever get old."

Tom looked at his mother, at her trim figure, her hair, silvery-dark, cut in a neat bob and the clear, unwrinkled skin. "You're not old, Mam. Even when you're old, you'll never be really old."

"Thank you," she said, truly pleased. "Come inside. I'll make a pot of tea and you can tell me why you wanted to see me *alone*." She pronounced the word as if it were mysterious, almost forbidden.

Fortified with a cup of tea and a healthy portion of

his mother's biscuits, he looked around the warm kitchen. There was something about a woman's kitchen, a brightness and a warmth that calmed the spirit, soothed the soul. Tea and biscuits, his mother's cure for whatever ailed. He watched her move from the stove to the refrigerator to the counter and back again. Susan Whelan never sat. She was constantly in motion, a condition that hadn't changed in all the years Tom could remember. He didn't know how to begin. It was difficult for him. It would be difficult for her.

"Tell me about Claire," he said at last.

She stopped in midstep. "I'm sorry?"

"I know you see her, Mam."

"I've never denied it."

"Does she ever talk about me?"

Susan was silent.

"Does she ever wish it was different?"

She was looking at him now, her eyes wide and blue and angry. "Claire never was a deep thinker, Tom. There's only the one thing you ever had in common."

"Heather?"

"I'm not talking about Heather. I'm talking about sex. You and Claire had that between you and that's all. I never thought you would get around to marrying."

"What did you expect me to do?"

"What everyone else in your generation did. Live with the woman. Get it out of your system and then settle down with someone more suitable." Susan slumped down into a chair. "Good lord. I didn't mean to say all that."

"Why do you visit her?"

Susan stared at her son. "She has no one else."

"They're paroling prisoners, you know. She won't be there forever."

Susan looked down at her hands. *"Sooner than you think,"* she said, "She's going to be released, Tom. Prepare yourself for that. It's a given."

"Will she come back here?"

"Why don't you ask her?" said his mother.

"We both know why."

"They have visiting hours at Maidenstone."

"I'm not going to her, hat in hand anymore, Mam. She left me. I'm over her."

"Are you, Tom?"

"Aye."

They were silent for a bit, staring out the window, sipping tea, lost in their own thoughts.

"I won't stay here," he said at last, "not if she does."

"If that's the way it is, you're not really over her."

"Do you think it shouldn't matter?"

"Aye. I think it shouldn't, not after all this time."

He was silent.

Susan sighed. Some things were beyond her control. One didn't reach old age without learning that. Tom would do what he must. She would have to trust that it would all come about. It usually did. "What of Kellie?"

"I don't know."

His mother's lips tightened. "You don't know much lately, do you, Tom?"

"You're hard on me, Mam."

Susan broke the biscuit on her plate into little pieces. It was a sin to waste food. Her mother had told her that long ago when she was a girl, but Ireland was different then. Now, it wasn't so important that she crumbled biscuits on her plate and washed them down the drain. "What are your intentions toward this woman?"

"My intentions? Does anyone ask that anymore?"

"I just did. Don't be fresh."

"I don't know. We're brand-new. We barely know each other."

"You don't know the specifics, but you know her. Living with each other should have told you enough."

"All right, Mam. I know her. I just don't know what to do about her yet."

"Does she make you happy?"

"Lord, yes."

"Then you know what to do."

"It isn't as simple as that."

"Why not?"

"She's a person. Her wishes matter, too. She's an educated woman. What kind of life would I be offering her here in Banburren?"

"You might give her the choice."

"And be rejected."

His mother looked at him astonished. "I would never have taken you for a coward, Thomas."

He'd had enough. He stood abruptly, kissed his

mother's cheek and strode toward the door. "Goodbye, Mam. I'll leave you to your garden."

"Think about what I said," she called after him.

She smiled, not just with her mouth but with her eyes, too, a woman slender and soft with eyes the color of light rain. She was cleaning the stove. "How is your mother?"

He laughed. "Filled with advice."

"Isn't that why you went to see her?"

Tom poured himself a cup of tea and sat down at the table. "Not exactly. I went for information, but she threw in a bit of advice as well. She always does."

"Mine, too. It comes with being a mother."

Tom was immediately caught. "Tell me about your mother."

She rubbed out an offending spot. "There's nothing to tell, really. There were seven of us, all troubled, except Connor and me. We were her pride and joy. She wanted me to go on to university, to leave Belfast, and I did."

"Do you see her often?"

Kellie shook her head. "Almost never."

"When is the last time you visited?"

"A few days ago, actually. While you were with Heather, I went to see her. She lives alone, now. I have one older sister. The boys are all gone, dead or emigrated to America."

She was so matter-of-fact. It couldn't have been pleasant for her, growing up, moving away, losing her first family. Expectations were low for Catholics in the Six Counties, but Kellie's were lower than most.

He watched her, appreciating her efficient movements, the tendency toward perfectionism. The hunger that affected him when she was near began again. What was it about the skin at the nape of a woman's neck, the dip at her waist, the curve where her shoulder met her arm? Tom recognized desire for what it was. He was thirty-seven years old and the last seven of those years had been dry ones.

She was attracted to him. He knew that. But he wanted more and he knew enough to realize that sex would only make it more difficult when she left, if she left. Still, the wanting was there and he knew, if she was willing, that he would take her, here and now, in his kitchen, while his daughter slept peacefully in the other room. Was she willing?

"Kellie," he rasped, the word catching in his throat.

She turned. Their eyes met and her cheeks burned. Deliberately, he stood and walked toward her. Taking her hand in his, he pressed his mouth to her palm. "Do you know what I'm wanting, Kellie?" he murmured against her ear.

"Yes." Her answer was soft, muffled.

He kissed her, gently at first, and then not so gently. His hands moved over her back and down, pressing her close, deepening his kiss. She reached for him, twining her arms around his neck. Heat flared between them. They stood for long moments, holding each other, familiarizing themselves with the weight of each other, the swell of breast, the length of muscle.

Her hands slid under his shirt, boldly exploring the lean, solid strength of him, the bend of his shoulder, the position of his spine, her hands moving, always moving, to the pelt of hair on the wall of his chest and down the flat plane of stomach. Her fingers moved below his belt, down to the hair-rough skin, curling around the smooth, thick heat of him.

He tensed and froze, wanting more, fearing more. What was it about her that made him want her so? Lifting her into his arms, he carried her down the hall and into his bedroom. Pushing the door shut with his foot, he laid her on the bed. She looked up at him, eyes wide and wise, neither resisting nor encouraging.

"What if I can't stay?" she asked him.

"Do you want to stay?"

She nodded. "Now, yes."

He brushed the hair back away from her face, following with his lips where his fingers touched, the side of her neck, her ear, her cheekbone, the slide of her nose, the seam of her lips.

She reached up and pulled him down on top of her, opening her arms and her mouth, helping him with her clothes. It was incredibly easy, the preparations for loving, the separation of buttons, the cool smoothness of sheets, the mounting anticipation, fingers walking across sensitive skin, the length and heat and strength of a man's desire, sensations found and lost and found again in the swirling moments before it all came together, the purpose for life, the simple amazing act that made everything possible.

"Do you love me?" he asked when it was over.

"Yes."

He laughed softly and pulled her closer so that her head rested on the bulge of his shoulder. Her breath was warm against his skin. The hair under his hand was silky and tangled. The memory of Claire was very far away. She was Kellie, his Kellie, a woman finer and deeper than Claire had ever been.

"Well?" he heard her say.

"Well, what?"

"You asked me if I loved you. The logical response is 'I love you, too.' Do you?"

"Of course I do."

She sat up on her elbow. "That isn't enough for me, Tom. I need to hear the words."

He cupped her face in his hands. "I love you, Kellie. I want you to stay with me or I'll go with you. Whatever you like."

"Do you mean that?"

"I do."

She relaxed against him. "I've worried about that for a while now. I know it's ridiculous to worry about the future when nothing is settled."

Her tone, matter-of-fact and resigned, chilled him. He tightened his arms around her. "Don't say that. We'll sort this out."

"Do you have a plan?"

"I'm going to find Dennis McGarrety. He's not easy to track down, but I'll manage it somehow.

"Can you think of anything that might have happened in your past that might connect you with something?"

"Many things, but no one thing. I'm sure he'll enlighten me."

Kellie had had enough of darkness. She changed the subject. "I've never heard you play the pipes in public. May I?"

He stroked her thigh, enjoying the sensation of soft, smooth skin. "You're always welcome to come with me although it won't be much different than my practice sessions."

"I've read your poetry, but only on your computer. Will you show me where you're published?"

He kissed her ear. "If you like. Don't be expecting another Seamus Heaney or William Yeats. I'm not in that league."

"Publishing alone is a tremendous accomplishment. You should be proud of yourself. I'm proud of you."

"Thank you. But this is Ireland. Everyone is published. Words are our strength."

She laughed and the sound settled, warm and right, around his heart.

"Everyone isn't published," she corrected him, "and you're much too modest. I want to read your poetry in an official publication. Tell me you'll show it to me."

"I will," he promised. It was lovely sharing with her, lovely to release the truth and hold nothing back, to hold her beside him in the middle of the day, naked and willing, lazy and sated.

Footsteps sounded in the hall. He felt the muscles of her shoulders tense.

"Heather," she whispered.

He pulled the sheet up, covering both of them.

The door opened and Heather peeked in. "Da," she said reproachfully, "I couldn't find you."

"We're here, love."

"Are you sick?"

"No."

"Why are you and Kellie in bed?"

"We took a nap."

She thought a minute and then nodded. "Are you rested?"

His voice was laced with amusement. "Are we rested, love?" he asked Kellie.

"I think so."

"Turn on the telly, Heather. We'll be up and about in a minute."

"I'm hungry."

"That's grand. Run along now and we'll be there in a minute."

They waited until she'd left the room. Kellie buried her face in his shoulder. "Do you think she saw the clothes?"

"It doesn't matter. She takes off her clothes when she goes to bed. Children are remarkably logical."

Kellie lifted her head. "You're not embarrassed at all, are you?"

"Not a bit. I'm only sorry she didn't sleep longer. But there's always tonight." He watched the smile begin at the corners of her mouth. She wanted him. The last lingering kernel of his doubt dissolved.

Heather's lower lip trembled. She stood at the door in a clean blouse and jumper, her jacket zipped, her book bag at her feet. "I don't think I'm well enough to go to school."

"Of course you are," Tom said bracingly.

"What if I'm sick at school?"

"Your teacher will call us," Kellie said.

"Will you come for me right away?"

"Immediately," Kellie promised. "We'll race right down there and pick you up straight away."

A reluctant smile tugged at the child's mouth. "You won't."

"We will," Tom assured her. "We'll take our marks and be there before you can say, 'God save Liam Parnell.'"

"His name isn't Liam, Da," Heather informed him scornfully. "Everyone knows that."

"Do they?" Tom looked amazed. "Isn't education a grand thing?" He appealed to Kellie. "My daughter is smarter than I am."

"Da, you're teasing me." Heather laughed and shouldered her bag. "I'm ready."

Tom took her hand. "Is there anything you need while I'm out?" he asked Kellie.

"Nothing," she assured him. "Don't rush back if you have something to do. I'm going to read that book you left out for me." She'd found a volume of his poetry on the nightstand when she woke that morning.

He grimaced. "Don't be too hard on me."

Her eyes danced and his heart lifted. She was happy. He was making her happy.

"I'll be as kind as possible," she promised.

* * *

Kellie shook out the damp dish towel and hung it over a chair, swept the floor and deposited the crumbs in the trash container. Settling herself in a chair close to the window, she decided against artificial light. She opened the slim leather-bound volume of poems and began to read. The words drew her in and for the next hour she was completely absorbed in the unique voice of what her training told her was a natural storyteller.

For Kellie, poetry had always been slow going. She took time to savor the words, look up and breathe deeply, think about the metaphors and the literal meaning, go back and read the forward and the credits. It was important to know what was in a poet's head before attempting his verse. In her hurry to read his words, she'd skipped Tom's forward, believing she knew him well enough. But now she changed her mind, flipping back to the beginning. The pages were thin, delicate, gold-embossed, a lovely package of a book.

Something fluttered to the floor. It was a photo. She picked it up. A woman with large, light eyes in a provocative pose stared back at her. An inscription was scrawled across the bottom. *May I always be your inspiration. Love, Claire.*

So this was Claire. A beauty by anyone's standards. *Love, Claire.*

The words bothered her. She wasn't a child, nor was she naive. Surely Tom and Claire had loved each other. Why would they have married? And just as surely, those feelings no longer existed between them. But why was her picture in the front of his book, published years after his wife was incarcerated? A cold fist closed around Kellie's heart.

Fifteen

Banburren was in the throes of preparing for its annual wedding festival. Entertainment would be in the form of musicians from all over Ireland. Every restaurant, convenience store and pub proprietor was polishing, painting and refurbishing his premises. Food preparation was at its peak. Kitchens and bakeries hummed with activity. Every lodging house, bed-and-breakfast and Banburren's single hotel was booked to capacity.

Kellie, in addition to her usual duties, had committed herself to a marbled cheesecake and three dozen butterscotch squares for the occasion. Three of Tom's guest rooms were booked with young women from America. They'd arrived the day before the three-day festival. With new sheets and towels and breakfast to prepare every day, neither Tom nor Kellie had a moment to think of anything else.

There was much more to running a guest house than Kellie had imagined. Silver had to be polished and linens ironed. Cereals and fresh fruit, dear this time of year, were purchased, sliced and set out. A hot breakfast of eggs, bacon, sausage, toast, juice and grilled tomatoes was offered in fine china every day. Fresh flowers sat on the dining table, now converted to a breakfast room, and brochures for sights within driving distance were displayed on a rack in the hallway.

Rising with Tom at six in the morning to prepare breakfast, Kellie didn't sit down to a cup of tea and hot toast until noon when the last bed was covered with new sheets and every pillow fluffed.

"Is it worth it?" she asked Tom the second morning after their guests had arrived. They had flown past each other in the hallway, he carrying laundry for the wash, she with clean sheets.

"I think so," he said. "The money helps. I could manage without renting the rooms, but a cushion is a grand thing to have."

"I suppose so." Kellie looked doubtful.

He laughed. "Don't try and convince me that twenty-five seven-year-olds are easier to manage than nine adults from America."

She thought a minute. "Oddly enough, they are. Teaching has rules and a curriculum that teachers must teach. Nothing goes as planned here. Someone is allergic to milk, another is a vegetarian. The water is too hot or there isn't enough of it. For pity's sake, this is Ireland. They're lucky to have hot water at all." Her lips twitched. "I sound like a dreadful complainer, don't I?"

"You sound like a woman who would never run a bed-and-breakfast."

She laughed. "That, too."

He reached out a hand to stroke her cheek. "Have you considered staying here in Banburren permanently?"

She caught his hand. ''That would be premature, don't you think?''

''No. I don't.''

She said nothing.

''Am I going too fast for you?''

''Under normal circumstances, no. We aren't children.''

''Something's troubling you.''

The picture of Claire was burned in Kellie's memory. She hadn't brought it up because, instinctively, she knew the discussion would be a serious one and there was a chance the outcome would not be the one she would have chosen. She smiled. ''No. It's nothing.''

His eyes moved across her face. ''You would tell me, wouldn't you?''

''Of course.''

He kissed her lightly on the lips. ''I love you, Kellie.''

She held on to the words. Throughout the day, she would recall them, savoring them, believing them. Could a man who touched her the way Tom did, who said the words he said still be involved with another woman? Her heart told her no. But her mind wouldn't let the doubts rest. She and Claire were similar in type, bone structure, eyes and coloring. An ugly niggling doubt told her that her resemblance to Claire was a good part of the reason Tom was attracted to her.

Reason told her it didn't matter. She wasn't Claire, not her mind, her interests or her actions. What did it matter why Tom had taken a second look as long as he liked what continued to unfold. There were huge chunks of the day when she didn't think of anything at all except that fate had brought her to this man, this child, this town. Her nearly rabid desire to rid herself of the taint of Northern Ireland was gone. Five years and the Good Friday Agreement had worked wonders. The hostility she'd grown up with no longer existed in Banburren. People lived, worked and prayed on their own side, but they shopped, visited and recreated together, regardless of religious lines. Quite simply, she was happy. She could see herself settling in, helping to run a bed-and-breakfast, loving Tom, caring for Heather, perhaps teaching at one of the local schools.

There was one large flaw in her plan. Tom was married. Claire Whelan would eventually have to be dealt with. Kellie kept up with the news. Prisoners incarcerated for political crimes were being released according to the terms of the Good Friday Agreement. Where else would a woman go, but home? There would be a reckoning. Either Tom was ignoring the obvious or he hadn't thought it through. Kellie wasn't and she had. There would be a time when he would have to choose. Until she was unconditionally sure he would choose her, she would hold on to the possibility that her months in Banburren would be a lovely memory to be dusted off and held up at some future date when she could look at it again without pain.

She was frosting the butterscotch squares when Heather walked through the door. Kellie kissed her cheek and handed her what was left of the bowl of butterscotch icing. "Hello, love. How was school?"

The child's cheeks were flushed and her eyes sparkled. "Grand. I'm to dance a solo tonight. Miss Mooney says my steps are graceful and confident." She mimicked the dance teacher's high voice.

"That's wonderful. Have you told your da?"

"Not yet. He's setting up tables on High Street." She fingered the material of the dress hanging on the coatrack. "Are you wearing this tonight?"

Kellie nodded. "It's the only dressy frock I have."

"It's lovely." She tilted her head. "Miss Mooney says my hair needs curling."

Setting the dessert pan aside, Kellie washed and dried her hands. "We'd better do it now. Your hair is so thick and straight it won't be finished otherwise." She glanced ruefully at her reflection in the window. "If you had my hair we wouldn't have to do any curling at all." She pulled at the strands above her forehead. "It's a fright."

Heather reached up to touch the bright, springy curls. "I love your hair. It's soft, like a cloud around your head. It makes you look happy."

Kellie laughed. "And I'm terribly jealous of yours, the way it hangs so smooth and straight no matter what the weather."

"Tonight it needs to curl," said Heather practically.

"So it shall." Kellie took the little girl's hand and led her off into the bedroom.

It was a cold night, crisp and clear except for the pockets of mist that settled in the flatlands like a gray blanket shrouding the low-growing shrubs. Banburren glowed with brightly colored lanterns, the streets illuminated, softer but no less bright than daylight. Tables groaning with food, crafts, clothing, trinkets, postcards and CDs lined the streets. Light spilled from the church where a stage and dance floor were set up. Musicians tuned their instruments. Dancers milled around, fidgeting with curls and checking shoes and costumes. Young people and others not so young gathered in groups, calling out greetings, flirting, smiling, laughing, making connections. Guinness flowed. Spirits were high and inhibitions low. It was a magical night.

Kellie hardly recognized the small town of Banburren. Unfamiliar faces met her at every turn. She was reminded of the stories she'd read about the fertility rites of the early Celts, the festivals of Beltaine and Samhain. The thought flashed across her mind that people hadn't changed significantly in two thousand years.

Balancing a plate of food in one hand and her pint of Harp in the other, she looked around for a seat. Susan Whelan waved frantically at her.

"Kellie, I've saved you a spot. Heather and the others will be on soon."

Climbing over a sea of legs, Kellie smiled and exchanged pleasantries as she negotiated her way to where Tom's mother sat. Sinking into the chair beside her, she breathed a sigh of relief. "Is it always like this?"

"Every year," said Susan. "It's our one claim to fame. I'm surprised you hadn't heard of it."

Kellie looked around. "This really is a lovely town," she said slowly.

"Lovely enough to stay?"

Kellie laughed. "I knew you wouldn't let me forget that one."

"You were so definite, letting me know in the most diplomatic of ways that Banburren simply wouldn't do for you. I'm glad you changed your mind." She smiled warmly at Kellie. "I imagine my son had something to do with your turnabout."

Kellie refused to be drawn in. "Look," she said pointing to the stage. "The dancers."

Heather, dressed in green and white, a green ribbon threaded through her meticulously curled hair, danced out onto the stage. The crowd roared its approval. Other dancers joined her, heels kicking, arms straight, hair bouncing, stage smiles pasted on their faces. One by one, they executed their moves in exquisite precision, every step appreciated anew by their adoring mothers, fathers, aunts, uncles and grandparents. Heather was indeed graceful and confident.

Kellie's heart turned over and the dark cloud that never quite left her returned. What if it wasn't meant for her to be here with this child? What if her mother returned to take her place in her husband's and daughter's life? That was really the bottom line, the final denouement. What did it matter if she was accepted by the Whelans or that she had friends in town or even that Heather loved her? What mattered was Tom and despite what he said and did, he was still largely unknown.

The dancers disappeared from the stage. Men carrying speakers arranged sound equipment and chairs for the musicians. Lights dimmed and a spotlight was focused in the center. Tom, a fiddler and a man carrying a tin whistle hopped up on stage. The audience cheered.

The moment the musicians struck up their first tune, the crowd was silent. Kellie listened to the music and forgot her food, the woman beside her and her reason for coming to Banburren. Completely caught up in music she hadn't heard since leaving Ireland, she closed her eyes and listened to the hand-clapping, foot-stomping tunes she remembered from childhood. They played a jig, then a reel, then a soft sweet ballad that brought tears to her eyes. When the last note died away, the room was silent for a brief moment before the deafening applause shook the rafters.

Taking their bows, the men disappeared from the stage. Susan wiped her eyes. ''My goodness, that was grand.''

Kellie simply nodded. Somehow it seemed profane to speak. She heard Tom's voice in her ear. ''Kellie, my love, save me a dance.''

She laughed and turned to him. ''My dance card is empty. I'll save you every dance.''

He grinned and pulled her up and out onto the dance floor. The music was soft and melodic and romantic. He slipped his arms around her. ''I was hoping you'd say that.''

This was what heaven must be like, thought Kellie. Good food, new friends, lovers swaying together in a church hall. The wedding festival. What a lovely idea.

What a lovely night. If only it would last. She rubbed her cheek against his chin. He smelled like the woods. "Do you know you have a wicked smile?" she said, pulling back to look at him.

"Do I?"

"Yes. It's one of the first things I noticed about you."

He pulled her close again. "What else did you notice about me?"

"You have lovely eyes, but your jokes are dreadful and the decor in the house needs a bit of work."

Tom threw back his head and laughed. When he'd settled her against him again, he rested his lips against her hair. "Do you want to know what I noticed about you?"

"Only if it's nice."

His voice thickened. "It's very nice."

"Tell me."

"You have the loveliest bum I'd ever seen."

"Did you really notice that?"

"Aye. A man notices these things."

"What else?"

"Your legs are perfect and you've a mouth made for kissing."

"Really? I've never thought of myself that way."

"What way?"

"I never thought a man would look at me and think of sex."

"Are you blind, lass? What else would a man think?"

She considered his question seriously. "I'm the wholesome type, the kind of woman a man confides in and befriends, not the kind he fantasizes about. I've always been considered something of an intellectual. Men don't often equate the two." The minute the confession left her lips she could have bitten her tongue. What a fool she was to be telling a man other men didn't find her sexy.

His answer surprised her. "You're a foolish lass, Kellie Delaney, to not know that a woman who is wholesome and intellectual, a friend and a confidante is exactly the kind of woman a man fantasizes about."

Tom Whelan had a silver tongue. But more than that, he was nice. She would hold on to that thought and what he'd said about her. And just for now she would think of nothing but the feel of his arms around her, the nubby texture of his sweater and the promise in the blue eyes so close to her own.

Sixteen

Maidenstone Prison, the women's high-security facility, was the stuff of gothic fiction, dark, brooding, lichen-covered, its lines thick and ugly, architecturally belonging to no particular period or style. It sat high on the edge of a Welsh moor, surrounded by forbidding gates, a ravine that was once a moat, and guard towers manned by high-powered lights and men with rifles who could pick a crow out of the sky at a thousand meters. Sixteen hundred inmates, all women, lived and worked and served their time within its walls.

Claire Whelan had called it home for seven years although she'd stopped counting long ago. Her sentence was life without parole. Because she had no reason to believe she would ever see the real world again, she'd retreated from the trappings that had once been so important to her: television, radio, newspapers, magazines. Books were the exception. She had not given up books. Books were her solace, her escape. She'd read her way through the prison's respectable library, taking comfort in fiction, in philosophy, history, psychology, ethics and theology. Within three years she'd earned the equivalent of a Leaving Certificate. It gave her pleasure to stretch her mind, even though she was reconciled to never using her knowledge for practical purposes. Humans, she reflected, were amazing creatures. They could adapt to anything. She was a prime example. She wasn't settled. She would never be settled in Maidenstone, but she had accepted her fate. Therefore, she was completely unprepared for her summons to the warden's office that Tuesday morning and even more unprepared for the news that followed.

Flanked by two female guards, Claire listened to her captor's incredulous pronouncement. Under the terms of the Good Friday Agreement, all political prisoners were scheduled for release. Her papers had been processed. Tomorrow, she would walk out of Maidenstone a free woman.

She slept less than usual on her last night. Catholic fatalism brought on her insomnia. Surely such good fortune would be coupled with a terrible price. Somewhere in the night she would be murdered in her bed or, even worse, her release would be a cruel joke perpetrated by even crueler prison guards.

But neither of the two occurred and in the bitter cold of an English dawn, she was sent on her way in the denims and leather jacket she'd exchanged for a prison jumpsuit seven years before. Twenty pounds in cash, and a check for another four hundred, gratis of Her Majesty's government, was her allotment for seven years of labor. The matron handed her a paper bag with her comb and a toothbrush. Then she unlocked the door and spat at Claire's feet.

A slow smile spread across Claire's face. "And a good life to you, too, Mrs. Metz," she said. Stepping over the spittle, she walked across the courtyard and out the front gate, free to go home.

The signpost indicated the town of Warrington was three kilometers away. Claire bent her head and, keeping to the side of the road, covered the distance in less than an hour. Stepping into a phone booth, she punched in the number of the woman who had been her only friend for seven years. "Please, answer," she whispered.

Susan Whelan's familiar voice picked up on the third double ring.

Claire cleared her throat. "Hello, Susan. It's Claire."

Silence and then, "Claire? Where are you?"

"I've been released, but I need some money to come home. I've got a government check but I can't cash it just yet. Can you help me?"

"Can you get to the ferry?"

Bless Susan, always so practical, no questions, no recriminations. "Aye. I'm near the coast. I've twenty pounds in cash. I'll catch a bus to Liverpool and another one to Banburren once I reach Ireland."

"I'll reserve a ferry ticket with my credit card. Have you enough for bus fare when you reach Ireland?"

"I think so."

"Claire?"

"Yes?"

"I'll be waiting for you."

Claire pressed her fingers against her eyelids to hold back the tears. "Thank you," she whispered.

* * *

Claire spent the night in a deck chair on the ferry, sleeping the thick, mind-drugged sleep of the unconscious. It was her first uninterrupted night in seven years. The ferry docked in Dublin Harbor in the morning. For three hours she walked the streets, listening to Irish voices, drinking Irish tea, feeling Irish soil beneath the soles of her shoes. Finally, when she'd absorbed enough of her homeland to move on, she found the bus station and asked about the route to Banburren.

There was a queue of three at the stop, a sure sign that the bus was about to arrive. She kept herself back, away from the man in front of her, wanting to discourage conversation. When the bus arrived, she paid her fare and sank, gratefully, into the first empty seat.

Claire stared out the window at the Irish countryside, the tangle of bog-myrtle, the hills bright with gorse and golden fronds of bracken. It had rained recently and there were potholes in the road, silvery in the sun, lovely to look at, difficult for the bus to maintain a smooth ride. No one complained. One did not expect comfort while traveling on a bus through Ireland.

She would have slept but the stopping and starting of the vehicle prevented her. Near Ballybofey a large woman with a bag sat down beside her. Nodding at Claire, she pulled out a thermos, unscrewed the lid and poured out a measure of tea. Then she offered it to her.

Claire took the cup and drank. "Thank you," she said, returning the lid.

"You're welcome. Would you like more?"

"Yes, please."

The woman poured another cup and watched her drink it down.

"You look like you could use a bit of nourishment. I'm sorry I don't have anything more to offer you."

Claire smiled. "That's very kind of you. The tea was wonderful."

"I'm Maggie O'Hare," the woman said conversationally. "My sister is in Ardara. I'll spend the week with her."

Claire slid her tongue across her bottom lip. Her comment required a response. She held out her hand. "Claire Whelan."

The woman smiled and her eyes nearly disappeared in the crease between her forehead and cheeks. "People travel nowadays, don't they? It's a different world."

Claire liked her immediately. "I'm not much of a traveler."

"Are you visiting family?"

"Yes. I've family in Banburren."

"Will you be there long?"

"I'm not sure."

"Does your husband not mind your being away? Or maybe you're not-married. Women don't always marry like they used to."

Claire thought for a minute and then decided on a partial truth. "He doesn't mind my visiting family as long as I don't do it very often."

Maggie nodded as if she understood. "Mine was the same way after the children left home. Before that, he wouldn't hear of my going away, not unless I brought them along and I could hardly bring seven children with me on the bus, now could I?"

Claire agreed that she couldn't.

"It was a relief when he passed on," the woman confided. "I loved him dearly but he was ill for a long time. The cancer took him and at the end it was painful. He was in hospital for nearly thirty days. Took his time dying, he did. Poor soul. They gave him morphine to ease his pain, but it wasn't enough. Even the priest was praying for his release."

"I'm sorry."

"Don't be. He had a good life." She smiled, and again her eyes disappeared. "And now I'm having one. It's restful to be alone and eat and sleep whenever I please. The children come, now and then. But I tell them I've raised them all up and I'm not about to do it again with my grandchildren. Love them I do, but not enough to take them in every time their parents have a mind to go on holiday. We never went on holiday without the children. Why should they?"

Claire acknowledged that they shouldn't.

"Would you like more tea, dear?"

"There will be none left for you."

She patted her bag. "I've another thermos right here. I always bring an extra."

"You're very kind, but I've had enough, thank you."

"Do you have children, Claire Whelan?"

Claire lifted her chin. "I do," she said, "a daughter. She's with her father."

Maggie sighed. "My husband wasn't much of a father, God rest his soul. Fathers are different today, aren't they, with all the feeding and diapering they do. In my day, children were a mother's worry."

Claire shuddered to think what would have become of Heather without Tom.

"Do you have only the one?"

"Yes, just the one."

"It's better that way, I suppose. Large families aren't practical, what with everyone needing an education and wanting their own telephones." She brightened. "We had grand times with all nine of us in the house at once. There was never a moment to spare."

Claire laughed. "I can imagine."

The woman pointed at a signpost in the distance. "We're nearly at your stop. My goodness. It came quickly."

Claire stood. "Thank you for the tea and the conversation."

"I enjoyed the company," the woman said. "Take care if I don't see you again." Maggie settled her bag on the seat beside her and waved. Claire waved back. She stood at the stop and waited for the bus to disappear down the road.

She hiked the back way, across the turned-over peat bog to Susan's house. The earth was dark and rich, the thick slabs of peat still wet and oozing from an eternity spent hidden from the day. Claire stooped down and dug her fingers into the turf, bending her head, kneading the earth, inhaling the unique, familiar smell of bog. Never again would she take a peat fire for granted.

She stood and faced west, toward the Whelan Bed-and-Breakfast, squinting her eyes. It wouldn't do to go directly home. Heather would be there. Maybe Tom would have guests. He would need time to adjust to her return. Tom wasn't good with surprises.

Susan's porch light was on and a flickering candle sat on the window ledge. Claire smiled and recognized the gesture for what it was, a welcome home, the only one she could reasonably expect. Tentatively, she knocked on the door and stepped inside. Susan would be in the kitchen. Claire followed the delicious smell of afternoon tea prepared as only Susan Whelan could prepare it.

Her mother-in-law's eyes warmed when Claire walked into the kitchen. Susan Whelan wasn't normally demonstrative but the embrace she gave Claire was no less satisfactory than if it had been offered by a more effusive woman.

"You're too thin," she said, pulling away and running her hands up and down the younger woman's arms.

Claire laughed. "You always say that."

"This time I mean it. Do you work at it or don't they feed people in that place?"

Claire shrugged. "I ate enough to survive. The food wasn't the best."

"Are you hungry, lass? I've enough to feed the village."

Claire breathed in the delicious meaty smell in Susan's kitchen. "I am," she said, surprised that it was true.

Susan led her to the table and pulled out a chair. "Sit down. I'll have it served up in a minute."

"Are you expecting anyone else?" Claire asked.

"No, love. I thought you might want some time alone."

Claire nodded. "I want to see Tom and then Heather."

Susan pulled a roasting pan out of the oven. "You'll do that soon enough, but first fill your stomach. There's no rush. You've been away seven years. One more night won't change anything."

"Tell me about Heather."

"You'll see her soon enough."

Claire frowned. Susan wasn't looking at her. Was it her imagination or was she trying to keep her away from Tom and Heather? "Is there something I should know?" she asked.

Susan ladled soup into a bowl and set it in front of Claire. "Seven years is a long time, Claire. People change."

"What are you saying?"

Susan hesitated. "This isn't easy for me."

"Say it."

"Tom has someone else."

Claire stirred her soup and concentrated on breathing evenly. "I see."

"You refused to see him. Did you expect him to wait?"

Claire didn't answer. What had she expected? A

forgiving husband waiting for her with open arms? No. That was what she wanted. It was not what she expected. It wouldn't be that simple. She didn't deserve for it to be that simple. She wet her lips. "Who is she?"

"No one you know. She's a teacher from England, born in Belfast."

"What is she doing here?"

"She came for a holiday and ended up staying."

Claire's eyebrows rose. "A holiday? Here in Banburren?"

"Does it matter?" Susan asked softly.

"I suppose not." Claire stood. "I'm going home, Susan. I'm not hungry after all."

"Does Tom know you're coming?"

"No."

"Do you think it's wise to simply show up?"

Claire's lips tightened. "I don't care."

Susan shook her head. "I wish you would stay here tonight. You'll look at this with a clearer head in the morning."

"Thank you for your help, Susan. I don't know what I would have done without you for all these years."

"You always were stubborn, Claire Donovan," her mother-in-law said fiercely. "I loved your mother and I love you, but I wish you had left my son alone."

"We have a daughter together," Claire reminded her. "Whatever we've done, there is that. She deserves to have a mother."

Susan turned away, defeated. "Take care," she said.

* * *

Claire quietly opened the back door of the house that had once been hers, stepped inside and walked down the hall into the kitchen. A woman sat at the table reading a newspaper. No one else was in sight. It was late. Heather would be in bed, but where was Tom? Claire took a moment to really look at her competition. Her eyes widened. She couldn't help the expletive that burst from her lips. "Holy shyte. Wherever did he find you?"

The woman turned and wide gray eyes met Claire's. She could be her sister, she was so similar, except that she had more hair and that delicate ripple marring the bridge of her nose. Her spirits improved immeasurably. If this was Tom's new love, he'd certainly stayed true to type. Was he living with her? The thought brought an involuntary twitch to her lips. Tom Whelan living in sin. Imagine.

Claire sauntered to the refrigerator and opened it. "Well, well, well," she said. "This looks well-stocked. Do you cook, too, Miss—?"

"Delaney," Kellie said automatically, "Kellie Delaney. What are you doing here?" Kellie asked.

"Don't you really mean who let me out?"

"Yes," Kellie said, "assuming you're Claire."

Claire helped herself to a wedge of apple pie and closed the refrigerator door. "I am. I've been paroled."

Kellie's color returned. "Then you're here legitimately?"

"Yes."

"What do you want?"

Claire bit into the pie, leaned against the counter

and crossed her arms. "What kind of a question is that? I live here. I'm home. I've come to reclaim my life. What are *you* doing here?"

Kellie opened her mouth, but no words came.

"Let me guess," Claire continued. "You've moved in to take over my life, my child—" she licked her finger "—and my husband."

Claire didn't miss the color flooding Kellie's face or the shaking hands and averted eyes. So, it was true. The woman was in love with Tom. Claire dismissed her. It didn't matter. The real question, the important question was, *Was Tom in love with her?* The answer would come soon enough, as soon as she saw them together. She could handle it if he was. Tom and she had been through worse. It was Heather who brought the ground-glass feeling to her stomach. Heather, the child she'd borne, the one she'd thought of every waking moment for seven years. It was imaginary conversations with Heather that had seen her through the agonizing brutality of prison, given her strength, created the desire to maintain, to endure the nightmare of Maidenstone. She dreamed of her daughter, straight and tall and lovely, welcoming her with open arms as if the years, the empty, silent years, had never come between them.

"Not exactly."

She'd said something. Claire wasn't paying attention. She spoke bluntly. "I want you to go."

Kellie lifted her chin. "What if I refuse?"

She had courage and she wasn't stupid. Claire had to give her that. "Why would you stay where you're not wanted?"

"Are you sure of that?"

Claire smiled. "I've known Tom Whelan all my life. He'll take me back. He always has."

"Maybe he's changed."

They were silent for long seconds, staring at one another, two women alike and yet nothing alike.

"Did he know you were coming?" Kellie asked.

"No."

Kellie drew a deep, shaky breath. "How will you tell him?"

"I'll handle him." The conviction of her words was sheer bravado. She no longer knew Tom. Over the years, he'd faded into the back of her mind where all bad memories were stored. She didn't know what to do if he refused to take her back. Surely he wouldn't. After all, she was the mother of his daughter.

"And Heather?"

"Heather is my daughter," Claire said coldly. "Did you really think I would hand her to you without a fight?"

Kellie smiled slightly. "It's been seven years. Forgive me if I doubt your motherly instincts."

"Never mind that," Claire said impatiently. "Will you go?"

"I can't go yet."

Claire shrugged and changed her tactics. "There are plenty of rooms. As long as you know how things stand, I don't mind your staying."

"I beg your pardon?" Kellie Delaney had a temper after all. "Do you really think we can all stay here together?"

Claire sighed. "This is my house. If anyone goes it will be you."

Kellie's lips tightened. She had a point. "Tom will be back soon. He's taken the dog out."

Claire nodded. "I'll wait upstairs in the room overlooking the garden. You can tell him I'm here."

Kellie's face was white, pinched. "This is a nightmare. You can't possibly mean for me to tell him his wife is home from prison?"

"What I'd like," Claire said pointedly, "is to see him alone."

Kellie stood, her face frozen. "I'll leave you to him," she said, and left the room.

Claire watched her leave. Was Kellie Delaney really so cool and collected, or was there more beneath her reserve?

She sat down at the table and crossed her legs. Coming home had shaken her. The idea of seeing Tom again left her brain befuddled and her hands clammy. What would he think of her after all these years? Would he help her or reject her completely?

Claire forced herself to think objectively. She hadn't been much of a wife to him when he'd come home after Long Kesh. She'd been absorbed with the life she'd made for herself. She pushed the thought aside. Too many regrets. She wouldn't go there, not now, perhaps not ever. She had today to get through, today and tomorrow. That would be difficult enough. She didn't like to depend on people. They rarely came through. But this time she had little choice. Her mind wandered. If only she could talk to Heather. It was absurd, of course, to imagine that Heather would want

her. The child knew only Tom and now, Kellie. She
had to think of her. It wasn't good to uproot a little
girl no matter how much one wanted it. Not even a
mother had a right to do that. She would reassure
Tom that she had no such intention. Perhaps, then, he
would help her find her place again.

When had it all become so complicated? How had
she come to this point in her life, a fugitive with no
place to go and no one to care? There had been moments when she'd had it all, when she was Claire
Donovan of Banburren and all of life was ahead.
When had it changed for her? How could anything
have been more important to her than her freedom?
What had drawn her in? She thought back. Nothing
came to her. Christ, it was cold. She closed her eyes
and concentrated, taking herself back and back, further back, her mind settling on a spring day when she
first became aware of Tom Whelan.

She'd always known the Whelans, of course. There
wasn't anyone on the Taig or Nationalist side of Banburren who didn't know everyone else. She assumed
it was the same on the Loyalist side although she had
no way of really verifying that. She'd never known a
Protestant, never even spoken to one other than to
hurl insults across clumsily constructed barricades.
Children's games that fed adult hatreds, feuds that
spanned the centuries. Did they think it would all go
away because a few men had signed a piece of paper?
They could mandate jobs and housing and education,
but that was all. It would go no further because as
long as the drums rolled in July and men gathered to

march wearing orange sashes and bowler hats, the anger would endure.

Tom Whelan was different from the beefy lads who slouched on street corners, smoked incessantly and swore vengeance on those from the other side who walked away with the jobs. She remembered the first time their eyes locked, the slow magic of his smile and the lean, spare look of him that stopped the breath in her throat.

Claire was no stranger to admiring glances. She knew she was pretty, the prettiest girl in Banburren except for Maggie Whelan and she didn't count because she was Tom's sister. But when Tom looked at her and then looked again, she felt a stirring inside that she'd never felt before.

He wasn't forward like the others. Neither was he shy or self-conscious. Rather it was his reserve, a serious sort of calm, that she'd noticed. It was as if he valued himself too much to allow anyone close to him who, when all was said and done, wouldn't matter.

Claire became the aggressor, arranging to be where she knew he would be, pretending it was all mere coincidence. Whether he knew or not he never said. It took time, nearly a year, but Claire was tenacious and in the end she won him. Tom was a one-woman man and a terrifyingly traditional one. She bound him to her by giving him her body, willingly and frequently. Looking back she should have known that a man so single-minded in such matters would be the same in other ways as well. It was his single-mindedness, his regimented focus that allowed for no other way but his own and, in the end, that drove her away.

Uncomfortable with her memories, Claire looked around, struggling against the claustrophobia of closed doors. She'd had enough of those for a lifetime. The walls were covered with family photos, mostly of Heather at various stages of her life. There was Lexi as a puppy and Susan with her brood. Her own mother and father smiled at her with Heather balancing on unsteady legs between them. The entire family was represented with one exception. Claire's mouth twisted. How he must despise her to have eradicated her so completely from his life.

Was Tom a different man than he'd been seven years before because he'd changed or because he was with a different woman? An interesting question. One that should be explored, but not now, not in this room that was growing colder as the minutes passed.

She'd given no real thought as to where she would go if Tom wouldn't have her back. Canada, perhaps, or America. She couldn't stay in Banburren, not with Tom here. The thought of leaving Ireland was like a fist closing around her heart. She was a revolutionary, not a pioneer. She wanted to fix the old, not take on the new. Ireland was in her blood, its rhythms a part of her, ebbing and flowing, always present even in the prison cell that had been her home for the last seven years. What would she do if she had to leave, how would she live, a stranger in a strange land? She swallowed hard. Sometimes survival carried a price and she would survive. She would return someday. Nothing was forever except death.

She glanced at the clock and ran her tongue over her lip. For the first time in years she wished for lipstick. What did one say to a husband after seven years in prison? She finger-combed her hair and pushed it behind her ears. If only she could take back the wasted years.

Suddenly, the door opened and he was there in the room with her. She stared at him, her eyes wide and dry in the pale thinness of her face.

He stepped forward and gripped her shoulders, his fingers hard and hurting, his gaze searching, fierce, urgent. "My God," he said harshly, "it really is you. I stopped at Mam's and she said—"

Claire nodded and would have replied, but he pulled her against his chest and held her in a tight, impenetrable embrace.

"Claire," he said, brokenly, "Claire."

It was the sound of her name on his lips that broke her reserve. Nothing had prepared her for this. She'd expected anger, sarcasm, coldness, even rejection, but never this hurting sorrow that came from a place deep inside of him.

Pain and regret and loss welled up and spilled over. The tears flowed and flowed, tears for the years of separation and all the years before that. She cried for hope that was lost, for what she had given up and could never bring back. She cried until her eyes were beyond swollen and her nose ached and she no longer felt anything at all. It was only then that she stepped away, wiped her eyes and nose with the hem of her shirt and looked at him.

What she saw shocked her beyond tears. Seven

years had changed him. She'd left behind a boy and come home to a man. Silver threads softened the dark hair at his temples and fine lines radiated from his eyes. He was still lean and spare of flesh but sorrow and experience and time had taken their toll and the bones of his face had hardened into the man he would be until the end of his days. He allowed her inspection with a quiet stillness that was new to him.

"They let me out," she said at last.

"Aye."

"Are you pleased?"

"Very pleased."

"Will you send her away?"

Something flickered in his eyes. He spoke carefully. "I'm happy that you've been released, Claire, but we have a great deal to settle."

She wanted to ask if he was in love with Kellie but the words wouldn't come. How did a woman ask her husband if he loved another woman?

"You haven't asked about Heather."

"I was coming to that."

"I assume you'll want to see her."

"Of course."

"Who will you say you are?"

Color flamed in Claire's cheeks. "I'm her mother, Tom. She has a right to know that."

"Does she?"

"What do you think?"

"I think she has a right to know why her mother hasn't asked to see her in seven years."

He was bitter after all. The back of her throat was

very dry. It was difficult to breathe. "You know why."

"I know you wanted no part of me, but your own daughter? Why, Claire?"

"Don't do this, Tom."

"How could you? Is there anything more reprehensible than to ignore the existence of your child?"

Her eyes filled. "I'm not going to discuss this with you, not now after all this time."

"When should we have discussed it? Before she was born or at some point during the last seven years?"

"Don't blame me for that." Her voice shook. "You have no idea what it was like for me."

"You wouldn't see me. You refused my help."

"You brought a barrister, a *British* barrister."

"I wanted to help you."

"I didn't want *his* help."

"We both know you served seven years because you wouldn't implicate Dennis McGarrety. Your friends were no help to you, Claire. I wanted to help you. What was wrong with fighting British injustice with a British barrister?"

She tightened her lips stubbornly. "You don't understand. You never did."

He sighed. "Whether I do or not is beside the point. The issue at hand is more important. What do you want from me and what do you expect from Heather?"

"I want my daughter," said Claire fiercely. "What I didn't want was a little girl visiting a prison, knowing her mother lived there. Until very recently I had no hope for parole. There was no point in knowing my daughter. I did it for her. Do you think I wouldn't have rather seen her if I was thinking only of myself?''

''What do you want now?''

''I want to know my daughter. I want to be her mother all the time.''

''That's a tall order, Claire.''

She lifted her chin. ''A person can change.''

''Have you changed?''

''I'm not the person I was. If you give me a chance, I'll prove it to you.''

He shoved his hands into his pockets. ''What exactly is it that you want from me?''

''I want to come home.''

''For how long?''

She wasn't getting through to him. He wasn't understanding. She drew a deep breath. ''Permanently.''

Seventeen

For a third time Claire walked around the play-ground. Little girls in plaid skirts and blue jumpers skipped rope, bounced balls or hung upside down on monkey bars. She'd spotted Heather immediately. It was as if everyone around her moved in a blur of slow motion and her own child was the only sharply defined image in her vision. She would have known her anywhere, a slightly built little girl, all arms and legs with lovely bones, too large eyes and thick straight brown hair that hung together and swayed like a curtain when she moved. Heather Whelan wasn't pretty or even cute, but she had the promise of growing into someone unusual. Claire was de-lighted with the looks of her and petrified of meeting her face-to-face, hence the surreptitious walk around the grounds, the quick glances, the hope that no one would take notice and report her for suspicious activity in the vicinity of junior school.

So engrossed in the lovely, illicit pleasure of watching her daughter, she didn't notice the nun over-taking her. Not until the woman tapped her on the shoulder did she realize she wasn't alone.

Claire turned around, startled, her hand over her heart.

"May I help you?" the nun asked in a firm voice.

She looked familiar. Claire frowned. "Sister Mary Carol? Is it you?"

The blue eyes narrowed. "I don't—"

"It's Claire Whelan."

Recognition and then shock froze the nun's features. "My goodness. Claire. You've changed. I wouldn't have recognized you."

"Yes," said Claire.

"What are you doing here? I thought—" She stopped embarrassed.

"I've been released."

"How long have you been home?"

"Since last night." She nodded toward the playground. "I wanted to see Heather."

"Heather. Of course. Does Tom know you're back?"

"I'm staying with Tom."

"I see." The nun held out her hand. "Welcome home, Claire." Her smile didn't reach her eyes. "Under the circumstances, I can't release Heather to you without her father's permission."

"Of course not," said Claire softly, turning away. "I didn't expect it. I just wanted to see her."

The nun's voice stopped her. "This is rather embarrassing, Claire, but your interest has been noticed. A few of the parents who live in the neighborhood are worried. I'll have to ask you to leave."

"I understand." She walked away, conscious of the nun's eyes on her back.

Claire hadn't expected to slip back into her past life without some reservations from the local community, but she hadn't expected it to hurt. Her own reaction puzzled her. She had never been particularly concerned about appearances. Somewhere that had changed without her realizing it. She wanted to fit in somewhere. She wanted to walk down the streets of the town where she was born and smile and wave at her neighbors. She wanted to bake soda bread and drink tea and wash sheets. She wanted to hold her daughter's hand and tell her stories and admonish her for eating too many sweets. She wanted her husband's eyes to light up when he saw her, just as they had years ago. For the first time, the magnitude of what she'd thrown away was clear. Tears formed in the corners of her eyes. Horrified, she brushed them away. She never cried. What was the matter with her?

Tom was waiting for her when she arrived home. She knew what that white line around his lips meant and braced herself.

"May I ask what in bloody hell you thought you were doing?"

She didn't pretend to misunderstand him. "I wanted to see my daughter. Is that so unusual?"

"Why couldn't you wait a few more hours until she came home?"

"Because I wasn't sure you would allow me to see her," she shot back.

"Are you insane?"

"No," she said calmly, "just desperate." She opened the refrigerator. Where was Kellie? He wouldn't show this side of himself if she were around.

He'd followed her into the kitchen. "If you are going to live in this town—" He stopped. "If you are going to be accepted in this town, your behavior must change."

"That's the real question isn't it?"

He ignored her comment. "You can't simply go your way and not consider the consequences."

"Why not?"

"Because, damn it, you have a daughter. She has friends who have parents who don't want their children associating with a child who has a strange mother."

"If you're referring to my prison years, may I remind you that you are an ex-felon as well."

"Don't be stupid. You know perfectly well why that's different. Unfortunately the world isn't as kind to women as it is to men. I'm sorry if you think it's unfair. I do, too, but it's Heather who will suffer unless your behavior is that of a completely rehabilitated woman."

She stared at him poker-faced. "May I see my daughter?"

"Don't push me, Claire. I'm not predisposed to giving you the benefit of the doubt."

"May I see my daughter?" she repeated.

He sighed. "Of course you may. I'd never intended it otherwise. She'll be walking home soon. We'll meet her halfway and then I'll leave the two of you alone."

"Where's Kellie?"

"Out," he said tersely, without elaborating.

Wisely, Claire kept silent. She wasn't interested in where Kellie was, only that she wouldn't be interrupted when she was with her daughter for the first time. She would allow Tom to arrange the details. He was the one who had complicated their lives with another woman. Let him work it out.

Heather stared at Claire and clung to her father's hand. Tom had said all he could. The rest was up to Claire.

"Hello," she said softly and held out her hand. "It's lovely to finally meet you. I've thought of you every day since you were born."

Heather, formally polite, took her mother's hand, gave it a brief shake and let go. "Are you really my mum?"

"I am."

"You're very pretty."

"Thank you. So are you. In fact I think you look like me. What do you think?"

Heather tilted her head, her eyes moving over her mother, from head down. "Yes," she said at last. She looked at her father.

Tom cleared his throat. "I've a few errands to run, Heather. Your mum will walk the rest of the way home with you."

"Where's Kellie?"

Claire didn't miss the note of panic in the child's voice. "Tom, surely your errands can wait. I think Heather would like you to come with us. Isn't that right, love?"

The little girl nodded. Claire could have wept at the look of relief that crossed the small features.

Tom looked confused but he didn't argue.

Heather slipped her hand inside her father's and Claire fell into step beside them.

"Why haven't you ever come to see me?" asked Heather.

"I wasn't able to get away, even though I wanted to very much."

"Where do you live?"

Claire glanced at Tom. "I live here now, in Banburren, with you and your da."

"Where did you live before?"

Claire drew a deep breath. She willed Tom to look at her. Somehow, he felt her need. *What shall I do?* Her eyes asked the question.

Tom squeezed his daughter's hand. "Do you remember when Sean Dougherty's father came home last year?"

Heather nodded. "He was sent to prison for fighting the British."

"That's right. He spent a long time away and then he came home again. The same thing happened to your mother. She fought the British and, because of that, they put her in prison. Now she's home again. Do you understand, Heather?"

She thought a minute. "I do," she said at last.

"We thought you should know the truth," continued Tom, "because your friends may hear things from their parents. We wanted you to hear it from us."

Heather looked at her mother. "Will you stay here long?" she asked.

Claire was nonplussed. This small, poised stranger shook her to the core with the questions she asked.

She swallowed and, like Tom, decided on the truth. "I came back to Banburren because you are here, Heather. Wherever I go, I won't leave you again. I want to know you that. I'd like us to be friends. If I move away, I would love to have you visit me as much as you like. What do you think of that?"

Again, something she'd said brought that look of painful relief to the child's face. Heather reached out to hold her mother's hand. "Sean Dougherty's mum and da don't live together. He lives with his mum."

"Oh." At first Claire didn't see the logic.

Tom cut in quickly. "That's because Sean has always lived with his mum. His dad came home only last year. It's the same with you. Your mum and I won't be living together but you'll stay with me because you always have. You'll visit her, of course, whenever you like, as she says, but you'll stay with me."

The firm deliberate tone of voice was like the lid of a pot clamped securely down. There was no room for deviation, disagreement or even suggestion. Claire would be allowed her daughter on a part-time basis and that was all. More to the point, Tom had delivered an irrefutable message: he and Claire were finished. They would not be making a home together. Claire wondered if she should believe him. Perhaps she should wait until his shock wore off before she pressed him for a definite answer. Meanwhile, Heather would be shared, unequally, but not unfairly considering the circumstances.

It wasn't what she'd hoped for, but it wasn't the worst case either. Tom could have tried to keep her from Heather altogether. Not that he could have done so permanently, but she would have had to hire a solicitor to see her daughter at all and that would have taken time and money she didn't have. No, she was satisfied. A part-time daughter was better than no daughter at all, and she knew Tom Whelan. If Heather was happy when she visited Claire, he would allow the child to visit as often as she pleased.

Suddenly Claire was content, more so than she'd been in a long time. She didn't want to go back to Tom's house. She didn't want to see Kellie, the woman who had taken her place. "Would you like to go out to dinner with me, Heather?" she asked impulsively. "I know it's early yet, but you could give Da your book bag and we could go for a walk first."

Heather's eyes widened. "May I, Da? May I go out to dinner with Mum?"

Tom's steps slowed. Claire could see his reluctance but she wasn't backing down. He'd promised her time alone. Heather was agreeable.

"All right," Tom said. "Remember that you have school tomorrow and homework tonight."

She clapped her hands. Her eyes shone. The promise of a treat was stronger than her natural reticence at being left with a stranger.

They waited until Tom turned the corner before walking back in the direction they'd come from.

"Where would you like to go?" the child ask amiably.

"The beach," Claire said promptly. "For seven years I never once walked on sand. I'd like to do that first."

Heather laughed. "We should have brought Lexi. She loves the beach."

"Next time," Claire promised.

"Are you really going to stay here?"

Claire wanted to promise her the world but she was done with fabrication. "I don't know, Heather. That's up to your da."

Heather considered her answer thoughtfully. "What will you do if Da says no?"

"I'd like to go on to university. I never knew that I was smart until I was sent to Maidenstone. I took classes there. No one ever told me I could earn a degree and do something important. I'd like to try."

"Aunt Mary went to university."

"Aye." Claire nodded. "Mary Catherine always was a bright one. She went to Galway."

"I've been there," said Heather. "Da goes to play the pipes sometimes and I go with him."

"It's a lovely city, isn't it?"

"It's a huge city." The little girl extended her arms. "Much bigger than Banburren. Won't you be lost in such a city?"

"Perhaps, at first. But after a while it will be just as familiar as here. Would you visit me there?"

"Can Da come, too?"

"If he wants to."

Killean's Beach was windswept with wild grass struggling through the dunes. It was a beach too cold for swimming and too windy for bathing, a walking and thinking beach. Claire had always loved it because it was solitary. Many a decision she had made walking the shores of this beach. Now she was here with her daughter. Only a few days ago she would never have believed it was possible.

Heather stepped carefully to avoid sand in her shoes.

Claire sat down on the sand and began to remove her shoes and socks. Heather watched her for a minute and then did the same. Hand in hand they approached the crashing surf. Standing just at the edge of the encroaching tide, they waited for the icy lave of ocean water to cover their toes.

Heather couldn't stand still. Dancing on the balls of her feet, she ran backward and then forward and backward again.

Claire watched her, laughing. When the rise and fall of the waves no longer held their interest, they found an abandoned foam cup and began heaping wet sand into a pile. Claire dug a tunnel through the mound and around it. "Wait for a moment and then watch," she told her daughter.

Within minutes, seawater rushed through the dugout and around the moat. Heather giggled, delighted. She found twigs and bits of shells to decorate their creation.

Claire sat back on her heels, heedless of the cold wind and damp sand. Heather's cheeks were flushed with color and her eyes shone.

She looked at her mother and laughed out loud. Then her lips quivered. "I'm cold," she said.

Claire brushed off her feet, tied her shoes and stood. "Let's find somewhere to eat. What would you like?"

"Spaghetti and chips," the child said, without thinking. "It's my favorite."

"Spaghetti and chips, it is," said Claire as she helped Heather with her socks and shoes. "Where shall we go for good spaghetti?"

Heather held out her hand. "I'll show you."

Together they walked down the darkening streets into town. Heather pointed out a cozy restaurant with checked cloths and candles on the tables. Claire ordered salad and wine for herself, chips and pasta for Heather. Then she looked around. It was crowded for a weeknight, nearly every table filled and a large group took up the center of the room. She recognized several of the women from her school days. One of them glanced in her direction. Claire smiled at her but the woman looked away, commenting to the man beside her. He waited a decent interval and then turned around to look. This time Claire didn't smile.

Self-conscious, she sipped her wine and listened to Heather chatter about her friends and school. *They're only people,* she reminded herself. *Don't let them bother you. This is enough: freedom, your child, all of life ahead.* The self-talk helped. She'd learned it in prison. Thinking positive thoughts was a survival technique. It turned one's mind in the right direction. Claire knew it wouldn't be easy making her way in Banburren. She'd come for Heather, to know her daughter, and to see if there was the possibility of a life with Tom. The last was still up in the air.

Tom was angry with her, but his anger would fade in time. She would give him a chance to think about what he truly wanted. If he wanted her back,

she would make a go of it. She owed him. She'd
wronged him.

With a sense of relief, she watched Heather eat her
ice cream. Finally, after seven years, she had a plan.
Tom and Heather came first. There was something to
be said for keeping a family together, for belonging
to something. She was tired of having no one care
whether or not she came home at night. But if that
wasn't to be, then she would make a new life for
herself with people who hadn't known the old Claire
Whelan.

Eighteen

Tom released Lexi from her leash, pulled the ball from his jacket pocket, and threw it in a wide arc across the field. Immediately the dog streaked after it, the white and gold of her coat blurring into the long green grass. Like a homing pigeon, she bounded toward her prize, picked it up in her mouth and strutted proudly back to her master, dropping it at his feet.

He rubbed her head. "Good girl. You're a grand lass, Lexi. Shall we try it again?"

The dog whimpered. Tom picked up the ball and threw it, watching as the setter raced across the grass, sniffed it out and brought it back to him. Lexi was a champion, her limbs strong and healthy, her coat gleaming and her teeth in remarkable shape for a nine-year-old dog. In the beginning she had been Claire's pet and protector, never leaving her side, emitting a menacing growl whenever anyone questionable came too near. Then Claire was gone. For a long time Tom had worked to win the loyal animal over. It wasn't until Heather's second birthday, nearly three years after Claire had left, that Lexi had capitulated. Tom still remembered the night Lexi nudged the door to the study open and stretched out at his feet. He'd felt triumphant that day, as if something of much greater importance had occurred than the acceptance of a four-legged animal. For Tom it was a sign that life would go on, that he would find contentment with his child and his dog, no matter that his wife would never return. Now that Claire was back Tom took a good deal of pleasure in knowing that Lexi still preferred him.

Not that the dog mattered to Claire. He had no clear idea of what did matter to her. Her sudden reappearance in his life had unsettled him, angered him. It was damn awkward, Kellie and Claire together in the same house. Claire was still his wife and yet he felt disloyal to Kellie. It was as if the last few weeks with Kellie had never happened. They'd fallen back into habits begun when she'd first come to Banburren. He knew they needed to talk but he was afraid they would come together and speak of inconsequential things until finally their time was over and they would leave each other with nothing resolved, more frustrated than ever. His mother was right. He should have ended his marriage long ago. But he hadn't and he was paying a price. The trouble was he had no assurances for Kellie. He didn't know how long Claire would be staying and there was Heather to think of. She had attached herself to her mother and Tom couldn't refuse Claire's reasonable request to know her daughter.

Meanwhile Kellie was silent, completely uncommunicative no matter how he tried to draw her out. She attended to the business of the bed-and-breakfast—cooking, washing linens, booking guests, but there was no joy in her step, no smile on her lips.

Claire behaved as if the entire charade was completely normal while Heather was around. Later she disappeared into the sitting room and fell asleep on the floor in front of the telly after Heather had gone to bed. Tom spent as much time as possible away from home on ridiculous errands. The only one unaffected was Heather and she seemed quite comfortable with the new situation. Tom marveled at the resiliency of children, both grateful for and envious of their ability to adjust. *Why did Claire have to come home and spoil everything?* The thought came to him unbidden. Immediately he was ashamed. Where else would she go?

He couldn't come up with a clear solution. Everything he thought of came with obvious difficulties. He needed time to sort it out.

Lexi looked up at him with soulful eyes. Tom ruffled the hair on her head. Lexi was a constant, one of the few he could count on right now.

The two women sat across from each other at the kitchen table. Claire drummed her fingers on the wood. This whole situation with Kellie was bloody awkward. She wanted nothing to do with the woman. She fumbled in her pocket. Where had she left her cigarettes? "What is it that you need to tell me?" she asked, annoyed.

"I want you to understand why I'm here in Banburren."

"Go on," Claire said, interested despite her resentment of the woman.

"My brother Connor and his son were murdered,"

Kellie began. "Connor was an Intelligence Agent. He worked for Scotland Yard. No one would tell me why someone wanted my brother dead." Kellie's voice shook. She cleared her throat. "They were simply going to sweep his murder under the carpet. That wasn't acceptable to me. I found an invoice in Connor's coat pocket with Tom's name on it. I had nothing else to work with so I took a chance and came here. I found out that Dennis McGarrety was involved. I believe he ordered the murders."

She leaned forward. "My brother and my nephew, Danny, were my whole life. Surely you can understand that. I must find out why they were targeted. Tom doesn't remember a specific incident in his past that would lead Connor to him. Do you?"

Claire's expression was flat, emotionless. "Tell me exactly what Dennis McGarrety said to you."

Kellie repeated her conversation with the brigade leader.

"He specifically told you that Tom and Heather were in danger and that your brother was killed?"

"Yes."

Claire frowned. The expressions that flitted across her face revealed her quick intelligence. "Dennis McGarrety may have gotten it wrong," she said slowly. "He's no longer in the mainstream. Murder isn't popular with the rank and file. Nationalists are voting. They need patience, not violence."

Kellie nodded. It was odd, this communing with Claire. The woman was intelligent and articulate and marvelously patient with Heather. Kellie was both attracted to and repelled by her. In different circumstances, she might have been willing to strike up a friendship. Obviously, that was out of the question. One didn't befriend a woman whose husband she'd slept with. "If I could bring an end to this—" She stopped. What would she do? Leave Banburren? Leave Tom to Claire? Every instinct screamed out against it.

Claire pulled out a cigarette, struck a match and drew deeply. Smoke curled around her head. "Tom wasn't involved. I hope you know that. He hasn't the stomach for murder. He never did."

Kellie nodded, hating her for her intimate knowledge of her husband. "I know."

"Do you need specifics or will you be satisfied with general information?"

"I don't understand."

"Do you need a name?"

"No," Kellie said shortly. "I already know the who. I want to know why."

Claire's eyes, wide and gray and very like her own, met hers. "I'd like to strike a bargain."

"What kind of bargain?"

"Promise me you'll leave if I give you the why."

Kellie stirred her cooling tea. "I thought you didn't want Tom. Isn't that the way it was before you were sent away?"

Claire didn't answer immediately, but when she did, it wasn't the answer Kellie expected. "Seven years is long enough to shift priorities. What I want is this life, the normalcy of it. I want my child. Tom is a good man. I can make him happy."

Something was missing. Kellie pressed her. "Will *you* be happy?"

Claire looked at her, brows lifted in astonishment mixed with a good portion of contempt. "How dare you ask me such a question, you with your job and your education, and a whole world to go back to? I don't require happiness, Kellie Delaney. We aren't put here to be happy. What I have will be enough."

"What if Tom doesn't see it that way?"

"I have a feeling he may be suffering from a conflict of interests."

"What conflict?"

"My husband believes he's in love with you," Claire said bluntly.

Kellie flushed but she refused to look away.

Claire hesitated. "I know this is awkward, but it isn't unusual. You needn't be embarrassed. It's only natural after the way the two of you have been living. Tom isn't a womanizer. He would never go looking for anyone else. You were thrown at him, so to speak. I don't blame either of you."

There was so much more to say, but Kellie's mouth refused to work.

"I know what you're thinking," Claire continued. "But don't make more of it than there really is. You're convenient and there's our obvious resemblance." She leaned forward. "But don't make the mistake of thinking it's enough. You told me why you came here. Your relationship began with a lie. You have no shared history, no memories, no family. Tom and I were children together. I don't want to hurt you, Kellie. There's no reason for it. But I don't want you to harbor delusions, either. Tom, Heather and I will eventually work this out.''

Kellie's words were soft, but deliberate, as if she'd thought about the question for a long time. "Is that what you want, to work it out? Have you changed that much?''

"Aye.''

"How?'' Kellie knew she was pushing the edge, but she had to ask.

Claire looked surprised. "I want my daughter and a normal life. I've not wanted that before.''

"What about your husband?''

For the briefest second, Claire's eyes flashed with heat. "Are you a Catholic?'' she asked instead.

"Yes.''

"Then you'll understand that Tom is my husband. That can't be changed, no matter how much you want him. If I find the answers to your questions, you must leave Banburren.'' She ground out her cigarette in the ashtray. "It goes without saying that Tom must never know of our bargain.''

Kellie pushed her chair away from the table and stood. "I won't tell him. I want nothing that belongs to you.''

The Crispin Road was well traveled, mostly by trucks carrying goods from Dublin and Belfast to the west of Ireland. A modern shopping center complete with a petrol station and fast-food restaurants stood at one corner. Claire stuffed her cold hands into the pockets of her jacket and sat down on one of the benches. She looked around and wrinkled her nose.

A young mother with a cigarette in one hand and a soft-drink can in the other shouted at her toddler to keep the pace. Workers operating jackhammers had opened up the main road holding up traffic in both directions. Loud music blared at a decibel level designed to destroy eardrums, and two young men, every visible orifice pierced and tattooed, conversed and ate their Gyro King wraps with no consideration for manners. So this was progress, Ireland's answer to unemployment and immigration. Claire didn't approve. But, perhaps every country had to go through such a metamorphosis before it could join the world as a modern contributing nation.

Claire didn't begrudge her country its successes. She only hoped that the fast-track modernization and technology sweeping through Ireland could be tempered with an appreciation for its cultural roots. History and music and literature also had a place, as did sleepy villages and country roads, sheep dotting green hillsides, traditional music filling the minds and lifting the spirits in smoke-hazed pubs, lone tractors chugging down rutted paths and mist settling over silver lakes and disappearing into rich bog lands shimmering under a reluctant sun. Her appreciation for her culture and homeland ran deep. She wasn't ready to let that go.

It hadn't been easy arranging this meeting. But McGarrety owed her. Not once in her seven years in Maidenstone had she implicated him in the murder for which she'd been sentenced. Yes, he owed her a great deal, seven years to be precise and she didn't intend to let him forget it.

Claire still didn't know exactly whom she would be dealing with, but she was fairly confident that whoever it was would tell her what she wanted to know. She was no novice when it came to subversive operations. Despite the passage of seven years, her instincts were still good. Therefore, when an older sandy-haired man carrying a paper cup and a newspaper took up a position on the bus bench beside her, her radar leaped into ready mode. When he allowed two buses to pass, she knew she'd found her contact.

Claire knew the rules. She waited for him to acknowledge her.

Ten minutes passed. Finally he spoke. "What do you want?"

She resolved to speak as little as possible. "Why is Tom Whelan compromised?"

"Tom Whelan is the one with information."

"I'm his wife. I've been told he's in danger and I want to know if it has anything to do with the murder of Connor Delaney." She sounded more confident than she felt.

"Do you think I would be here if we didn't know you were Claire Whelan home from prison?"

"What information does Tom have?"

"Can you guarantee his silence?"

Claire wet her lips. "Aye."

"Kevin Davies must be reelected."

Faces flickered through her memory. Then it came to her. The IRA man who won the election. "Davies? The MP?"

"Aye."

Suddenly it all was beginning to make sense. Davies might be a popular politician today but he had a past that could destroy him. "What did Connor Delaney have to do with Davies?"

"He found out about the Davies murders but he needed witnesses. Tom is the only one left who was there."

"He was always the only one left. Why worry now? That was fifteen years ago. Surely you know that Tom wouldn't come forward?"

"We weren't worried until Connor Delaney started snooping around. We can't afford to have Davies run at reelection compromised. We know Tom wouldn't voluntarily talk, but we aren't sure what he would do in a courtroom."

Claire was silent. McGarrety was pathetic. Connor Delaney's murder was unnecessary. Tom would never have talked.

The man pressed her. "Will he talk if he's brought up in court?"

"No," Claire promised recklessly. "He won't say anything. We want you to leave us alone."

The man pulled out a cigarette, struck a match and lit up. He inhaled deeply. "I'll relay your message, both of them." He exhaled a cloud of smoke and waited for her to go. "It would be foolish to lie," he said quietly.

For the first time Claire looked at him directly. "It would be just as foolish for Dennis McGarrety to forget his debt to me."

He was gone. She'd weathered the meeting and now knew what she knew. If only Kellie Delaney would cooperate.

Her drive home was purposely slow. She decided on the back way, past the river and through the glen that in spring glowed with the golden light of a thousand daffodils. She didn't want to go home. It was cloying with Kellie silent as a post and Tom caught between two women, not knowing how to behave. She couldn't even be natural with Heather, knowing the two of them watched her every move. What did they think she would do, kidnap the child? In all fairness, she supposed it was done on occasion, but such an act held no appeal for her.

Claire was in a bind. As much as she wanted to give Kellie her answers and expedite her leaving Banburren, there was another more important issue to consider. Tom was in danger. He was the only witness to an unsolved brutal murder that now, fifteen years later, had been resurrected because of Connor Delaney. If Kellie's brother had traced the Davies incident to Tom, someone else would sort it out as well—sooner or later. The only way to ensure that Tom would never talk would be to silence him permanently. He must be warned. But by warning him he would want to know why she had involved herself, and then her bargain with Kellie would be exposed.

Claire lightened the pressure on the accelerator and enjoyed the gentle coast around the narrow road bordering the glen. She and Tom had come here as children. They were more than children, really, but in looking back, their eager innocence qualified them as no more than that.

She pulled over and stopped the car. Slowly she opened the door and stepped outside. Memories crowded in on her, conflicting memories of Tom, her years alone when she was swept up in the cause of Irish freedom, her prison years bringing her finally, now, to today. Where was she now? What was it she wanted? What was even possible for a woman with her past? Remorse and self-pity swept through her. She was thirty-three years old with nothing to show for it, not a single person alive in the world to mourn her passing and it was all her own doing.

She walked faster now, down through the fern-covered earth floor, beneath the trees toward the sound of water. Thirty-three was still young. She would start over, do it differently this time, maybe go on to university and earn her degree. She could marry again, have more children. It wasn't impossible. She reached the oak where Tom had carved their initials, artistically intertwining them in a unique design so that only those who knew what to look for could see the flowery letters. What did she want from Tom? Once she thought marriage meant forever. Now she wasn't sure that was possible, despite what she'd told Kellie. Not that she wasn't willing to give it another go, for Heather's sake, but she didn't think Tom was up for it.

Poor Tom. He was such a gentleman, with a highly developed sense of character. Through the years when he'd belonged to the Nationalist movement, and even through the prison years, he'd kept his integrity. How he must despise their current situation. Claire knew that infidelity chafed him like a shoe that pinched. She felt a deep sadness for what she'd lost now that it was too late. She'd been through enough to know that suffering could be measured in degrees and that, in the scheme of things, stepping outside of one's marriage wasn't an impossible obstacle to overcome. Petty jealousies, proprietary relationships, even the rules for acceptable behavior changed with circumstances. After seven years of humiliating degradation, of individual preference stripped away like feathers from a game hen, of unnatural cohabitation where even the most intimate details of one's toileting habits were common knowledge, sharing one's husband didn't seem so difficult to accept.

Claire was fairly confident that she could accept anything after what she'd been through, whether it was a husband who preferred another woman or no husband at all. Her only nonnegotiable was Heather. She wouldn't give up Heather to another woman. Heather was hers, born of her body, born after the years Tom was in prison. The child was her link to a normal life. Thoughts of her daughter had kept her sane. When the walls closed in and all the books had been read and the long hours of darkness were left to get through, she would think of her child and look at the pictures Susan sent. She would stare at her lovely hair and her light clear eyes and the freckles bridging her nose. She had long legs and a brilliant smile and ears like the fairies. No, she wouldn't give up Heather. It wouldn't be right for a mother to give up her child, no matter what the circumstance. Despite everything, Heather would know she had a mother who wanted her.

Claire sighed and began walking back to the car.

There was no help for it. She couldn't win no matter what she did. But at least her conscience would be clear if she told Tom about her conversation with McGarrety's man.

Nineteen

Tom cursed himself for dragging his feet. Kellie was hurting and it tore him apart. Why hadn't he divorced Claire years ago? What excuse did he have for falling in love with a woman when he still had a wife? The roil of emotions that began when she came home hadn't abated and now there was the McGarrety mess. He trusted Claire's judgment in the matter. Her description of the meeting and her assessment of his options were frighteningly perceptive. Kellie had stubbornly refused to accept information once removed and was insisting on a meeting with Kevin Davies. Tom had a few questions of Davies as well. Claire was right. If Connor Delaney had found him out, others would as well. He needed to speak to Kevin Davies personally and reassure him that their past association was forgotten. No one would learn anything from Tom Whelan.

Heather walked into the study, her mouth filled with bread and jam. "Da, Kathleen Mallory and I have to make a poster of the book we're reading in school. We were at her house yesterday, but her mum says we can't be underfoot today. May she come here tomorrow?"

He wasn't really listening. "Yes, love."

She climbed into his lap and rested her head against his shoulder.

"What are you doing?"

"Working." It was true. Ironically, the twisted dynamics of his life motivated him to write, giving him a direction he'd not yet explored. He was conscious of the slight weight of his daughter. She was still catching up after her illness.

"Kellie says we're to have stew for dinner, but I told Auntie Kate that I didn't like stew and she invited me to her house. I told Mum and she spoke to Auntie Kate and I can go."

Tom removed Heather from his lap and stood. "You can play a game on the computer if you like. I'll be back shortly."

"I have to go to Auntie Kate's for dinner. Mum said she would take me."

"Did she now?"

Heather nodded. "It's all right if I go, isn't it, Da? I love Auntie Kate and I haven't seen her for a long time."

"Be patient for a bit, Heather. I want to speak with your mother."

Satisfied, she climbed back into the chair.

Tom found Claire at the kitchen table reading a newspaper. Despite his good intentions he attacked immediately. "I'd rather you not tell Heather she can go somewhere else for dinner unless you ask me."

Claire looked up. "Are you mad? I'm not going to ask permission for such a thing. I'm her mother."

Tom's fists balled. Christ, she was selfish. Had she always been this way or had their seven-year separation opened his eyes? Deliberately, he willed himself to remain calm. "Have you thought about why Kate might be asking Heather to dinner?"

She folded up the newspaper and looked at him. "Are you angry with me, Tom?"

"I think you're insane," he said evenly.

"What brought you to that brilliant conclusion?"

She was nothing like Kellie. She didn't even look like her anymore. "I'm beginning to wonder if you want me to throw you out."

She flushed. "Don't be ridiculous."

"I'm not the one who is ridiculous. Surely you can see the problem."

"No," she said coolly. "Tell me."

He spoke slowly, deliberately, as if speaking to a slow-witted child. "Kate will talk with Heather. It's highly probable that someone like Kate, a teacher having a strong rapport with children, will encourage Heather to confide in her. Heather is an intelligent child. We don't know what she's picked up in bits and pieces from listening to us. I would rather the rest of Banburren not know of our situation."

"That makes sense," Claire agreed. "But you're the one encouraging gossip as well. Don't you think everyone is wondering why Kellie is still here now that I'm back? If you're so concerned about what people think, send her home."

Tom frowned. "Kellie came for a reason. When she's satisfied, she'll decide for herself whether to go or stay."

He watched her touch her tongue to her lips. She

was shaking. "Will you go after her, Tom, or will we all live happily ever after?"

"No."

"To which answer?"

"No, to both. Kellie needs time to think things through," he said slowly. "A great deal has happened in her life. I'm going to allow her that time, as much as she needs, away from Banburren and me. I won't go after her. As for you and me, we won't live happily ever after because our marriage is over. I'm not the person you left. I'll do the best I can to see that you're settled but that's all."

Her voice was fierce, territorial. "I won't give up my child."

"You gave her away easily enough seven years ago."

"I had no choice."

"The choice was yours when you first knew you were carrying a child. You decided your *work* was more important than a baby."

She dropped her head into her hands. "Must you always come back to this? I know you blame me. I'm sorry. I was wrong. You're not the only person who's changed. Why can't you see that?"

"It's too late."

Her cheeks were flushed with shame or anger. He couldn't tell which.

"You really are a cold bastard."

"Stop it, Claire. We were miserable together. You wanted out of our marriage more than I did. Nothing's changed."

"Except that you want to divorce me and marry Kellie Delaney."

Tom lost his temper. "You know nothing about this. It isn't as simple as that. But you're right about one thing. Kellie is worth a dozen of you. She's dying inside because she lost a nephew. You gave away your own daughter."

She shook her head, picked up the paper and began to read.

"I don't know what I ever saw in you," he said and left the room.

"Or I in you."

Heather, at play on the computer, was oblivious to the drama acted out a few minutes before in the kitchen. Tom stood at the door looking at her for several minutes before speaking. She was so like her mother, light-brown hair, clear gray eyes and a slightness of build that made everyone with a nesting instinct want to feed her. Apparently, he had brought very little to the equation. Still, she was his daughter and he loved her desperately. Nothing would make him give her up. Claire had no right to her. Marching in at the final hour and demanding parental privilege was absurd. He would help her get back on her feet, but on the condition that she leave Heather to him. He would give her freedom and financial security in exchange for his child. After that he owed her nothing. His debt would be satisfied.

Kellie was sitting in the garden, pruning shears in her hand, the late afternoon sun framing her in backlight. Her domestic side appealed to him. Everything she did appealed to him. She shook her head in amazement. "You can't be serious."

"Why not?"

"She's Heather's mother. Do you think you can simply take a child away from her mother without so much as an argument?"

"She hasn't been much of mother."

"What choice did she have?"

He hadn't thought she would take Claire's side so vehemently. Was there an unwritten rule that women had to stick together, stand up for one another even when they were on opposing sides? "She had a choice."

"She was in prison serving a life sentence. Be reasonable, Tom. What could she have done?"

"She could have stepped away from it all when she knew she was pregnant."

She sighed. "I don't remember many men stepping away for the sake of a wife's pregnancy or even when they had a slew of other children. Why is it always the women whose lives must change?"

"That's a ridiculous argument, Kellie."

She flushed but she wasn't finished. "Not really. Claire knew you were here to take care of Heather."

"Does that make it all right then, to bring a child into the world behind prison bars and then give her away for years? What difference does it make whether I was here or not? I'll not give my daughter to a person with so little feeling."

Kellie sat back on her heels and brushed the hair from her forehead with a dirt-stained hand. "I'm not suggesting that you give up Heather. You may have to compromise, Tom. Claire is the child's mother. She has a right to know her. Besides, she isn't the only one involved. There is Heather to consider. She should know her mother.''

There was no response he could make. He watched her walk into the house and wondered what he'd ever done without her or what he would do if she disappeared from his life. His head had been buried in the sand. Believing that they could continue to exist this way—the three of them, he, Kellie and Heather—as a family, without taking into consideration the forces at play that had brought her to him was nonsense.

Heather's uncharacteristic tantrum when Tom called Kate to refuse his daughter's dinner invitation cemented his decision. Something had to be done. He regretted the cozy camaraderie they'd shared at mealtime before Claire's return. Now they ate separately, Kellie managing a few bites while she made dinner, Tom in his study, Claire and Heather at the table by themselves.

Tonight he pushed his conflicting emotions aside and walked out to the shed. A few hours of quiet work on his pipes would help clear his mind. The set he'd carved out was a full set, expensive, finely honed. He sat down at his bench, running his hands reverently over the sanded ebony, the shiny brass, the brushed leather of the reservoir and the bellows. The next step was the reed. He would work the bamboo carefully, to be sure it matched the chanter. For now, he would use a tested one. Buckling the popping strap around his leg just above the knee, he adjusted the bellows under his right arm, strapping it on above the elbow and the belt around his waist. He adjusted the reservoir bag, attached the tube across his waist and settled the drones on his knees. A true piper needed more than a reasonable amount of natural dexterity and years of diligent practice.

Covering the holes of the chanter with his fingers, he tried the low notes first and then opening them up, one at a time, he ran over the scales. Lovely, lovely music. He only hoped the piper would do justice to the pipes he had ordered.

Music and poetry settled Tom's soul, righted his world, straightened his thinking. He wanted a new life with Kellie. She was unusual, one of a kind, an aberration, born into a family that didn't know what to make of her. Intelligent and focused, she managed to ignore her surroundings and excel in areas only recently available to Catholics in Protestant Ulster. How many, growing up with fathers and brothers in the organization, with British tanks patrolling the streets and soldiers in barbed wire guard towers on every corner, would have risen above it all to earn a university degree? Tom had never known or even heard of anyone who'd done such a thing. He was desperately afraid of losing her. His worst fear was that she would go back to England, marry someone worthy of her, someone who'd accomplished what she had, have children and resume the life she was suited for. The last months would be remembered as a painful, but brief, interruption. But in the interests of his own self-preservation, he wanted to convince her that she belonged with him. The problem was what to do with Claire.

Tom stood and walked to the window. A fine mist settled on the grass and fogged the windows. The gray matched his mood. Lexi lifted her head and whined. "I know, girl," he said without turning his head. "I don't like this, either, but I'll sort it out. We're survivors, the two of us." He picked up Lexi's lead from its hook on the wall and fastened it on the dog's collar. By the time purple shadows settled over the rise of Ben Bulban and the fog rolled in dark and thick and close, he had made his decision.

"It's time to face the music, Lexi, lass." He took the dog's head between his hands and rubbed the soft ears. "I'm in an awkward spot, Lexi. I'll probably lose the woman if I send her back to England, but I've no choice. We can't go on like this and I need time to settle Claire in a place of her own." He felt a small degree of optimism. Perhaps everything would work out after all.

Twenty

They were in his study with the door closed. It was the first time since Claire's arrival that they'd really been alone together.

Kellie rubbed her arms and walked to the window. "I don't know what to say. Surely you understand that I can't simply walk away and wait for Kevin Davies to contact you."

"What is that supposed to mean?"

"It means that I don't know you anymore. Perhaps I never did. How can I be sure you'll contact me at all? You could sweep this under the rug and hope I'll forget it."

He stared at her, aghast. "Do you really think so little of me?"

She wouldn't look at him.

"I love you, Kellie," he said, his voice low.

"Yes. So you say."

His hands clenched. "What in the hell is the matter with you?"

"Love is relative, isn't it? It can mean something completely different depending on who is saying the words."

"Now, it's I who don't know you."

"There is that," she agreed. "Perhaps neither of us knows the other."

"I'm going to pretend you didn't say that," Tom said evenly, "and return to the subject at hand. Kevin Davies has behaved decently and honorably for fifteen years."

"He had my brother and my nephew killed. Pardon me if I don't agree with your definition of decency."

Tom ignored her sarcasm. "I don't believe he had anything to do with your brother's murder. McGarrety could have worked that one out with others like him. They want Davies to be reelected. He's the only Nationalist candidate who stands a chance."

"And if he did have something to do with it? What then?"

"Then we'll know for sure."

"That isn't enough for me, Tom."

He gripped her shoulders and looked down into her face. She hadn't been sleeping. The wounded purple under her eyes was testimony to nights lived on the edge of her nerves. "You want justice served, but it won't be, Kellie. Nothing will bring them back. You said you needed answers. You won't find a name, an actual person who did the deed. Who will you blame? It's time for you to take hold of yourself and go forward. Your brother chose his life. Do you really believe he didn't know the risks?"

She pulled away from him and turned back to the window. He made sense. But the truth of it, the logic, angered her. This time *she* changed the subject. "By telling me to go forward, you don't mean here in Banburren, do you?"

She was a woman who stared directly into the truth, no matter the cost. "That's up to you."

"For God's sake, Tom. You're not even divorced. Your wife is here, living with you in the same house. You feel a responsibility for her. Do you have any idea how that makes me feel?"

"Yes, I do, and I have every intention of divorcing Claire."

She turned to look at him. "Really?"

He wanted to ask her to stay, to wait until he unscrambled his life, but he didn't. "I'm working on it, Kellie. It will take some time. There's Heather to think of. I can't simply throw Claire out in the cold. What would you think of me if I did that?" He'd never felt so helpless. "I wish I could make you understand."

"I do understand, more than you realize."

"If I could keep you here, I would, but it isn't working."

"Isn't it?"

"You know it isn't. We're all miserable."

She couldn't keep the bitterness from her voice. "No, Tom. All of us are not miserable. Your wife has come home and everything has gone her way."

"I don't think of her as my wife."

"How do you think of her?"

"She's Heather's mother. That's all."

"I see."

"No, you don't." He turned her toward him again. "This isn't a game, Kellie. It isn't what I want, but there's no other way. I won't ask you to wait for me until my life is settled. When that happens, and believe me it will, I'll have to take my chances with you. But until then I want you to trust me.''

She didn't believe him and he couldn't blame her. The obvious question would be for her to ask why he'd never bothered to divorce Claire in the seven years they were apart. But she wouldn't ask. Pride would keep her silent.

''I'm leaving tomorrow,'' she said.

Accepting the inevitable didn't make it any easier.

''When?'' he asked.

''The bus to Belfast Airport leaves at seven in the morning.''

''Let me drive you.''

''No.''

He didn't try to change her mind. ''Are you going back to Oxford?''

''Yes.'' She turned away, stopping at the door. ''Tom?''

''Yes.''

''I'm not leaving this alone. I came here for a reason. I'm going to finish it.''

His throat burned and the urge to pull her into his arms and damn the consequences had never been stronger. ''Be careful, Kellie,'' was all he said.

Kellie stood in the doorway and watched Claire read to her daughter. Her voice was lovely, raspy, low for a woman and emotion-filled, changing in tone and pitch with every character. Heather lay back on the pillow, her eyes open, staring at the ceiling. She was smiling.

Claire closed the book. "What do you think of her?" she asked her daughter.

"Who?"

"Tinkerbell."

"She's rather silly, isn't she?"

"Why is that?" asked her mother.

"She can't marry Peter. She's a fairy and he's a boy."

"Perhaps she wishes she were a girl and not a fairy."

"But she's not."

"She can still be jealous."

Heather frowned, deep in thought. "He's a little boy and Wendy is a little girl. It's silly to be jealous."

"Yes," said Claire. "I suppose it is."

Heather stroked her mother's cheek. "I like you. I'm glad you came back."

"Are you?"

"Yes."

"I'm glad. I love you."

Heather nodded. "I know. You love me and Da loves me and Kellie loves me and Gran loves me. Everyone loves me." She ticked her family members off on her fingers.

Claire laughed. "My goodness. You're a very popular young lady."

Heather laughed.

Kellie cleared her throat. The two on the bed looked up. Heather clapped her hands and sat up. "Kellie, we're reading *Peter Pan.*"

"I heard. It's a lovely story, isn't it?"

Heather nodded. "Have you come to read to me, too?"

"No, love. I just want to talk to you tonight, just for a minute, if I may?" She looked inquiringly at Claire.

Claire stood. "Of course," she said. "I was just about to say good-night. Take all the time you need." She kissed the little girl's cheek. "Sleep tight, darling. I'll see you in the morning." She brushed past Kellie without meeting her eyes.

Kellie sat down on the bed and took the child's hands in her own. Wouldn't it be lovely to be so young again and to assume that one was unconditionally loved for no other reason than mere existence? She breathed deeply and began. "I'm going away."

"Where?"

"I'm going back to England for a while, and then I'm not sure."

"Why?"

"I only came for a short holiday. But now I must go home."

Heather snuggled down into her comforter. "Are you leaving tomorrow?"

"Yes."

She stretched out her arms. "Kiss me goodbye now."

Kellie wrapped her arms around the little girl and kissed her. "I'll miss you," she said.

"Will you write?"

"Absolutely. If you'll write back."

"Will you have e-mail?"

"I will."

She grinned. "I'll e-mail you."

* * *

Claire sat on the back stoop smoking a cigarette.

Tom sat down beside her. "Those will kill you, you know," he said.

She nodded. "I know. At the moment I'm not terribly concerned with dying of cancer or heart disease."

"What do we do now?"

She ground out the cigarette. "What do you want to do?"

"Did you ever love me, Claire?"

Leaning her head back against the door, she smiled. "How can you even ask?" she said softly.

"I'm not sure of anything anymore."

She was silent for a long time. Finally she spoke and when she did her words shook him and he was more confused than ever.

"There was a time when I loved you so much I'd press my face against your shirts in the closet and just breathe in the smell of you. You had an electricity about you that left me wanting and anxious, insecure and vulnerable, quite desperate, actually, to be in your presence. I hated it when you were away or when you visited your mother or ran errands or read or walked or drove somewhere because it took time from us. The best part of every day was crawling into bed beside you and waiting and hoping that we would make love. For some reason, when we did that, when you concentrated only on me, the world was right. I don't think I ever felt that otherwise." She was silent again and then the words came out, low and earnest. "That's how much I loved you."

Tom stared at her, bereft of speech. She wouldn't look at him. Why hadn't he seen that she felt so strongly? Would he have done anything differently? What was it that made a man and woman walk together down the same path for a time and then change direction, part and go their separate ways? When did the fire, the excitement, the desire leave a marriage once embarked upon with such hope and joy? They'd started out with everything in place to make the journey together. When had it gotten out of hand? When did each of them decide the other would no longer do?

He thought back to the prison years. It wasn't the long separation with visits limited to one day a month. Claire had been incredibly loyal during those years, cheerful and loving and filled with hope, never once missing a visit. But when he came home, he felt the change. She was different, nearly a stranger, with habits she'd cultivated during his absence. Gone for long periods in the evening, she became surly when he asked where she'd been. Her association with the Nationals consumed her life. It was the kind of existence he no longer wanted to live. The rhetoric was dated and absurd. World opinion was with the Catholic population of Ulster. Sinn Fein was legitimized and given legal and political status. Everyone was permitted to vote. Finding housing, always difficult, became less so. The lure of peace had a harmonizing effect on the country. The organization was anachronistic. The pipe bomb had given way to the ballot box.

He had seen it clearly. Claire had not. She took

more risks. He became silent, unforgiving, bitter. She spent days, even weeks, away. Then she told him about the baby. He'd been naive. How could they, practicing their avoidance techniques on each other, have conceived a child? If he'd really thought about it, he would have suspected from the beginning that she had a lover. The concept of infidelity was so foreign to him he hadn't even considered the possibility. Now, he was the one who'd been unfaithful. He wanted to ask her if it hurt, but he said nothing. What did a man say when he preferred another woman to his wife? Would she be forever stunted because of his words or would she recover, a better, wiser woman? What did she want of him, this woman he'd once known more intimately than anyone else?

"What about now? Do you love me now?" he asked.

"Why do you ask?"

"It's the all-important question, isn't it? If you don't, everything would be a great deal easier to work out."

"In other words, you would feel less guilty."

"There is that."

"It's not a fair question, Tom."

"Why not?"

Her voice rose. "Because I don't know yet. Because we haven't had a chance to be alone. You've given me no time."

"There's no need to shout."

She began again. "We've known each other our entire lives. Is nothing salvageable? Is your ego so fragile that everything we've done, everything we've been to each other, all the good we've shared is erased because I didn't see things your way?''

He stared at her. ''You're amazing. Somehow you've managed to convince yourself that you're the victim.''

''I am the victim. I'm the one who was sent to prison.''

He shook his head.

She sighed. ''All right, Tom. What do you want me to do? I can't go back. There's a great deal I regret, but how does that help us now? Would it make you feel better if I wrung my hands and groveled? I can do that. At this point I'll do just about anything.''

He stood, wooden-faced. ''It's late. I'm going to bed.''

''Tom.''

He waited.

''Are you still writing?''

''Aye.''

''May I read some of the new poems? I've read everything already published.''

''If you like. I'll print some out for you.'' Once he would have asked her to tell him what she liked. But that was a long time ago. Now, her opinion no longer mattered.

Claire sat down again and stared into the inky darkness. If she were a betting sort of woman she wouldn't give her hopes for a new start even a one percent chance of happening. Tom was through with her and, like it or not, she must accept it. She wouldn't be one of those clingy women who refused to acknowledge that their marriages were over, the kind who kept intruding into their ex-husband's lives and marriages with inconvenient phone calls, tears and accusations. She'd known women like that. Ireland was filled with them. Divorce was new in the Republic and even in the North, Catholic marriages were rarely dissolved. More often, men left their wives and took up with new women, even living with them for years and starting new families. No, she decided, she had her pride. She wouldn't go where she wasn't wanted. If she couldn't have her husband back, at least she would have his respect.

She looked at her reflection in the clear glass of the windowpane. She was older than she would like to be, with the ravaged, wary expression of a prison inmate. But she was still attractive; attractive enough that a bit of grooming would make a difference.

Filled with new resolve, Claire stood and walked back into the house, through the kitchen warmed by peat still glowing in the hearth, through the sitting room, down the hall and past the room that belonged to Kellie. Why hadn't the woman shared Tom's room? Perhaps they had until her return. To continue to do so would have been insensitive and awkward. Claire's appreciation for Kellie rose grudgingly. She didn't want to have positive feelings about Kellie Delaney but it couldn't be helped. She was the kind of woman Claire aspired to be.

Twenty-One

She found Susan at the kitchen table, writing a letter to her sister. She put it aside the minute she saw Kellie. "Hello, love," she said. "Sit down. It's good to see you."

Kellie's eyes burned with the effort of holding back tears. She had come to love this woman. "I came to say goodbye," she said immediately, before the words could no longer be formed. "I'm leaving tomorrow."

Susan stood and mechanically began her ritual for making tea; scouring the pot with hot water from the kettle, spooning in tea leaves, assembling milk, sugar, cups, saucers and spoons, all without saying a word.

Kellie sat down and waited. She knew she wouldn't be let off so easily.

At last, when Susan had filled two cups with steaming tea, she sat down across from Kellie. "You're giving up, just like that."

"I have no choice."

"I thought you had more spunk, Kellie Delaney."

Kellie bit her lip. "Tom isn't helping me, Susan. If I thought he was through with Claire and wanted me, I could wait. But that isn't the case. She's settled in again. He's always wanted her. I know that now."

"You're not seeing the situation clearly. Claire Donovan was never right for my son. I knew it from the beginning. She's not one for marriage. Trust me. I know her better than anyone."

"She's changed," said Kellie.

"No one can change that much. She thinks she can come back and start fresh, but I know better. She was never happy here. Claire isn't the kind of woman who is satisfied unless everything is about her."

"She wants Heather."

"And so she should. But she won't like it when Heather's difficult or when she needs shoes or clothes or a mother to go to parent night at school. Claire doesn't have it in her to nurture. If Tom gives Heather to her, he'll find the child on his doorstep before six months are gone."

"That's very harsh."

"It's the truth. I don't want you leaving my son and my granddaughter because you think she's better for them."

Kellie stared at the older woman in amazement. "You saw her all along when she was in prison, all those years. Have you no affection for her?"

Susan's eyes filled. "More than you know. I've known Claire Donovan since the day she was born. Her mother and I were friends. I love her. She can't help what she is. But I love my son more and she's not right for him. You are. Don't leave him to her."

Kellie shook her head. "You don't understand. Sometimes a woman can't always be the pursuer. Sometimes she needs a bit of encouragement. I'm not getting it. I have some pride, Susan. Is it too much

for him to show he wants me the way he once wanted
her?''

Susan reached out to grip Kellie's hand. ''You're
a strong woman, stronger than most I've seen. You
came here for a reason and you turned Tom's life
around. Are you really finished here, love? Can you
walk away and leave them behind?''

Kellie wanted to scream, to cry out that she was
the one who'd been left. She'd trusted Tom Whelan,
fallen in love with him and with his child, but it
wasn't enough. Yes, he would miss her. Yes, he
would be better off with her. Kellie knew it. Susan
knew it. But all the knowing in the world didn't matter if the woman Tom wanted was Claire. A woman
could only take so much suffering and Kellie had had
enough.

Susan's eyes, clear and bright as blue glass, softened. ''There, now.'' She patted Kellie's hand. ''I've
said all I'm going to say. Drink your tea and we'll
talk of other things.''

Kellie boarded the bus to Belfast at seven o'clock.
By one that afternoon she had rented a car in the city
and was driving up the Antrim coast by way of the
glens.

Her eyes burned from the effort of holding back
tears. There was a tightness around her mouth and a
grim determined set to her shoulders that discouraged
even the casual passing bike rider from lifting his
hand to wave her on.

She allowed only a single direction to her thoughts

and that was her destination, the residence of Antrim's member of Parliament, Kevin Davies.

Davies's address was a matter of public record. She hadn't bothered to call first. She knew he wouldn't speak with her if she asked politely on the other end of the telephone line. She would have to show up unannounced. Hopefully, the element of surprise and her own determination would ferret out the truth. Antrim was an odd county for a member of Parliament with Nationalist sympathies to reside in. It was overwhelmingly Protestant and quite expensive by Irish standards.

She pulled into the circular driveway and turned off the engine. The house wasn't quite a mansion, not by European standards, but it was definitely large enough to qualify as a country estate. Set back on a lush green lawn, the gray slate gables and white trim gave the house a stately, elegant quality.

Kellie swallowed and walked up the brick drive, climbed the stairs and pressed the bell. Minutes passed. Steps sounded behind the door. Kellie tensed. The door opened and she was face-to-face with a small woman, beautifully coiffed with arctic-blue eyes.

"May I help you?" the woman asked politely.

"My name is Kellie Delaney and I'm here to see Mr. Davies."

The woman shook her head. "I'm sorry. He's in London for the week. Can I help you?"

"Are you Mrs. Davies?"

"I am."

"May I have a moment of your time?"

For a fraction of a second the woman hesitated. Her eyes moved over Kellie once again and then she nodded, "Please, come in."

Kellie stepped into the wood-paneled entry.

Mrs. Davies closed the door. "We'll be comfortable in the parlor," she said. "Follow me."

Kellie passed by a series of elegant, tastefully decorated rooms. Kevin Davies had done very well for himself. She was struck by the similarity to Connor. Her brother, too, had lived above his apparent means, not quite so lavishly but certainly better than a public servant could afford.

She followed Mrs. Davies into a sun-washed room with long windows framing a spectacular view of the ocean. Kellie gasped.

The woman smiled slightly. "Everyone who comes here has the same reaction. It's lovely, isn't it?"

"Very."

"Please sit down." She waved Kellie to one of the comfortable cream-colored sofas on either side of the fireplace. "May I get you anything?"

"Tea would be lovely."

Mrs. Davies spoke into the intercom. "Mrs. Sims, please bring a pot of tea to the family room. There are two of us. Perhaps something sweet as well." She sat down across from Kellie. "Now, tell me, did I miss something? Did my husband have an appointment with you?"

Kellie shook her head. There was nothing left for her to do but confide in the woman and hope she would be as horrified as any innocent woman would be to know her husband was not what he seemed.

"I know this might seem very strange to you, but I felt I had nowhere else to go."

"I don't understand."

"I'm in trouble, Mrs. Davies. I don't quite know where to begin."

The disapproval lines around the woman's mouth deepened. "What kind of trouble?"

"Perhaps I'd better start at the beginning."

"Yes. That would help."

Kellie sighed. The woman was already bristling. There was every possibility that she would be shown the door when her interview was over. "My brother and his four-year-old son were murdered three months ago," Kellie began. "The brakes on Connor's car were cut."

The woman gasped. "I'm terribly sorry, Miss Delaney, but what does that have to do with my husband?"

"My brother worked for British Intelligence. He was conducting a murder investigation that occurred nearly fifteen years ago. The incident involved your husband and a man named Tom Whelan."

Mrs. Davies looked puzzled. "I'm not familiar with anything that happened that long ago. Kevin and I have only been married for six years."

"Several people were killed. I don't know many details, but I do know that. Tom Whelan is the only witness still alive."

"I don't believe I've ever heard Kevin mention a Tom Whelan."

Kellie believed her. "Do you know who Dennis McGarrety is?"

Again Mrs. Davies shook her head.

Kellie sat forward, her elbows on her knees. "He's an assassin. He also supports your husband's candidacy."

Mrs. Davies flushed. "That isn't Kevin's fault. He's the only Nationalist candidate who has a chance of winning. Naturally, there are factions that support him whose methods he doesn't condone."

"Dennis McGarrety murdered my brother because his investigation hit too close to home."

The woman stood. "I don't believe this. You're suggesting that my husband is implicated in a murder. Leave my house immediately. If you knew my husband, how decent he is, you would never have come here. Get out!"

"I need to know if your husband had any part in my brother's death, Mrs. Davies. His son was with him, his four-year-old son." Kellie's voice cracked.

A soft knock sounded at the door followed by a stern-faced woman bearing a tea tray.

Mrs. Davies composed herself. "Thank you, Mrs. Sims. Tea won't be necessary after all. Our guest is leaving."

The woman nodded and left the room without speaking.

"I'm going to tell my husband what you've told me. I'm sure he'll contact you. Meanwhile, please have the courtesy to keep this to yourself. Slanderous rumors can ruin a politician."

Kellie's control broke. "What is the matter with you people? Do you understand that keeping silent could cost people their lives?"

"What are you talking about?"

"What if your husband isn't the man you think he is? What if you tell him and then you read my obituary in the paper one morning? What will you do then, Mrs. Davies?"

"Don't be absurd. Kevin is my husband. I know him. He's nothing like that. He simply couldn't do the things you've said."

Kellie gathered her purse and stood. "I hope you're right. I hope your confidence is justified, because this won't go away. Very soon you're going to see exactly what your husband is made of. I'll give him a week, Mrs. Davies. He has one week to contact me before I go to the police."

Her voice shook. "Where will you be?"

"I'll wait at the Black Swan in Oxford, next Thursday, at one o'clock."

"I'll tell him."

Gillian, her mainstay, had picked her up at the airport and had driven her back to her flat and gone on to work. Kellie would have to find a place to stay. Her own flat was leased for another three months.

Meanwhile, she was hungry. She opened the pantry cupboard. As promised, it was well stocked with every spice imaginable and enough canned and packaged foods to last for weeks. Kellie found the tea, loose the way she liked it, and a can of evaporated milk. The pot was already on the counter. She filled the kettle, set it on the burner to boil and pulled two graham crackers from a fresh package.

Assembling a tea tray, she carried it into the living

room, set it on a low table and sank into Gilly's comfortable couch cushions. She was alone, really alone with no chance for interruption. She would use her isolation as an opportunity to clear her mind, to add in the thoughts one by one, sort them out and come up with some kind of plan.

Everything depended on her meeting with Davies. If he had nothing to hide he would call her bluff. More than likely he wouldn't bother to meet her. Then what?

She crumbled the graham cracker until it was no more than a small pile of brown powder on the white plate. Without some sort of confession from Davies she had nothing, no evidence whatsoever, to cause John Griffith to look any further into Connor's murder. Davies was the key. Everything depended on Thursday. Until then, all she could do was wait—and work at forgetting about Tom Whelan.

He'd hurt her terribly. It was as raw and simple as that. She'd allowed herself to be vulnerable, to care for him, to trust him. All the rationalizing in the world wouldn't wash away the truth; he'd never divorce his wife and now she was back where she'd started. The very thought sent a fresh wave of hurt down into her stomach, weighting her, preventing her from movement. It was odd, really, this new pain that drove the other one, the greater one, into a subservient position. Kellie had no experience being the other woman. She wanted all of Tom, his quiet regard, the glint of humor behind his eyes, his level mind, his way with words, his mother, his daughter. For a few brief weeks, she'd believed it could all be hers. Rationale told her she'd lost nothing—it wasn't hers to lose. But her heart told her differently.

She no longer had any interest in her cooling tea. The sun had disappeared into the ocean, streaking the sky with copper, pink and gold. Purple clouds rolled in settling like lumbering elephants over a swimming hole. Kellie walked to the wine rack, knelt down and looked at the three bottles that consisted of Gillian's selection. She recognized nothing. Choosing something red she found a corkscrew, opened the bottle and pulled out a wineglass. The liquid slid down her throat, warm, full, decadent. She poured another glass and carried it and the bottle back into the living room. Already she could feel the alcohol flush in her cheeks. She welcomed the warmth and the dulling of the sharpness in her middle.

The second glass disappeared as quickly as the first. She considered having another. When was one legally drunk? Did it even matter? She filled her glass again. Perhaps with a bit more alcohol she could even tolerate the subject of Tom Whelan. *Tom Whelan. Tom Whelan. Tom Whelan.* Repetition was desensitizing. She'd learned that long ago. Tom was a horse of a different color, as her mother would say.

She was attracted to Tom because he appreciated her. They complemented each other without competing. Despite her air of confidence Kellie needed his admiration and his love. If anything, she decided, she had been love-starved. Her childhood had been fairly typical by the standards of West Belfast, but for Kellie, a sensitive, introspective child, to have an absentee father and a mother so overworked that signs of overt affection were a luxury not to be expected, it was severely lacking.

The wine took effect. Her head felt thick, fuzzy. Her thoughts were no longer clear. The room circled around her. Seriously dizzy now, she clutched the arm of the sofa and positioned one leg on the floor. Kellie lay back on the couch and looked around. It could be worse. This was a lovely room with its wealth of books and tasteful furnishings. Perhaps she would stay here forever. She would work her way through the wine closet and the library. It was rather comforting, really, the aimlessness of it all. Low expectations. That was the key. Never expect too much. Too disappointing. Kellie's tongue was thick and dry. She was drunk. Even thinking was difficult. She would lie here for a while until she felt better, whatever that meant.

Twenty-Two

It was Thursday—at last. Would Kevin Davies meet her at the Black Swan today or would he call her bluff and allow her to go to the police? Kellie was conscious of warmth and light, the slow slide of the sun across a windowpane, a warmer, yellower sun than the one that belonged to Ireland. She pulled the covers over her head. Surely it was too early to be up. Besides, there was no reason to rise early. She'd been home for a week now. Her position at Silverlake wasn't available until the end of the term. Although she spent a good part of the day reading, one couldn't read forever. She needed activity, purpose, something more than wandering through the familiar streets of Oxford waiting for Thursday and her meeting with Davies. What was she doing here? When would her life begin again? She felt odd, like a fish out of water. For the first time in years Kellie began to seriously consider going home for good when this was all finished.

Minutes passed. Forcing herself, she crawled out of bed and made her way to the shower.

Standing under the hot spray, she wondered how she would make it through the morning until it was time to go to the Black Swan. Nothing came to her.

Panic rose in her chest. She fought it, toweled herself dry, dressed, found her purse and ran down the stairs. She would take her tea and read the newspaper somewhere other than Mindy's today.

It was chillier than usual. Kellie increased her pace. Against her will she thought of Banburren; wet mist against her face, soft rain curling her hair, Lexi's breath, Heather's quaint ways, white clouds disappearing into the gray and Tom—she wouldn't go there.

Oxford, on Thursday, was unusually bright and crisp. Men and women dressed in dark business suits passed each other on the streets. Restaurant menus were posted on billboards in anticipation of the lunch hour. Shops with inviting window displays lured shoppers inside and vendors hawked their wares on every corner.

Simone's, a designer dress shop offering only originals, sat back on an inconspicuous street near the financial district. Kellie had passed it several times during her early explorations of the city. Recognizing the clientele and the merchandise as well above her means, she had never ventured inside. Obvious wealth made her uncomfortable. Perhaps it was time to change her habits. Her share of Connor's estate had significantly increased her bank account. She could certainly afford a dress from Simone's and it would pass the time until her meeting with Davies—if he showed at all. Kellie stepped inside the shop and smiled tentatively at the woman who greeted her.

"May I help you?" she asked politely.

"I'm looking for a dress," Kellie began.

"For what occasion?"

"A dinner party," she improvised.

The woman's smile became ingratiating. "We have some lovely things that came in yesterday." She cocked her head. "With your coloring may I suggest something in cream or a pale yellow? Follow me. I have the perfect dress. In fact I have several perfect dresses."

"One will do."

An hour later, Kellie walked out of the shop carrying a buttery yellow sheath that fit like nothing she'd ever owned and bone-colored, strappy, high-heeled sandals. She looked at her watch and her heart beat accelerated. It was nearly time to head toward the Black Swan.

The pub was filled with the usual lunch rush. A harried waitress motioned Kellie to a table in the corner facing the door. She handed her a menu. "It will be a bit before I can get to you. I hope you're not in a hurry."

Kellie shook her head. "I'm expecting someone. Would you bring me an ale? Take your time."

The waitress was back in no time with her drink and then she disappeared into the kitchen. Kellie glanced at the menu and put it aside. All of her attention was concentrated on the entrance to the pub.

A man, between fifty and sixty, with gingery hair and a pleasant smile entered the pub. He looked around, saw Kellie, and made his way to her table. "Kellie Delaney?" he asked.

She nodded.

"My name is Kevin Davies."

She motioned toward the chair beside her. "Please, sit down."

He ignored the menu. "My wife told me you wanted to see me."

"Did she tell you why, Mr. Davies?"

He leaned forward. "I'm sorry for your loss. I want to assure you that I had no knowledge of the tragedy, nor would I ever allow or condone such an action."

Kellie sipped her drink. "Please don't be offended, Mr. Davies, but anyone would say that. Tell me why I should believe you."

He sat back and folded his hands on the table, a pleasant-looking man with blunt features and bright blue eyes. "I'm going to tell you a story, a dreadful story, that will incriminate me far more than the murder of your brother and his child. What you do with the information will be up to you."

"Does this have to do with Tom Whelan?"

"It does."

"Will I need another drink?"

"Are you a drinking woman, Miss Delaney?"

"No."

"Alcohol doesn't really solve anything." His smile was kind. "I've done a number of things I'm not proud of, but this one, if made public, will destroy my way of life."

"Why tell me?"

"Because you're angry and angry women are dangerous. I would rather be denounced for what I did than for what I didn't do. Besides, you've upset my wife. When this is over, I'd like a favor of you."

She was intrigued. "A favor?"

"I'd like you to tell my wife that we've spoken."

He was too controlled, too suave. She didn't trust him. "Please, go on."

"I came of age in Portadown in the sixties. There was nothing for the lads and I in a Loyalist town but to join up."

Kellie nodded. "I'm from Andersonstown. My brothers were the same."

He frowned. "Surely not the brother who was killed?"

"No. Connor was different."

Davies smiled briefly. "There were a few of those, shining lights who left as soon as it was possible."

"Please, continue."

"I was clever and managed to avoid prison. By the time I left for Belfast, I was a hard lad, up for almost anything. McGarrety and I set up the Belfast Brigade together."

"Was Tom Whelan part of that life?"

"Aye, he was indeed. But Tom was from Banburren. Lines are drawn but not so sharply in the small towns near the sea. He wasn't angry enough and he was married."

Kellie felt the pinch in her heart.

"He was caught before he earned himself a harsh sentence. That was enough for him."

"What did he have to do with you?"

Davies pulled out a handkerchief and wiped his hands. "We were on a mission together," he said, his voice level. "On a chance, we thought we'd found three Prods we were looking for in a local pub in Sligo. We blindfolded and cuffed them. The checkpoint at the border was manned. We didn't expect it, but when we saw the lights we knew we couldn't cross with our prisoners. I told Tom to get out of the car, to make his way over the hills. I drove them, cuffed and blindfolded, mind you, to within fifty yards of the checkpoint. I crawled out and waited for the guards to approach the car. Then I detonated the bomb that killed them all.''

Minutes ticked by as Kellie stared at the man beside her. His face was smooth, his manners gentle. She tried to imagine him in the situation he'd recreated and couldn't. ''Did Tom know what you'd planned to do?''

Davies shook his head. ''No one knew. I didn't know myself until I did it. Our automobiles were equipped with bombs just in case.''

Kellie wet her lips. ''I don't know what to say. What you did was terrible, unfortunately, but not unusual. Belfast was a war zone for a long time.''

''What was unusual was that two of the Protestants from the pub were women. We didn't normally set out to kill women.''

Her face whitened. ''Dear God.''

His eyes never left her face. ''There's more.''

She waited.

''The women weren't the right ones. They weren't involved at all. I murdered two innocent women because they were in the wrong company.''

''Please.'' Kellie shook her head. ''You've said enough. I can't hear any more of this.''

He leaned forward. ''There is more, Miss Delaney, but my role is finished. I imagine, when you think this through, that you will have questions.'' He reached into his pocket and handed her a card. ''Call me when you're ready for the answers and, please, do me the courtesy of telling me what you decide to do with the information I've given you before I read it on the front pages of the *London Times*.''

Kellie didn't watch him walk away. She waited a full fifteen minutes before paying the bill and making her way back to Gillian's flat. It was three o'clock and she was restless. She needed something to take her mind off her meeting with Davies.

In Banburren, Heather would be walking home from school. Tom would be looking at the clock, anticipating her arrival home, fixing her tea, or perhaps that task had fallen to Claire. Kellie bit her lip. She wanted to hear Heather's voice. Tom hadn't said she wasn't to call. She picked up the phone. Quickly, before she changed her mind, she pressed the keypad numbers and waited for the familiar double ring that signaled Ireland.

A woman answered. Claire. Kellie resisted the impulse to hang up. ''Hello,'' she said. ''This is Kellie.''

Silence.

She began again. ''I'm calling for Heather.''

Claire came right to the point. ''I wish you wouldn't.''

''Why?''

Claire's voice lowered. Kellie could barely hear her.

''It should be obvious. She's my daughter.''

''How is she?''

''Very well, thank you. We're all fine.''

Kellie's heart hurt. "I'm glad."

"Are you?"

"Yes."

"Is there anything else you wanted?"

"No. Nothing at all."

"You can't have them."

"I beg your pardon?"

"I won't give you my husband and child."

"Of course not. Goodbye, Claire."

The click of the phone was firm and final.

Kellie hung up the phone, stared at it for a long time and then picked it up again. Then she punched in the number she'd committed to memory. A man answered after the first ring. "John Griffiths, please. This is Kellie Delaney."

Claire replaced the phone, poured herself a cup of tea and sat down at the table. Normally she loved winter afternoons. It was her private time, a world of gray mist and muted sounds and solitude. Wrapped in a plaid blanket, she carried the cup outside and sat down on the steps. Heather and Tom wouldn't be home for a while yet. She would have time to mull over her miniconversation with Kellie.

The woman was hurting. It was evident in her voice, in the phone call itself. What it must have taken for her to make such a call? Kellie Delaney had her share of pride. She wasn't one to go where she wasn't wanted. Claire had seen it immediately and had the grace to feel some responsibility over her role in complicating Kellie's life. Not that she'd had a choice.

Tom's voice broke through her thoughts. "It's cold out here."

Claire turned around. He stood in the doorway, hard eyed and handsome in faded jeans and a pullover, his arms crossed against his chest to ward off the chill.

"I'm used to it," she said. "Where's Heather?"

"Playing with Kathleen Mallory for the afternoon."

Claire's heart sank. They would be alone.

"I heard the phone," he said.

She thought of lying and decided against it. "It was Kellie."

"What did she want?"

He said it casually, as if it didn't matter to him. But Claire wasn't fooled. "She asked about Heather."

"How is she?"

"I don't know. We didn't discuss that. I told her we were all doing well."

Tom laughed. It was a hollow sound.

Claire, who knew him as well as she knew herself, winced. After all these years, his pain shouldn't bother her. "Why did you let her go, Tom? Obviously you care for her."

He didn't deny it. "I don't deserve her. I'm a married man, not formally educated, with the added complication of a wife who has nowhere else to go."

She didn't contradict him. Instead she tried to make him understand. "I needed to come home, Tom. I needed a place where I felt safe. You have no idea what I've been through."

"Don't I?"

She stared straight ahead. "It's not the same in a women's prison. We aren't housed with political prisoners. We don't study our language or Irish history or military strategy. We're with felons, murderers, psychotic personalities. It's a fight to survive."

He sat down beside her. She felt the edge of his knee against her thigh. When he spoke his words were unexpected and cruel. "I'm not responsible for your decisions and I refuse to feel guilty because you destroyed what we had."

She stared at him. "What are you saying?"

"I didn't want this for you," he said. Bitterness lined his face. "I wanted you to come home, have our child and settle into some semblance of normal family life. You didn't want that and you paid for it. Perhaps there was a time when it could have worked between us, but not any longer. I feel nothing for you but contempt. Christ, what you could have done if you'd channeled your energies differently, what we both could have done." He shook his head. "You have nothing to show for your adult life."

"Do you?"

He looked somewhere beyond her. "No."

She bit her lip. Nothing mattered except the words she refused to leave without saying. "I never stopped loving you, Tom."

"How convenient," he shot back. "When did you decide that, before or after you destroyed our lives?"

She sighed. "All right. I understand. I'll go as soon as the dole comes in."

He stood, straight, merciless, a man who knew his

own mind. "I'll check around and see if I can move your appointment up on the calendar."

"I could insist that you sell the house."

He looked at her evenly. "Is that what want, to sell my home?"

She corrected him. "Our home."

"You lived here for seven months. I've been here nine years."

She sighed. "I'm not much for tea this afternoon."

"I'll manage on my own," he said.

Claire was about to remind him that Heather had begun to dislike milk, but decided against it. They had managed before her and they would manage when she was no longer here. She would miss the child terribly. It wasn't fair. She'd known the minute her baby was born that she'd wanted nothing more than to go home, raise her daughter and leave the life she'd known behind. It wasn't easily done. Claire had wanted the chance to try again, but it wasn't meant to be.

Twenty-Three

She should have stayed away from the bakery. It was Susan's favorite but in previous years her mother-in-law had been an early riser. At this hour Claire was certain she could make her purchases and vacate the shop safely. She'd miscalculated. Both Susan and Maggie bore down on her, smiles wide, purpose stamped on their Whelan features.

"Hello, Claire." Susan smiled at her. "It's been a week since we've seen you. Where have you been?"

Claire cleared her throat. "Has it been that long? I didn't realize it."

"We were coming to invite you to Sharon's first communion," Maggie said. "I've mentioned it before but you may have forgotten."

Sharon's first communion. Who in the name of heaven was Sharon? "Of course I haven't forgotten," she lied.

"You will remind Tom?"

"Aye. I'll tell him."

"We'll be having a luncheon after it's over," Maggie continued. "I have you down for a pudding. Is that all right?"

"Perfectly."

Dear God. A pudding. Did these people know her

at all? How would she manage it? Perhaps she could buy something that looked homemade at the bakery. Her smile was brittle. "A pudding it will be."

Susan had said nothing beyond her first greeting. She was looking at her strangely.

Claire moved toward the door. "Lexi is outside. I've got to get her home. I won't forget to remind Tom about the celebration."

Outside, Claire whistled to the dog, set her package in the basket of her bicycle and pushed away from the curb. The bike wobbled precariously, refusing to right itself. Frustrated, Claire climbed off and looked at the front tire. It was flat.

Behind her, Susan spoke. "That won't get you anywhere."

"No," Claire replied. She stared straight ahead.

"Is something wrong?"

Claire saw no point in pretending. "Aye."

Susan sighed. "I've known you your whole life, Claire. Let me help you."

Claire shook her head.

"Why not?"

"There's nothing to say. Everything's grand."

"You're a liar, Claire Donovan. You've always been a liar."

Claire turned and met her mother-in-law's contemptuous glance. She ignored the challenge. "Where's Maggie?"

"Gone home."

Curiosity got the best of her. "Why did you visit me all those years?"

"I diapered your bottom more times than I can count. You married my son. I loved your mother."

Claire's eyes filled. She clutched the handlebars, unable to speak.

Susan stared at her. "What's got into you, Claire? Is it tears I'm seeing? What have I said that's upset you so?"

Claire shook her head.

"Come now," Susan said in her determined way. "I'm taking you home. I deserve a few answers and someone is going to give them to me."

"Tom will be home."

"I'm taking you to my home. I want you alone for a bit."

Claire allowed herself to be meekly propelled along the streets and down the road. Susan maintained a soothing flow of conversation that required no response. Claire was grateful. Hearing without listening, she forced herself to keep up, matching her mother-in-law's pace, placing one foot in front of the other. After an interminable walk, much longer than Claire remembered, they were there.

With a grateful sigh, Claire sank into the comfortable couch that hadn't changed since she was a child. It was comforting to lean back, close her eyes and absorb the well-being that she'd always associated with Tom's mother.

Susan left her alone to disappear into the kitchen. After a bit she returned with a tray piled with biscuits, cake and the makings for tea, Susan's remedy for all ailments. Claire smiled. Some things never changed.

"There now." Susan sat across from her, fortified

with a cup of sweet, milky tea. "Don't argue with me, Claire. I want to know everything."

"Everything?"

"Aye. Don't tell me it's none of my business. After what I've done for you I deserve the truth."

The truth. Which truth did she want? Would Susan be happy with her truth or with Tom's? Perhaps it was Kellie's truth she preferred. "I don't know what that is."

"Of course you do. Tell me how you rousted Kellie Delaney."

Claire's hands shook. She lifted the cup to her lips. Some of the liquid sloshed over into the saucer. She set it down on the low table in front of her. "Why do you assume that I've done it?"

"Because you're here and she's gone."

Claire looked down at her hands. "I think that was more Tom's doing than mine. He wasn't terribly enthusiastic about her staying and she's a woman with more than her share of pride. A woman like Kellie, attractive, educated, doesn't need to put up with a man's indecision. She'll find someone else."

Susan pursed her lips. "Maybe not. Sometimes it doesn't work that way."

Claire looked away. "Are we here to talk about Kellie Delaney?"

"I want to know your intentions. Will you stay here in Banburren?"

"Why wouldn't I?"

"My son doesn't want you here."

"That's his problem."

Susan looked resigned. "Claire. What will you do with your life? You were never happy here."

Claire ignored the question. "You're very angry with me, aren't you, Susan?"

"Very."

"Do you miss Kellie?"

"Aye. She was good for Tom and for Heather."

"What was she really like?"

"Strong and sweet at the same time. Spunky and yet sensitive. There was something that set her apart. Tom said she didn't belong here." Susan tilted her head to think. "But I think she did."

"Is he in love with her?"

"Aye. I see no point in sparing you, Claire. You brought a great deal on yourself. My thinking is that you deserve a bit of pain after what you've caused."

Claire's eyes filled with tears. "I'm sorry, Susan. You have no idea how sorry I am."

Susan softened. She reached across the distance that divided them and squeezed her hand. "I'm sure you are, lass. I'm sure you are. I'm not one to place blame. We all have something to be sorry for."

Tom was conscious of a bitter taste in his mouth. It had been there since he left home this morning. He had no stomach for his errand. But it was unavoidable. Kellie needed answers and she wouldn't wait forever. Dennis McGarrety was a law unto himself. He had nothing to lose. Tom wanted to assure him of his silence. He hoped that would be enough and that Kellie would be left alone.

McGarrety ground out his cigarette and motioned

Tom to a chair. They were in a house in West Belfast, shabby on the outside, comfortable within. "We have a bit of a problem."

Tom sat down and waited for him to continue.

"Kellie Delaney has approached Davies."

Tom felt the heat rise from his chest to his face. Had there ever been a woman so stubborn? He'd specifically told her to leave it alone. He willed himself not to react. "So?"

"She's made a nuisance of herself, Tom. We can't have her making accusations about Kevin Davies."

"She knows nothing about him," Tom said. "I've told her very little. She's harmless. Without me, no one has anything."

McGarrety smiled thinly. "Why are you here?"

"I've built a life for myself. I want no part of the past. Kevin Davies is a decent man. I've no reason to tell anyone anything."

"What if you've no choice?"

"How could that be?"

"What if you're called into court and sworn to tell the truth?"

"That isn't likely to happen, Dennis. No one knows that Davies and I worked together, no one except you."

"True." McGarrety stared at the wall. "And Claire and now Kellie Delaney."

Tom's head spun. Somewhere, outside this room, normal people went about the business of living. They woke to the alarm, ate their porridge and tea, kissed their wives, went off to work on the train and traded jests with other blokes. He wanted to be there, but first the ugliness here must be sorted out. "Are you suggesting that Kellie would bring up a suit?"

"I'm saying that Kellie Delaney has reason to want this matter exposed. She's proven that by going to Davies."

"If she had anything she wouldn't have bothered to go there. She would have called the police."

McGarrety thought a minute. "Good point." He looked at Tom. "Will you keep silent even if you're called up in an investigation?"

Tom looked his nemesis directly in the eye. "Aye."

McGarrety nodded. "Your word is good enough for me, Tom."

"There are conditions."

"There always are."

"I don't want Kellie hurt."

"Then she'll have to keep her mouth shut."

"I'll tell her."

"Davies is having a dinner party for his contributors. Kellie will be there."

"How do you know?"

"Caroline Davies was quite upset over Kellie's allegations regarding her husband. She wants her to see Kevin in a different light. She issued her a personal invitation and Kellie has accepted."

Tom didn't ask how McGarrety came by his information. He already had a good idea. "Will you be there?"

McGarrety smiled thinly. "I wouldn't miss it."

A flock of sheep blocked the single lane road leading to Banburren. Tom relaxed his hands on the wheel and mulled over his conversation with Dennis Mc-Garrety. Objectively, he could see the man's point. Kellie was a threat and a man like McGarrety would not be threatened. In fact, McGarrety would likely want to solve this problem the old-fashioned way—with a bullet.

He stared out the window at the lad herding the sheep, a country sort with freckled cheeks, wild hair and a grin that brought the sun with it. Had his own life ever been so simple? Perhaps, once, a long time ago. As he gazed at the scene before him, Tom's resolve hardened. He *would* reclaim that simplicity and he would start with Claire.

He would begin with trying to expedite Claire's dole agreement and find her a safe haven, and then he planned to get on with the rest of his life.

The road was now nearly clear of sheep. The boy lifted his hand. Tom waved back and pressed down on the gas pedal. Banburren was twenty miles away. With luck he would make it before dark. It would still be early enough to arrange for a flight. He was going to England. If Kellie insisted on taking matters into her own hands, he would tell her exactly what she was up against.

Kellie drummed her fingers on the table and stared out at the Thames. The tea she'd ordered twenty minutes before was tepid and her temper was beginning to rise. John Griffith was already late by nearly thirty minutes. She would give him another five and then—what? What would she do? Go to the police, or better yet, the press? The BBC would crucify Kevin Davies. The thought calmed her. She had alternatives to John Griffith and Scotland Yard.

She was nearly out the door when he walked in. "I'm terribly sorry, Miss Delaney. I underestimated the time. I hope you weren't waiting long."

"As a matter of fact, I've been here for quite some time."

He frowned. "You're angry. Shall we reschedule our appointment or do you have time to see me now?"

Damn the man. She needed him. Already he had the advantage over her and he knew it. "I am angry, Mr. Griffith. My brother was murdered and your department has done nothing at all to bring in his killer. I don't understand. Why am I the only one who cares? I've told you about Kevin Davies. Why can't you move forward with the information I've given you?"

Griffith pointed to a bench near the water. "Shall we sit down? I've an idea I'd like to share with you."

When they were seated he explained. "If we confronted Mr. Davies, he would deny that he'd ever spoken to you. It would be his word against yours and, Miss Delaney, the result would be in his favor. He's a popular politician and you are—" He paused.

"Not that important," she finished for him.

He nodded. "I'm afraid so."

She was beyond taking offense. "You said you had an idea."

He nodded. "I'd like you to wear a wire to the Davies' dinner party. Engage Davies in conversation. Get him to refer to the murders he told you about. If he says something incriminating on tape, we'll have grounds for an investigation.''

"How would that work?"

"You'll wear a small microphone taped to your chest underneath your clothing. It will transmit your conversation to a tape recorder.''

"Where will the tape recorder be?"

"Inside a lorry parked near the Davies' home.''

"Where will you be?"

"There will be three of us inside the lorry—a driver, a technician and me.'' He ticked them off on his fingers. ''I must warn you that it could be dangerous. On occasion the microphone has malfunctioned.''

"What does that mean?"

"It makes a whistling sound.''

"How often does that happen?"

"Hardly ever, but it is possible.'' He smiled at her. ''Are you up for this, Miss Delaney?''

"Is it the only way?''

"I believe so.''

"All right. I'll do it.''

Kellie stared into the full-length mirror and widened her eyes in surprise. How long had it been since she'd looked at herself? Had she lost weight or was it the dress she'd found at Simone's? The straight lines and tiny darts at the waist emphasized her slimness and the sandals lengthened her legs. She looked tall and slender and quite put together. She'd even gone to some effort with her hair, using a volumizing shampoo and blowing it dry until the edges curved around her face in feathery layers. The small microphone taped to her chest was completely invisible under the soft silk.

"Understated," Gillian paused on her way into the kitchen, "and gorgeous."

Kellie applied a touch of mascara and lip gloss. "I'm nervous."

"Don't be. You look wonderful. Think of it as parent night at Silverlake. There are enough posh people there to make anyone afraid of using the wrong fork. Irish expatriates can't be all that stuffy. I'm impressed that you got an invitation, even if you do have to go all the way to London."

Kellie shrugged. "I'm not complaining. I've decided to take my car." She said nothing to Gillian but she knew exactly why Caroline Davies had called her and why she'd accepted. If John Griffith needed evidence of the MP's duplicity, she would give it to him.

"Good idea," replied Gillian. "That way if you decide to stay the night, there won't be any worrying about train schedules."

The Davies' London town house was awash in light and laughter. Gillian was right. It was very like Silverlake. Bearded gentlemen in dark suits and ladies artfully painted and manicured conversed in groups. A caterer offered Kellie a glass of sparkling wine. She accepted and moved toward the group where her hostess held court.

She was ushered into the circle immediately. "Kellie," said Caroline Davies, "I'm so pleased you came. Allow me to introduce you."

Kellie smiled, glanced at one inquiring face after another, and blanked. After the woman's introductions, she had no idea who anyone was, but apparently no one expected it. Moving from one group to the other, she made her way around the room until she'd said something to everyone. Then she excused herself to go to the washroom. The plush carpet muffled her footsteps. The hallway was dimly lit. On a cabinet in the hall sat an array of family photos. The Davies' marriage was obviously a joining of families and Caroline was definitely English. Kevin Davies had come a long way from Portadown. She didn't blame him for not wanting to go back. He looked every inch the English gentleman.

After locking the door to the powder room Kellie checked her wire—it was still safely secured and completely invisible. Looking up Kellie stared at her reflection in the mirror. She didn't belong here with these glittering people who knew nothing about her. Oddly enough the evening had cemented her decision. She was going home to her own kind, if not West Belfast, then to somewhere else in Ireland.

Back in the dining room she was seated between a nondescript woman and a man whose name she couldn't remember. The woman picked up a three-pronged fork and spoke first. "I can never remember what this one is for."

Startled, Kellie looked at her. "Shellfish," she said automatically. "We're probably having shrimp."

"I suppose you're used to this kind of thing," the woman said.

"Not at all." Alcohol had loosened her tongue. "I'm more like a poor relation come to visit."

"You don't look like a poor relation."

"Thank you." Kellie introduced herself. "I'm Kellie Delaney. I don't remember meeting you earlier."

The woman smiled and extended her hand. "I'm Jessica Hammond. I'm the acting dean of Dresden Academy. I understand you're a teacher."

Kellie was startled. Had she mentioned her profession? "I am," she said slowly, "although I'm on leave for the term."

"I'm looking for an English teacher until the end of the term. Are you interested?"

Kellie's eyebrows rose. "Just like that? You know nothing about me."

"Caroline Davies is an alumna. Her recommendation is enough. If you could commit to the end of the fall term, I think I could use you."

Caroline Davies had recommended her! "May I think about it?"

The woman pulled a business card and a pen from her purse and wrote on the back. "Take a week. As soon as you've decided, let me know."

"Is Dresden nearby?"

Jessica shook her head. "Not really, Dresden is in Salisbury, but the salary is exceptional." She named a figure so out of the ordinary that Kellie could barely swallow. *What did it mean, this invitation and a cushy job offer? Was Davies actually bribing her? Did he really think she would look the other way, forget the murders of her brother and nephew for a job?* Her food tasted like steel wool in her mouth. If she did nothing else in her life, she would spend it taking this man down.

Dessert and coffee were served in the formal living room. Kellie was so intent on her thoughts she barely glanced at the man who stood in the entry. When she recognized him, her hand moved to her throat. The air felt suddenly thin and she fought the dizziness that closed in on every side.

Twenty-Four

Kellie waited until he made his way to her side. He reached her at the same time Kevin Davies did.

"Hello, Tom," he said smoothly. "I didn't realize you were in England."

"I just arrived." Tom's eyes never left Kellie's face.

Davies lowered his voice. "We need to talk."

"When?"

Kellie moved closer.

"Not here. Where are you staying?"

Tom looked at Kellie.

"He'll stay with me," she said, very conscious of the microphone attached to her chest.

Davies nodded. "I'll be in touch." He looked around. "Have some coffee. Blend in." He clapped Tom on the back. "Good to see you, old friend."

Kellie waited until he left them. "What are you doing here?"

"I might ask the same of you."

His eyes were intensely blue and the hot white flare in their centers frightened her. "What's wrong?"

"I told you to leave this alone."

"I'm going to finish it."

"No, you're not," he said evenly.

"Who do you think you are?" she asked, her voice trembling with anger.

He pitched his voice so that only she could hear. "They're dead. You're not. However, if you continue to stir the pot, you very well might be. Connor Delaney died because he got close to something very ugly."

"I know all about that."

"Then you must know what will happen if you do the same."

A voice came close to her ear. "Listen to the man, Kellie."

She turned around and stared into the face of Dennis McGarrety. He smiled brilliantly.

Trying to remain calm she forced the words through her teeth. "My goodness. Is this a coincidence, Mr. McGarrety?"

"You've been very busy," McGarrety said.

"I have nothing to say to you."

"Perhaps not, but I have something to say to you. You've been warned once already," he said. "This is your second notice. You won't be getting another." He walked away.

Kellie waited until he disappeared into a circle of people on the other side of the room. She turned to Tom. "Tell me again that Davies is a decent man and that he has nothing to do with McGarrety."

"That doesn't matter," said Tom. "The warning stands. You're in danger, Kellie. Let the professionals handle this."

"The *professionals* won't touch it without evidence. Davies is a popular politician." Kellie's voice was thin and hard.

"What are you saying?"

She looked around. People were beginning to stare. "We can't discuss this here."

"Where?"

"I'll leave first. My car is outside about halfway down the street. It's a white Rover. I'll wait for you."

"Give me fifteen minutes to arrange a meeting with Davies."

Kellie's heart pounded. "I want to be there."

Tom nodded. "Wait for me."

Kellie looked at her watch several times to be sure the battery was still working. Huddling down inside her coat, she refused to look at it again. He would come as quickly as he could.

Finally, the passenger door opened and he climbed inside. "Sorry. I couldn't get away."

Kellie pulled out of the parking space and headed toward the motorway.

"Where are we going?" he asked.

"Back to Oxford to a friend's flat. That's where I'm staying."

He looked at his watch. "That's quite a drive."

"It's only ten o'clock and neither of us has anything to do in the morning. Besides, it will give you plenty of time to explain why you've come."

She edged through a late-turning light and he winced. "Christ, Kellie, be careful."

She ignored him. "Start explaining."

"McGarrety is dangerous. He had your brother

murdered. He already knows you've approached Davies. What do you think he'll do to you?''

"Kevin Davies did a despicable thing and everyone hushed it up. Why didn't *you* say anything?''

"You can see where it got Connor.''

"Are you saying you didn't talk because you were afraid?''

Tom rubbed his chin. "Aye,'' he admitted. "I was afraid, but not at first. It was only after I came to my senses that I was afraid. People were dying all around me. At first I thought I was immune. Then I realized I was just lucky. That's when I began to be afraid. After six years in prison there was no need to talk anymore. In the meantime Kevin had reformed. He was a politician making his mark. I was hardly one to point fingers.''

He looked at Kellie, her profile pure and clear in the moonlight. "I'll warrant that your brother had more than a few things to hide. If he worked for British Intelligence, he saw his share of death.''

She'd thought of that herself and rejected it. She refused to have her image of Connor tarnished. "I won't allow this to go unpunished.''

"Give it up, Kellie. For God's sake, what will it take to make you understand how dangerous this is for you?''

"They offered me a job,'' she said bitterly. "They invited me to dinner to bribe me to keep my mouth closed.''

"They're afraid of what you'll do and *I'm* afraid of what they'll do when they realize there's no stopping you.''

"It's none of your business," she said primly.

"Of course it's my business," he shouted. "Connor was killed because he'd located me, the only living witness to an event that could destroy a politician's career. You located me as well. You're in danger because of me."

Her heart flip-flopped in her chest. She hoped John Griffith was hearing every word of this. "Do you feel responsible?"

"Completely."

She was silent for a long time. "How is Heather?" she asked at last.

"Well, thank you."

"And Claire?"

"Claire is Claire." He turned to her impatiently. "What difference does it make how Claire is? I want to know your intentions."

"Why?"

"Damn it, Kellie. You know why. Don't go on with this."

She stared straight ahead.

He sighed. "What will it take to satisfy you?"

"I want McGarrety charged with Connor's murder."

"That won't happen," Tom said flatly. "It never does."

"I want Davies to step aside," she continued. "He doesn't deserve his position. It's one of public trust. I certainly don't trust him. Who could trust a man who allows others to murder for him?"

"We don't know that."

"Don't we?" This time it was her voice that was

raised to an angry pitch. "Do you really believe that McGarrety wouldn't be reined in if Davies gave the order?"

Tom didn't answer.

"Kevin Davies knows what's going on, Tom. He isn't the least bit sorry for what he's done. He's only sorry that he's been found out."

"That may be true, but it doesn't lessen your danger. Why do you have to be the one to expose him?"

"Because you didn't do it," she shot back. "Because you didn't reveal what he'd done, my brother was killed."

"That's a twisted way of looking at things."

She shook her head and maneuvered into the far right lane to overtake another car. "I don't think so."

Tom leaned back against the headrest and closed his eyes. She was right but she was also wrong. "We'll see him tomorrow," he said after a minute, "and we need McGarrety there, too."

"Why?"

"Because then I'll know what's going to happen next. When I see them together, I'll know."

"What will you do then?"

"I'm not sure."

"Are you afraid now?"

"Terrified."

"Why? They won't hurt you. You spared them."

"Not this time. Not if they hurt you."

She was having trouble concentrating on the road. The lights on the motorway were always inadequate at night and she was more than a little interested in the way the conversation was going. "Why did you come here, Tom?"

"I worry about you."

"Now, or just in general?"

"Every bloody waking moment. I wonder how I could have let you go. I worry that you'll meet someone else, someone wonderfully suited to you. I worry that you'll never forgive me for Claire. But most of all I worry that if you don't come back, I'll never get over you." He looked at her. "Are you coming back, Kellie?"

She waited some time before answering. "I can't think about that now. I'm in the middle of this and I'm still very angry with you."

He nodded. "I don't blame you."

"She's still there, isn't she, living with you?"

"She's sharing the house, Kellie. She's not living with me. I haven't touched Claire in eight years and I have no intention of ever doing so again."

Her question was a whisper. When he heard the words every instinct told him to lie.

"You considered it, though, didn't you?"

He'd lost. He knew it before he answered. But if he was to go down, he would go down honestly. "Yes," he said, "for exactly one minute, I considered it, but that's all."

"You don't have to explain, Tom. It's all right. I understand."

He could see her hands on the wheel, tight, white-knuckled. "Does it matter that I'm quite sure I've never loved anyone the way I love you?"

"That's very nice," she said mechanically, "but I

wish you wouldn't say things like that to me. It makes everything that much harder. Let's just stick to the business at hand.''

He stared out the window. "Will your friend mind my staying with her? I can find a hotel.''

"Gilly won't mind and, besides, I'd rather you be with me. That way we'll both know what's happening at the same time.''

He nodded. "Fair enough. Tell me, Kellie, why did you attend the dinner?''

Strange how circumstances compromised one's character. She'd never known how skilled at lying she was. "Curiosity, and because he asked me to speak with his wife. I told her about Connor and Danny. Apparently she was quite upset at the thought of her beloved husband committing murder.''

"Did you speak to her this evening?''

"No. You showed up and there was no opportunity.''

They were in Oxford now, heading toward the north end of town. Kellie pulled into a charming brick complex, obviously modern but built to look like it had weathered the ages. It was a few minutes past midnight.

"Will your friend still be awake?''

Kellie looked up at the window overlooking the garden. "Her light is on. She'll want to meet you.''

Gillian, wrapped in her bathrobe, was watching the last minutes of a late-night talk show. Her eyes widened when Kellie introduced Tom. She stood and held out her hand. "My goodness, it's grand to meet you. I've heard a great deal about you and your daughter.''

Tom grinned. "I'm not sure how to take that, but since you're still speaking to me, I'll accept it as a compliment."

Kellie stared. She'd never seen this side of Tom Whelan before. He wasn't exactly flirting, but he had definitely charmed Gillian.

"Kellie thought it might be acceptable for me to stay overnight here in your living room. If that's not convenient I can find a hotel."

Gillian shook her head. "I wouldn't think of sending you away. I was just about to go to bed anyway. I'll bring out some blankets and towels and you'll be set. Can I get you anything first? Maybe a cup of tea?"

"Not for me, thanks," said Tom.

Kellie followed Gillian down the hall to the linen closet. "Thank you, Gillian. He showed up after dinner. I had no idea he was coming."

"He doesn't have to stay on the couch, Kellie. You're both adults and under the circumstances—"

Kellie shook her head firmly. "Nothing's changed. He's still married and living with his wife."

"He's very attractive. You didn't tell me that."

"Yes," said Kellie slowly. "I suppose he is."

Gillian stared at her. "What is it?"

"I'm not sure." She chewed the inside of her lip. "A month ago, I wanted him desperately."

"And now?"

Kellie looked at her friend, her eyes bright and hard. "He rejected me. From one day to the next everything changed. He told me he loved me and then Claire came home and it was as if nothing had ever happened between us. When I needed reassurance the most, he let me down. How does one get over something like that?''

"Kellie." Gillian gripped her shoulders. "We're all human. People make mistakes. The man is here. If he wanted to be with his wife, he would be there."

Kellie sighed. "I want this to be over. I can't think of anything else besides Connor and Danny and Kevin Davies. It's consumed my mind."

Gillian handed her a set of snowy sheets, two towels and a washcloth. "You're a strong woman, Kellie Delaney, one of the strongest I know. Your background has done that for you. You'll get through this. Whatever decision you make about Tom Whelan will be the right one."

Kellie kissed her friend's cheek. "You're a wonderful friend, Gilly. Thank you for being here."

"Don't mention it. And if you're truly not interested in Tom Whelan, be sure to let me know first."

Twenty-Five

Claire was cleaning the kitchen floor, reluctantly. Housework had never appealed to her. Only the tacky feeling wherever she stepped prompted her to take on the unpleasant task of crouching on her hands and knees to scrub the pathway and corners where food and spills had collected.

The ring of the phone was a welcome respite. When she listened further she was concerned and then angry. "I'll be right there," she said tersely.

Replacing the phone, she grabbed her jacket and ran out the door. *Damn Tom Whelan. Where was he? What was so important that he needed to absent himself for days at a time?* She was tempted to call his mobile phone, but pride kept her from it. She wouldn't give him the satisfaction of knowing she couldn't cope.

Mother Mary Patricia had come up in the world, Claire reflected bitterly. Years ago she'd been an eighth-level teacher. Now she was principal of the school Heather attended. Claire hadn't cared for the nun when she was a student in her catechism class. And she wasn't looking forward to this meeting.

A mousy woman dressed in gray wool ushered her into the principal's office. The nun sat at her desk, elbows perched on top, hands touching in a pyramid. Heather stood before her even though there were two empty chairs in the room. Claire gritted her teeth. She wished she had bothered to change clothes.

"Hello, Mrs. Whelan," said the nun. "Please sit down."

How long had Heather been standing? Suddenly Claire was angry. "I *will* sit down." She pulled over one of the chairs. "Heather, love, you've been very ill. It isn't good for you to strain yourself. Come and sit with me."

Obediently, the child climbed on Claire's lap.

Claire kissed her cheek. "Don't worry, love," she whispered. "It can't be that bad. No one's dead." She looked at the nun. "Now, Mother. What exactly is the difficulty?"

"It isn't *one* difficulty, Mrs. Whelan. Heather isn't herself lately. She's done quite a few things that are uncharacteristic. Perhaps you can explain."

"What exactly has she done?"

The woman ticked Heather's transgressions off on her fingers. "For one thing, she pulled the fire alarm. When I asked her why she'd done so, she told me she *felt like it.* Then she refused to pick up the crayons and markers she was using for an art project. Her teacher asked her to clean up around her desk and she told her *she didn't want to.*"

Claire's eyebrows rose. "Is that all?"

Mother Mary Patricia exploded. "No, as a matter of fact, it isn't all. But it is very unusual. Heather is normally a very polite, accommodating young lady. Lately, I would hardly describe her that way. We can deal with it, of course, but we're not here to do that. We work with the total child. I, for one, would like to know if there is a reason she's acting out.''

Claire's heart pounded. ''Heather, love, please wait outside in the front office. Tell the secretary that you need to sit down.''

Again, the child did as she was told.

When the two women were alone and the door was tightly closed, Claire began. ''I think my return has been a difficult adjustment for her. After all, to have a mother again after seven years is traumatic.''

''I would think having a mother would be a positive addition to her life.''

Damn the woman. ''I didn't realize you had a degree in psychology, Mother,'' Claire said sweetly.

Mother Mary adjusted her glasses. ''I'll be blunt, Claire Whelan. You were difficult as a child. I didn't tolerate it then and I won't now. This is a respected private school. We can't have unacceptable behavior here. It isn't good modeling for the other girls. I'm willing to give Heather a chance, given her previous record, but I have to know what I'm working with.''

Claire's instinct was to stonewall, but Tom's advice about fitting in stopped her. There was Heather to consider. She sighed. ''Heather is confused,'' she explained. ''My husband and I are having difficulties. I don't know how long I'll be here. I'm sure it's affecting my daughter. Unfortunately, there isn't a thing I can do about it. Please, be patient with her. I'll do whatever I can.''

The nun was silent for long seconds. ''Thank you,'' she said after a bit. ''I appreciate the honesty and I'm sorry for your situation." She hesitated. "As long as we're having this discussion, may I ask if I should speak to Heather's father?"

Claire shrugged. "Not unless you're a marriage counselor."

"Hardly, although there are those who are influenced by the clergy. Susan Whelan is one of those."

"I don't think her son is."

The nun leaned forward. "How are *you,* Claire? We've all been quite worried about you."

Claire stood. "I'm weary, Mother, and dreadfully worried about my daughter. If you can help her, I would deeply appreciate it."

The nun nodded approvingly. "We'll do what we can. Take a minute to talk with Heather and then send her in to me."

Claire was only too anxious to leave. In her haste to close the door and reassure Heather, she nearly bumped into a young woman standing at the copy machine.

She smiled. "Hello, Claire."

Dear God, what now? "Hello," Claire replied cautiously.

"How are you?"

"I'm well, thank you, and you?"

"Fine."

The woman was lovely in the dark-haired, creamy-skinned way of Irish women. She looked familiar. *Who was she?*

"I noticed Heather waiting outside on the bench. Is something wrong?"

Claire cleared her throat. "A little misunderstanding, that's all."

The woman lowered her voice. "If I can help, let me know. Even though James is gone, I'm still her aunt."

Shocked into silence, Claire stared at the woman. *A relative, her sister-in-law, and she didn't recognize her.* Another reminder of how she no longer fit. "You're Kate Whelan from Dublin, James's wife?"

"Actually, I'm his widow."

Claire flushed. "I'm very sorry."

"Thank you."

Kate had asked her something. She had no idea what it was. "I can't stay," she said. "I've got to find Heather. Mother wants to speak with her again and so do I." She moved purposely toward the door.

"I meant what I said," Kate called after her. "Call me any time."

Claire didn't answer. She would find Heather and then she would call Tom. Something had to change. She was tired of waiting. She wanted her own life.

The lovely old building where the Irish members of Parliament had their offices was set back on Penbrook Lane across from Big Ben. Wooden benches, mature trees and a garden gave it a pastoral quality in a city where green trees and grass were relegated to Hyde Park. Tom opened the hand-carved oak door and motioned Kellie in ahead of him. Together they climbed the stairs to the second floor.

Kevin Davies, casually dressed in tweed and khaki, stood and held out his hand first to Tom and then to

Kellie. "Thank you for coming," he said. "Please, sit down."

The office was plushly decorated. A Persian carpet covered the wooden floor, expensive draperies bordered the windows and a collection of fine art and family photos added color to the walls. The furnishings were comfortable and modern.

"I was surprised to see you, Tom," began Davies. "It's been a long time. We've lost touch."

Tom nodded. "It was better for both of us that way."

"I want to assure you, as I've assured Kellie, that I don't condone Dennis McGarrety's actions."

"Where is McGarrety?" asked Tom. "I thought he would be here."

"He had to leave," apologized Davies. "I'm sorry."

Kellie broke in. "You might not condone Mr. McGarrety's actions, but you don't condemn them, either."

"Actually, I do, Kellie. But I can't take responsibility for every disenfranchised group that supports my candidacy. These people, unless they're felons, are allowed to vote. They vote for whom they please. I can't control them."

Kellie had to admit that his logic sounded sensible, but she was still angry. "My brother and nephew are dead because Connor was closing in on the details of the incident you told me about. How can you absolve yourself of responsibility?"

"I had no knowledge of McGarrety's plans. We don't move in the same circles. We don't speak or communicate in any way. I finished with all that years ago. Isn't that right, Tom?''

Tom Whelan, his eyes narrowed, forehead furrowed, shook his head. "I thought so, but now I'm not sure. You moved in the same circles last night. Kellie's right. He's acting with your implied consent. He knows your every move. It is your responsibility and you must do something. If that means revealing the truth about what happened, so be it.''

"That's easy for you to say." Davies voice shook. "I'll be ruined.''

Kellie needed him to say much more than that. She interrupted. "The incident happened fifteen years ago. Surely there's a statute of limitations.''

"There's no limitation on murder," Davies said. "The women were innocent victims. I'll lose my position and go to jail.''

"Are you sure they were innocent?" Kellie suggested.

"Whether they were or not, they didn't deserve what I did to them." He shuddered. "I can still see that car going up in flames.''

She pressed him. "Was that the first time you killed anyone?''

Tom looked at her strangely.

"Lord, no," said Davies, "but I'd never killed a woman, no matter what her affiliations were.''

"It happened, Kevin," Tom said gently. "You did what you did. Perhaps losing your position is your penance.''

"There has to be another way.''

Tom shook his head. "I don't think so. I came here

to warn Kellie that she may be in danger. McGarrety knows she approached you. How would he know that, Kevin?''

"I have no idea," he blustered. "Perhaps we were seen together or perhaps there is a leak somewhere else." His eyes widened. "You don't think I told him?''

"Aye," said Tom. "I do. He knew about your dinner party. He knew Kellie would be there.''

"That's absurd. Why would I tell him that?''

"To warn her away.''

"Why would I arrange a high-paying position at an exclusive girls' school if I wanted to threaten her?''

"To throw her off the scent," Tom replied promptly.

"I'm not taking the job," said Kellie. "You can't buy my silence. My brother was killed along with his four-year-old son. Do you have children, Mr. Davies?''

"I do, and believe me, I understand your pain. There was no buying intended. I merely wanted you to know how appreciative I am for your cooperation.''

Kellie wet her lips. "That's just it, Mr. Davies. I'm not going to stay silent. I'm going to the authorities with what you told me. Dennis McGarrety must be stopped. If you won't do it, I will. I'm sorry that your past may be exposed, but I'm not backing down.''

Sweat beaded on the politician's brow despite the cool temperature. "How long do I have?''

"The longer I wait, the more dangerous it is for me.''

"Is there anything I can do to dissuade you?"

"No?"

"What if I resign?"

Kellie looked at Tom.

"You would do that?" she asked.

"If you agree not to implicate me."

"Why?"

"I'd rather go out with my name clean and my pension intact than fight public disapproval and financial penalty after it's smeared."

"What about McGarrety?" Tom asked.

"He'll have no reason to harm Kellie. He's not a psychopath, just a man with a mission. I'll handle him."

"If we don't tell anyone, what guarantee do we have that Kellie and I won't be targeted?"

"I won't tell McGarrety what's happened here today. He'll have nothing on Kellie."

Once more Tom shook his head. "Dennis isn't stupid. He'll figure it out. We have to think of something else."

Kellie was done with thinking. She had Kevin Davies's confession on tape. It was all she needed.

"What if, instead of resigning, I decide not to run again?"

Kellie was finished. She stood. "That is your choice to make. I appreciate your time and your sacrifice, Mr. Davies. But I must tell you that I'm not through with Dennis McGarrety. He had Connor and Danny killed. I want to see him go to prison."

Davies passed his hand over his eyes. "Dennis

McGarrety is a survivor. He's also very lucky. Be careful. He hasn't a great deal to lose.''

Kellie drove Tom to the airport at Heathrow. She pulled up to the pavement outside the domestic departure area. "Goodbye, Tom. Take care," she said brightly.

"Do me a favor," he said.

"Of course."

"Don't go after McGarrety alone, Kellie. You've won a major victory. Davies is finished. I don't agree with his assessment of McGarrety's character. He's an assassin. One more dead body makes little difference to him."

"All right," she said. "I won't go after him alone."

"It's very important that you wait on this. When Dennis learns you've had anything to do with Davies giving up the race, he'll come after you."

"I understand, Tom," Kellie said impatiently. "You're repeating yourself."

He swore under his breath, unbuckled his seat belt, leaned over and kissed her hard on the mouth. "For an intelligent woman, you're very stupid sometimes. When you're finished here, call me."

With that, he opened the door, reached into the back for his bag and disappeared into the terminal without looking back.

Twenty-Six

When he pulled the car up to the front of the house, Tom could see through the window that his mother was in the kitchen with Claire. Swearing softly, he turned off the engine and climbed the front steps. He didn't want to have this conversation in front of an audience.

"Hello," he said more easily than he felt. "I'm home. Where's Heather?"

"In her room," said Claire. "We've been doing schoolwork. She's nearly finished."

Tom kissed his mother and picked at the carrots she was peeling. "What are you doing here?"

Susan slapped his arm. "Is that any way to greet your mother? Claire invited me to dinner. She's cooking."

"Another treat," he muttered under his breath.

Claire's mouth tightened. Quickly she turned to stir something on the stove.

"What are we having?" asked Tom.

"Stew," she said without looking at him. "If you don't like it, help yourself to something else."

"Stew is fine. Do we have everything or shall I go out?"

Claire turned, hands on her hips holding the ladle,

stew dripping on the floor. "You just got home," she hissed. "There's no excuse for you to leave."

Tom frowned. "What are you talking about?"

"You're never here. I'm doing everything. This is ridiculous."

He looked pointedly at the ladle. "You're dripping on the floor."

Claire exploded. "To hell with the floor. Damn you, Tom Whelan. There are more important things than a clean floor."

He grabbed the ladle from her hand. "Obviously. What's gotten into you? You're hysterical."

"And why not!" she shouted at him. "I should be hysterical. I'm terrified of every knock on the door. I have a nonexistent husband and a daughter who is acting out, most likely because she doesn't know who she's going to lose next."

"Stop it, Claire," Tom glanced at his mother who stood at rigid attention near the sink. "Heather will hear you. What are you talking about?"

Tears spilled over and ran down Claire's cheeks. "Your mother already knows everything and you know perfectly well what I'm talking about. I can't take this anymore. I thought you were through with this and now that woman has dragged you into it all over again."

"If you're referring to Kellie, she was the one who was dragged into it. I was already there."

"They left you alone for fifteen years, Tom. Now, coincidentally, they decide to resurrect the Kevin Davies incident? Don't make me laugh. Kellie isn't the only one in danger. Without you, nothing Davies did can be proven. Have you thought of that?''

He sighed and ran an unsteady hand through his hair. He wouldn't ask how she knew where he'd been. He wasn't ready for that yet. "What's this about Heather?''

Claire lifted her hands and dropped them. Turning away, she shook her head.

Susan stepped forward. "Mother Mary called Claire in today. Apparently Heather is being defiant at school.''

"Heather?'' Tom was incredulous.

"Children react differently to things, Tom. You can't assume that she's unaffected because she doesn't say anything. This situation isn't a good one. Kellie came into this house and she's gone. Now, Claire is leaving. From what I understand you haven't been much help lately.''

Tom struggled to control his temper. Did no one understand what he was going through? "I'll see to Heather,'' he said. "Don't wait dinner on us. We're going out.''

He left them in the kitchen, standing frozen in their places, and he realized that he didn't care. His daughter was the one who mattered.

Heather had to be coaxed into her jacket. Tom looked at his child, his love, at her rosy cheeks, her shiny light-brown hair, her eyes clear and pale as glass. She didn't look defiant. She looked sweet and clean and lovely.

Brennan's, Banburren's only claim to a real restaurant, was exceptionally busy for a Thursday evening.

Instead of being seated immediately at a table, they were ushered into a sitting room, handed menus and drinks and left alone. Heather sipped her lemon fizzle and Tom his ale. Neither spoke for a long time. Finally Tom broke the silence. "What would you like to eat, love?"

She shrugged. "I don't know. Where are Mum and Gran?"

"I didn't want to share you tonight," Tom explained.

"Mum was shouting."

"Sometimes people shout. She's all right now."

Heather shook her head. "I don't think so." She tilted her head. "She cries when she thinks no one is looking."

"Does she now?"

"Why can't she live with us?"

"Because she was gone for too long. She wouldn't be happy with me nor I with her."

Heather's eyes clouded. "I don't want her to go. I like her."

Tom sighed. "I'm sorry, love."

"Why must she leave us?"

It was a feeling he experienced quite often lately, this sense of shame, almost a dislike of himself. "She needs to find a place of her own where she can be comfortable."

"Is Kellie coming back?"

He choked on his ale. "Why do you ask?"

Heather shrugged. "She said she would e-mail me, but she hasn't."

Tom looked at her downcast eyes. "I'm sorry, I don't know," he said again, helplessly.

Susan was still there when he brought Heather home and tucked her into bed. Claire had already gone up. The door to her room was shut and the tiny space near the floor was dark as pitch.

Tom returned to the kitchen and poured himself a mug of tea. "Say it," he said flatly.

"I have every intention of doing so," replied Susan. "What in the name of Mary and all the saints do you think you're doing?"

"Be specific, please."

"If you don't want any part of the woman send her away. Look what you're doing to your child."

He turned around and frowned at his mother. "I want to but where do you suggest I send a woman with no money and no job prospects? I can't support two households. She wants to go on to university. She's applied for dole money. We're waiting for the approval to come through."

Susan tapped her fingers on the table. She shook her head. "Your father would be turning in his grave to know that one of his own took the dole."

Tom struggled for patience. "Claire isn't one of his own, Mam. She's my estranged wife. I've also filed for divorce."

"That's the first sensible thing you've said tonight."

"Thank you," he said bitterly. "Meanwhile, what do I do with her?"

Susan thought a minute and then drew a deep breath. "She can stay with me."

He stared at her. "You can't mean that."

"I do. I've thought about it for some time now. She isn't happy here and you're miserable. Heather is feeling out of sorts because the two of you are. It's a difficult situation. I can help. I'm alone. The house is big enough for the both of us. Claire can leave when she's ready."

"Have you told her about your offer?"

"Not yet. I wanted to talk with you first."

Tom wrapped his arms around his mother. "Thank you. You're a saint."

"Not quite."

"Almost."

"Well—" Her eyes twinkled. "Almost."

Kellie sat in John Griffith's office in London. It was dusk and throughout the city, lights warmed the deepening night.

"You've done a marvelous job, Kellie," Griffith said, pouring brandy into her glass. "You're very brave and, I might add, relentless."

She wasn't ready to forgive British Intelligence. They'd dropped the ball in this investigation. She'd done their job for them. "Will it be enough?" she asked shortly.

"It will. At this very moment, an order for the arrest of Dennis McGarrety is being processed. Davies has already made a full confession in exchange for no prison time. He's finished politically and I imagine when the papers are through with him, he'll be finished socially as well.''

"It's too bad for him and his family," she said. "The press are running with the story. It's on the front page of every newspaper."

"Don't feel sorry for him. The man never paid for his crimes. It's past time."

"What will happen to McGarrety?"

"We have to find him first. When that happens he'll be charged with Connor and Danny's murder. You should understand that until he's caught, you're in danger. What are your plans now?"

"My bags are packed. I'm off to Liverpool and from there I'll take the ferry over to Dublin. I've been offered a position at the National School for next term." She finished her drink and stood. "I'll be leaving now."

He shook her hand. "Stay out of sight, Kellie. Tell no one where you're going and don't go anywhere near Belfast until McGarrety is arrested. Please, keep in touch. Good luck to you.''

She waited in the queue for a taxi to Heathrow. Her mind was far away. Seeing Tom again had shaken her. She didn't want to suffer over Tom Whelan and his child along with everything else.

What was it that her mother had once told her sister who was bemoaning a broken heart? *If a man doesn't recognize what he has, then he isn't deserving. If a man is what you want, there are more out there.* It wasn't that Tom didn't recognize what he had, it was that he'd done so too late. The entire situation wasn't clean. Why, then, couldn't she leave it alone?

Kellie swallowed the lump in her throat. She wanted to see her mother, hear her no-nonsense voice, listen to her practical philosophy for managing the days, feel the aura of the house where she'd grown up, drink tea as only Mary Delaney could make it, eat her soda bread dripping in sweet butter, breathe in the yeast smell that hung over the kitchen.

She closed her eyes and thought of Tom. No matter how badly she wanted to, she would not stop in Banburren on the way home.

Tom's fists were clenched. ''We've gone through all of this already.''

Claire sat at the table and shivered, completely helpless, dependent. Despite everything, all of their conversations and their acrimony, she had fallen apart when the day came for her to move on without Tom.

Trust had become foreign to Claire. The past seven years had eradicated the very idea from her consciousness. Every encounter outside her comfort zone was a potential trap. Danger lurked behind every greeting, every handshake, every casual question. Her mind and body were desperate for a level existence where simple tasks were carried out with the tedious, rhythms of boring regularity.

She yearned for normalcy, perhaps a small house with a garden, a job, friends, a glass or two on Fridays at the local pub. She craved security, safety, regular meals, and simple things like hand lotion and skin cream. And here was her husband telling her it wasn't to be, that she had to take a few risks—that it was time to try something new.

Scooping out a ladle of oats, Tom dumped them in a bowl and pushed it in front of her. Obediently, like a child, she picked up her spoon and began to eat.

"There's sugar in the bowl." He gestured toward the middle of the table.

"It doesn't matter," she said, forcing the food into her mouth, swallowing without tasting, recognizing her body's need for sustenance.

He poured the tea, added sugar and passed it to her. She drank it. Tom sat down across from her, his own oats neglected. "You can stay there for as long as you like. My mother wants you."

"No, she doesn't," Claire said tonelessly. "Susan is being kind. She's tolerating me because you don't want me."

"Damn it, Claire. You don't want me, either."

Claire's eyes filled. "How do you know?"

"You need someone. You're afraid, but you don't really want *me.*"

"What about Heather? Will I see her?"

"You're her mother." He sighed and leaned back in his chair. "I realize how important that bond is. Kellie helped me see that. You should be a part of your daughter's life. You love her. Somehow we'll work it out between us."

"What of Kellie? Will you work things out with her?"

Tom stared at something over her head, considering his reply. At last he spoke. "The circumstances aren't right for us now. I had hoped—" He stopped. "Never mind. I'll wait while you clean up and talk to Heather. Then I'll walk you to Mam's."

*   *   *

She was ready in less than ten minutes. Her no-nonsense style, no makeup, sensible hair and rough hands required little grooming. He remembered the way she had been when she first wanted him, long fluttery eyelashes and pink lips, a softly feminine woman. She must have cultivated her current habits during her prison years when softness was not a virtue. Tom recognized his own detachment. He had no feelings left for her, other than the regard of one human being toward another. Regret for mistakes of the past was pointless. He knew that. Still, he would have given a great deal to live his youth over again.

They'd decided Claire should be the one to tell her.

Heather Whelan nodded her head as if the news that her mother was moving out of her house and in with her grandmother happened to her every day.

"Do you have any questions, love?"

"No."

"Are you sure you understand?"

"Yes."

"Tell me, in your own words"

"I'll stay here with Da and you'll live with Grandma," Heather replied flatly.

It was such a small part of what Claire had explained to her. "What else?"

"You'll see me as much as I want. I'll have two homes."

Claire reached out and lifted Heather's chin with her hand so that the little girl was looking directly at her. "Is that all right with you, love? Do you mind that I won't be here?"

Heather's eyes, clear and gray, stared at her mother. "Why can't you live here with us?"

"Da and I don't want to live together," Claire explained patiently.

"I don't want you to live somewhere else. I want us all to live here."

I do, too. The words leaped into her mind. She caught them before they were out. "That isn't possible. Your da and I are divorcing."

"What's that?"

"People who were once married decide not to live together anymore."

"Why?"

"Because they're different and the other person makes them unhappy."

"I don't know anyone who is divorced."

"Neither do I, but that doesn't mean it isn't happening. People make mistakes when they're young and then they wish themselves back to the place where they were before the mistake was made. Surely you've made a mistake before and wished it never happened."

Heather nodded. "I wished I'd never given Christina Murray my Henrietta doll. I wanted it back and she wouldn't give it to me."

Claire hid a smile. "Well, there, you see. You do understand about mistakes."

"I think so," Heather said slowly. She looked at her mother. "What about me? Am I a mistake?"

"Of course not," Claire gasped, horrified. *Lord,*

deliver me from intelligent children. "You are the best thing in the world. Think how sad Da and I would be without you."

Again Heather nodded. "That's what Da says. I just wanted to be sure."

Relieved, Claire closed her eyes and drew in a deep breath.

"You aren't going away again, are you?"

Claire reached out and drew her child's slight body into her arms. "No, love. I won't go away again, not like the last time."

Twenty-Seven

Rain slanted against the roof of the ferry, running down the windows, washing clean the deck, forcing all but the most seasick passengers to take refuge inside the cabin. Gusts of wind moaned, waves crested and the deck tilted at an alarming angle, making it impossible for the kitchen to serve tea and its renowned oxtail soup. It was an intense storm and the ferry was behind schedule. Kellie shivered and burrowed down inside her jacket.

She must have slept because she didn't remember the man sliding into the seat beside her. He sat with his arms folded against his chest and the hood of his parka pulled low over his face. She yawned and would have closed her eyes again when he slipped off the hood, turned to her and spoke.

"It's lovely to see you again, Kellie."

Speechless, Kellie turned to look at Dennis McGarrety. She was sure her heart had stopped pumping blood to her arms and legs because, try as she might, she couldn't move them.

"Don't say a word, lass. I've something to tell you."

She waited, paralyzed with fear.

He smiled. "Good girl. This ferry will dock in less

than an hour. You'll come with me. Don't try anything foolish, Kellie, lass, or the wee girl will be hurt.''

Kellie wet her lips. "What wee girl?"

"Why, Heather Whelan of course."

"Are you going to kill me?" she whispered. Her words sounded polite, vacant, as if she were asking for milk for her tea.

McGarrety shook his head. "I've no taste for murder anymore, although I've done my share in the past. But there are those who don't mind so much. I leave it to them."

"What do you want from me?"

"You're my ticket out of Ireland, Kellie Delaney, the only one I've got. I want a new passport and free passage to the States, and you're going to make sure I get them."

"Where are you taking me?"

"We'll take your car and drive to County Clare where I've a house near the sea. From there I'll notify the authorities."

The question had to be asked. "What if you don't get what you want?"

"That isn't an option."

"What if they say no? What if I'm not important enough to allow you to get away?"

"Then it will be up to Tom. It will be Tom Whelan who has the final aye or nay."

"I don't understand."

"You don't have to understand, Kellie, love. Just do as I say."

"What if I won't do it?"

"I beg your pardon?"

"What if I won't go with you? Will you shoot me here on the ferry, in front of everyone?"

"No, lass," he said softly. "I wouldn't do that. I'd simply place a call to Banburren and the wee lass, Heather Whelan, will have her throat cut."

Kellie gasped and whitened.

McGarrety smiled. "Now, then. Are we agreed that you'll come with me without commotion?"

Kellie nodded. "I'll do whatever you ask. Please just don't hurt Heather."

"Not if it can be helped," he said and looked out the window. "The storm's settled itself. Would you care for a cup of tea?"

Heather waved goodbye to her friend and turned the corner toward home. Ahead of her the street was empty. She frowned. Where was Mam? She was supposed to meet her near the bakery. Shrugging off her disappointment, she quickened her pace. Mam was always late. Heather would run home and surprise her at the gate.

A shadow crossed her path and then a large man stepped in front of her. "Hello, Heather," he said.

Heather looked at the man doubtfully. She'd never seen him before on her walk home, and she'd been told not to talk to strangers. "Hello."

He smiled. "Your da had to go away for a bit. He wants me to take you home."

She brightened. "My mam is supposed to come for me. She's staying with my granny. Will you take me there?"

"Aye. That's exactly where I'll be taking you, to your mam who's staying with your granny." He picked up her school bag and held out his hand. "Come along now."

She slipped her hand inside his. "What's your name?"

"Colin," he said.

"How do you know my da?"

"We worked together a long time ago, before you were born."

Heather skipped along beside him until the village was behind them. When they passed the bend in the road that led to Susan's house, Heather stopped and looked around. "This isn't the way."

"I'm taking a shortcut. We'll be there faster."

"But you're going the wrong way."

"It will be faster." He smiled. "You'll see. Trust me."

Heather tugged at his hand. Something was wrong. "I want to go the other way."

The man's smile faded. "We're going this way."

Tears spilled down her cheeks. He wouldn't let go of her hand. "I don't like you. I'm not going with you."

"Heather?" Claire's voice, frantic, called out from behind them. "What's going on? What are you doing with my daughter?"

Immediately, Heather was lifted off the ground. A hand was clamped across her mouth. The man began to run.

"Wait." Claire shouted. She chased after them. Fear lent her speed. "Please, wait."

Heather began to kick and squirm. The hand slipped across her mouth, freeing her lip. She bit down, hard, drawing blood. "Mam, Mam, please help," she screamed.

Cursing, the man pulled his torn flesh from Heather's teeth, slowed and waited for Claire to catch up. He was strong and fast, but no match for a struggling child and a desperate woman.

Panting, Claire stopped directly in front of him, her eyes on Heather's face. She forced herself to speak calmly. "Colin, what are you doing?"

"I need to borrow your daughter for a bit," he said, still struggling to keep hold of the squirming child.

"What do you want?" Claire demanded.

The man hesitated. Everyone would know soon enough. "McGarrety needs a hostage until he's given safe passage to America. I won't harm the lass. When McGarrety is safe, I'll bring her home."

Claire stepped forward. "Then take me," she said. "Leave my daughter, for God's sake. You know me. I keep my word. I kept it for seven years in Maidenstone. I'll come with you willingly. Let the child go."

He hesitated. Blood flowed from the bite. A grown woman who was willing and who knew the stakes would be easier to manage than a child. And she was Tom Delaney's wife. Tom wouldn't want her harmed.

Colin thought hard. He didn't usually make decisions like this. If only he could check with someone. But that wasn't possible. Carefully, he set Heather on her feet. She ran to her mother and clung to her waist. Claire held her close.

"If you try to run away, he'll send someone else.

You know that." He nodded at Heather. "She'll never be safe."

"I know, I know. I won't run away. I'll cooperate, just don't harm my daughter." Claire knelt down and took Heather's face in her hands. "Heather, go to Gran's. Tell her what happened. She'll know what to do."

"Are you coming with me?" Heather sobbed.

"No, love. I'm going with Colin. I have to go. He needs one of us. Do you understand?"

Heather shook her head and held on to her mother.

Claire set her away, keeping hold of her arms. "You must do as I say, Heather. Go home. Tell Gran and your da. Please." Her voice cracked. "Go now."

Heather broke free of her arms and ran back toward Banburren. Claire watched her for a minute and then forced herself to look away. "Where are we going?" she asked.

"Sligo. We have a house there."

Claire nodded. "I know it. Do you have a car?"

"Aye," the man said. "It's parked around the bend."

Heather lay on the floor curled into a fetal position, her thumb wedged tightly in her mouth, and stared at the telly. She hadn't said a word in more than two hours.

Susan was frightened. She had never seen the child so silent and still. She was nearly ready to pack her up and take her to the doctor. Tom was delivering a set of pipes to a man in Galway. She had no idea where Claire was, but she wasn't surprised at her lapse. Susan had little faith in her daughter-in-law's transformation. Mothering didn't come naturally to her. Claire was Claire, and sooner or later her real disposition would reveal itself.

"Can I fix you a bite to eat, love?" Susan asked the silent child.

Heather kept her eyes on the television and rocked her head back and forth.

Susan frowned, stepped over her granddaughter and turned off the television. "You'll answer me when I speak to you, Heather Whelan."

Heather stared blankly at her grandmother.

Susan sat down on the floor, worked the offensive thumb out of the child's mouth and held both small hands in her own. "Tell your granny what's wrong, love. Did something happen at school?"

"No," Heather whispered.

"Something must have happened," Susan insisted. "I've never seen you look so sad."

"Where's Da?" asked Heather.

Susan looked at the clock. It was nearly six o'clock. "He'll be home soon." She kissed the little girl's cheek. "Will you tell him what's troubling you?"

Heather's eyes filled. She nodded.

Susan turned the television back on and settled Heather on the couch with a blanket. "I'll call him on the mobile phone and find out exactly where he is." She walked into the kitchen and sighed with relief when she saw Tom's car pull up beside the house.

"Thank God you're here," she said when he was inside.

"Where's Claire?" he asked looking around. "She was supposed to pick Heather up after school and stay with her until I came home."

"I don't know where she is. Heather walked to my house after school and we came here to wait for you."

"Thanks for staying with her, Mam. I didn't expect to be so long."

"Something's wrong with the child, Tom."

He frowned. "Is she ill?"

"I don't know, but she isn't acting like herself at all."

The double ring of the telephone interrupted them. Tom answered it.

"Yes," he said, "this is Tom Whelan." A pause. "You're mistaken, Mr. Griffith. My daughter is here with me." He looked at his mother and, holding the phone to his ear, walked into the sitting room to satisfy himself that Heather was home. "She's here watching the telly." Another pause. His hand tightened on the phone. "I see." He picked up a pencil and jotted something down on a pad of paper near the phone. Then he ripped the top sheet off and stuffed it into his pocket. "Yes. I'll be in touch," he said before hanging up.

"What's the matter?" asked Susan.

"Dennis McGarrety has Kellie," he said tersely. "He's asking for safe passage to America."

"Dear God." Susan's eyes were huge and terrified. "Will they give it to him?"

Tom shrugged back into his coat. "Griffith didn't say. Dennis told him one of his men had Heather."

"That's ridiculous. Heather's here in your sitting

room. Where are you going?'' she asked, alarm in her voice.

''I have an idea where he's keeping Kellie.''

Susan grabbed his arm. ''What can you do, Tom? More than likely the man is armed.''

''I'll think of something on the way.''

Heather leaned against the door frame and spoke around the thumb wedged firmly in her mouth. ''Someone has Mam, too.''

Susan watched her son freeze up. It was odd, really, the way his limbs stiffened and all movement stopped. The silence in the room was absolute, shrouding the three of them in a private, ugly world.

Tom walked across the kitchen and knelt in front of his daughter. ''Tell me what happened, love.''

''A man picked me up at school. He said his name was Colin. He said you wanted him to take me to Gran's. I liked him in the beginning but he went the wrong way. I told him I didn't want to go with him and then I heard Mam. She ran after me.''

''And then what happened?''

''He picked me up and ran, too, but I bit him. Then he put me down and we waited for Mam. She said for him to take her, not me.'' Heather was crying now. ''I told her I didn't want her to go with him, but she told me to run home and tell Gran.''

Susan lifted her hands. ''All these hours and you said nothing. Why didn't you tell me, child?''

Heather shook her head. The tears were coming too quickly to wipe them away.

Tom drew his daughter into his arms. ''It's all right, love. I'll take care of it. We'll get Mam back, and Kellie, too. Don't worry. Gran will stay with you.''

"Will Colin come back?"

"No, Heather," Tom said firmly. "He won't be back."

Susan stepped forward. "I'll take her. Go on now, and keep in touch." She kissed his cheek and led Heather into the sitting room. "Choose a story, love, and I'll read it to you. We'll stay right here on the couch together."

Tom waited until they'd left the room before picking up the phone. He pulled the piece of paper out of his pocket and punched in the number John Griffith had given him. The man answered immediately.

"Heather is here with me," Tom said. "It is Claire Whelan, my wife, they have."

Griffith's reply was brief. "Do you know where they might have taken her?"

"Aye."

"Will you show me?"

"I'm going after Kellie, Mr. Griffith. McGarrety is the dangerous one. Colin Burke is the man with Claire. He won't harm her unless McGarrety gives him the order. Besides, Claire will know how to handle him. Meanwhile, I want protection for my mother and daughter. The RUC will act quickly on your orders."

"I'll arrange it. Where shall I meet you?"

"There are several possibilities. If I were McGarrety, I'd stay as far away from Belfast as possible, but close to an airport."

"My guess would be Shannon."

"Aye," agreed Tom. "There's a house outside of Ennis. I'd try that first."

"I know Ennis," said Griffith. "I'll meet you at the Lemon Tree Restaurant in the center of town. I've a few matters to attend to before I leave London. I'll be there in about three hours."

"How will I know you?"

"Don't concern yourself," said Griffith. "I'll know you."

Twenty-Eight

Tom stood at the entrance of the Lemon Tree Restaurant and looked around. He knew John Griffith immediately. He was typical of British agents, nondescript, chosen for his ability to blend in, a man of average height and weight, deliberately unremarkable.

Casually, he made his way to the bar, sat down on a stool beside the Englishman and ordered a Harp. Neither man spoke. Finally, Griffith walked to a booth in the corner and sat down. Tom followed him.

"What are you planning to do?" he asked.

Griffith turned his mug around on the table. "Talk to him. Try to get him to give Kellie up."

"What about his demands?"

The Englishman shook his head. "There will be no negotiating with terrorists. Our policy forbids it."

"Even when two lives are at stake and the terrorist is willing to be deported?"

"We don't foist our problems on the United States."

Tom's jaw tensed. "The hell we don't. Half the Provisional IRA lives comfortably in San Francisco."

"I know that." For an instant something akin to temper flashed in Griffith's eyes. Then it was gone. "When all is said and done, I'm an employee," he said slowly. "I've been told that I must remember that."

"What are you saying?"

"My hands are tied. I can't offer McGarrety anything at all."

"He'll kill Kellie."

Griffith nodded.

Tom thought a minute, weighed his options and decided he had no choice but to trust the man. "Will you look the other way for a bit?"

Griffith frowned. "Excuse me?"

"I'm going to bargain with McGarrety. I'm asking you to look the other way until Kellie is safe."

Griffith lifted his glass and drank deeply. He set his empty glass on the table. "What's your plan?"

"Negotiate with him. Make him believe you'll give him what he wants."

"What about my superiors?"

"Do they trust you?"

Griffith nodded. "They're waiting for a report before they send in more men."

"Tell them we have the situation in hand. Tell them McGarrety is listening to you and that more men will scare him."

"I don't know how long we'll have before the press figures out the link between Davies and McGarrety. They may already have."

"Tell your people that secrecy is crucial for the time being. Explain that McGarrety is being reasonable for now. It's all over if the newspapers focus on Dennis."

John Griffith looked at Tom thoughtfully. "I need more than that. Tell me what you're planning to do."

"Give him a passport and an escort to Shannon. Your people can pick him up at the airport."

"I'll agree to that. We'll follow him and make the arrest at Shannon before he boards the plane."

"He's got to think he has a chance."

"We can't risk losing him," Griffith said.

"What if you did lose him? You already have Davies, and you'll have saved two women. Do you really think Dennis will be a menace to society if he leaves Ireland?"

John shook his head. "If we lose him, I'm finished."

"You'll have your self-respect. Better that than your pension."

"You really mean that, don't you?"

"Aye. Six years in Long Kesh helped me set my priorities."

John Griffith held out his hand. "Good luck, Mr. Whelan. I'll go along with your plan, and I'll do my best to bring in Dennis McGarrety."

Morning dawned the way it always did near the sea, with the cry of gulls and the lap of the tide against wet sand.

Kellie came awake slowly, stretching the stiffness out of her arms and legs. She'd spent the night on a small couch in front of an inadequate peat fire, curled up against the cold. McGarrety had disappeared somewhere down the hall into another room. By the time they'd reached their destination she was too exhausted to care where her captor spent the night. All she'd wanted was a washroom, a blanket and a place to lay her head. McGarrety had provided her with all three, even throwing in a pillow.

Kellie stepped into her shoes and found the kitchen. She filled a kettle, set it on the stove and lit the pilot with a match from the box on the counter. She refused to think about the consequences if Dennis's terms weren't met. All she could do now was wait...and pray. She walked back into the living room and rummaged through her suitcase for clean clothes. Where was Dennis?

She walked down the hall and looked in the bedroom. He sat in a chair staring out the window. "Do you mind if I use the washroom?" she asked.

Keeping his eyes fixed on the view from the window, he shook his head.

Kellie locked the bathroom door, filled the tub and stripped off her clothes. The water was blessedly hot. She washed quickly, soaping and rinsing her body and then her hair, scrubbing away yesterday's dirt and exhaustion. Wrapping herself in the towel to conserve as much warmth as possible, she pulled on a thick sweater, socks and a pair of loose corduroy slacks. Her thick curly hair would take hours to dry in this dampness, but it couldn't be helped. She was ready to face the world and McGarrety. Perhaps she would come up with a way out of her dilemma.

The kitchen was surprisingly well-stocked. She hoped it didn't mean he'd planned on an extended stay. She poured herself a bowl of cereal and made the tea.

She was on her second cup of tea when Dennis joined her in the kitchen.

He sat in the empty chair across from her. "I see that you've settled in."

She shrugged. "I need to eat. Hopefully I'll be alive next week."

McGarrety stared at her in amazement and then he laughed. "You've a sense of humor. I didn't know there was so much of your da in you, Kellie Delaney."

"If you intended that as a compliment, think again."

"Brian Delaney was a grand lad, always one for a good laugh."

"And a pint all around if I remember correctly."

"We were sorry to lose him."

"My mother is better off without him."

McGarrety found a cup, poured himself some tea and drank it down in one swallow. "Those are hard words coming from a daughter."

Kellie looked at him steadily. "You're not behaving like someone who thought highly of my da. What do you think he would say if he knew you were planning to kill me if you don't get what you want?"

His eyebrows rose in astonishment. "Now, didn't I tell you I wouldn't be doing such a thing, Kellie Delaney?"

"You said you would have Heather Whelan's throat cut."

He poured more tea into his cup and shrugged. "I needed leverage to get you here. How was I to know you wouldn't go screaming to the captain of the ferry boat and have me arrested?''

"I would have," Kellie said promptly.

"There, now. I knew it. What was I to do?''

"Have you ever considered staying on the right side of the law? Don't you get tired of always being on the run?''

He thought a minute. "I haven't always been on the run, Kellie. I was managing until your brother stirred the pot. Why couldn't he leave well enough alone? Davies was reformed. The old ways were finished. Men who once carried rifles are now marching into Stormant demanding a share of the pie, and getting it, lass. We've come a long way in twenty years."

"Connor was doing his job," she said shortly.

"Aye, and what kind of job was that, working for the Brits? I'm sorry he was your brother, Kellie, and Brian Delaney's son, but he brought no glory to his family name. He was an Irishman gone bad, that's what he was, a man who turned on his own." Dennis nodded his head. "You won't want to hear it, but it's so. Your poor mam can hardly hold up her head in the Falls because of Connor."

Tears burned her eyes. "He was a good man and he had a little boy. Who are you to decide who lives and who dies?''

"Connor's murder was necessary. I won't apologize for it. I am sorry about the wee lad. Sometimes there are casualties.''

"I don't want Heather Whelan to be another casualty," she said.

A loud knock froze them in their places. Then McGarrety jumped up, pulled a revolver from inside his jacket and walked to the door. "Who is it?"

"Tom Whelan."

Kellie gasped.

"What do you want?" McGarrety said.

"Open the door, Dennis. I have an offer for you."

"Are you alone?"

"I am."

McGarrety unlocked the door, opened it a crack and pulled Tom inside. "Did you bring the police?"

"John Griffith is waiting in Ennis. He's a British Intelligence Agent. Otherwise, I'm alone."

"How did you work that one out?"

Tom ignored him. His eyes met Kellie's and he smiled. "Are you all right?"

She nodded. "Is Heather safe?"

"Heather is at home with my mother. McGarrety's man has Claire."

"Jaysus Christ," McGarrety swore. "Colin Burke is a fool. Claire Whelan's no good. She was one of us. The Brits know that."

Kellie looked at him strangely. "You came for *me* instead of Claire?"

McGarrety interrupted. "Never mind about Claire. What's going on, Tom? Why are you here?"

Tom sat down on the couch. "Put your weapon away."

McGarrety hesitated and then complied, setting the gun on the table close to where he stood. "Go on."

"The Brits won't give you what you want, officially."

"What does that mean?"

"I'm to give you a new passport and a ticket out of Shannon on the condition that you release Kellie. From there you can catch a plane to the States."

"What's the catch?"

"There's no catch."

McGarrety grinned. "That's it? That's the bargain?"

"Aye."

He laughed and clapped Tom on the shoulder. "You're a genius, lad, a bloody genius."

"Shall I tell Griffith you've agreed and that you'll tell Colin Burke to release Claire?"

"Aye. Tell him it's a sweet deal. I'll call Colin after I land in the States."

Tom stood. "I'll be back with your papers." He hesitated. "It may not work out for you, Dennis."

"Don't worry about me, lad. I'll risk it."

Tom nodded, then looked at Kellie. "Give us a minute, Dennis."

Dennis McGarrety picked up his gun and walked to the other side of the room.

Kellie left her chair and sat beside Tom. "This is dangerous for you, too," she whispered. "How do we know Dennis will let us go?"

"Don't worry." He took her hand and lifted it to his lips. "There isn't anything I wouldn't do to keep you safe. Will you be all right here until I get back?"

"Yes. Now that I know Heather is safe, it will be easier." She looked down at their intertwined hands. "What about Claire?"

"Colin Burke won't act without McGarrety's orders. She'll survive."

Kellie lifted shining eyes to his face. "Thank you, Tom."

He squeezed her hand. "I love you."

"I believe you," she answered.

They were seated in a small tea shop on a quiet street in Ennis. John Griffith looked uncomfortable. "My superior isn't in agreement. He's questioning whether we can guarantee McGarrety's capture at Shannon and I tend to agree with him."

Tom swore silently. "What does he suggest?"

"He wants to go in, guns blazing."

Tom lost his temper. "Call him back."

"I beg your pardon."

"I said, call him back."

"What are you going to do?"

Tom leaned across the table. "If you don't call him back now, I'll go to the press and tell them how you bungled the investigation of Connor Delaney's murder. I'll explain that Kellie Delaney, a schoolteacher from Oxford, solved the case after you and your superiors ignored it for months, and how, after she brought Kevin Davies and Dennis McGarrety to justice, you allowed her to die in a police shoot-out that could have been avoided."

Griffith dialed the number and handed the phone to Tom who repeated his threat to Cecil Marsh.

"Well?" asked John after Tom had disconnected.

"Marsh will close off Shannon Airport and cancel all flights."

Twenty-Nine

Tom was edgier than he'd been during his original meeting with Dennis. Kellie noticed it and didn't comment, but McGarrety did. "Is something troubling you, lad? You wouldn't be thinking of double-crossing old Dennis McGarrety, would you?"

"I owe you nothing," Tom said bluntly. "But I will tell you this. You haven't more than prayer when it comes down to it. You'll not get away. All flights from Shannon to the States will be canceled."

"You're not telling me anything I haven't thought of already."

"What will you do?"

"I'd better keep that one to myself. There are other ways to get where I want to go. I'm taking Kellie as far as the airport."

"I'm coming with you."

McGarrety shrugged. "Suit yourself. You'll do the driving if you come along."

"We'll be followed," Tom warned him.

"Not for a bit," said McGarrety. "They'll have to give me a head start before coming down on me. Otherwise I have no reason to give up my accommodating hostage." He looked at the passport. "This is excellent, Tom. I appreciate the effort. Too bad every

Brit on the island knows it for the forgery it is." He grinned. "We'll take Kellie's car."

McGarrety navigated while Tom drove, hugging the back roads, passing Clairecastle and Newmarket-on-Fergus. McGarrety maintained a constant vigil out the back window where the glow of headlights in the distance never quite disappeared. At Hurler's Cross the N19 met a narrow country road. "Turn here," he ordered.

Tom turned the wheel quickly and swung onto the gravel path. They bumped over the next five kilometers to another road, and still another, until the glow behind them was gone and they were completely alone on the road.

"Bloody Brits," McGarrety said. "Stop here."

Tom shifted into Park and pulled the hand brake. "What now?"

McGarrety opened the door and climbed out. He stuck his head back inside the car. "This is where I'll leave you." He nodded at Tom. "You've done a good job for me, lad. I won't forget you. Your job is to tell them you dropped me at Shannon."

"What about Claire?"

"You should see her back home by morning." With that, he slipped off into the night.

Tom turned the car around and drove back in the direction they had come from.

"Do you think he'll make it?" Kellie asked.

"He has a chance."

"What do you think he'll do if he can't get out tonight?"

"Lay low for awhile, a few months, maybe. Then find a ship out of Belfast Harbor."

Kellie rubbed her arms against the cold and looked out the window. "Why did he want the passport if it's useless?"

"To fool the police."

"I don't understand."

"They'll be thinking he'll use it. They'll be looking for the man whose name is underneath the photo. McGarrety will slip through the cracks."

"I hope they find him."

Tom rested his hand on her knee. "Either way, we won't be seeing him again."

"How can you be sure?"

"Intuition."

"Does your intuition usually serve you well?"

"Usually. I knew you were the one for me the minute I saw you."

"Really?" She stared at him, intrigued.

Tom's voice was low and serious. "Are you coming home with me, Kellie?"

Her answer was teasing and filled with laughter. "Where else would I be going?"

"I never know what you're thinking," he confessed.

"I suppose that's a good thing," she reflected. "You won't be bored with me."

"The idea never crossed my mind."

The following morning Kellie woke, still groggy from sleep. Tom was already up and about. Perhaps he had houseguests. She heard voices downstairs and strained to listen. It wasn't the radio. He had a visitor, a woman. She recognized Claire's voice. Her stomach twisted and the usual hollow, anxious feeling she recognized as jealousy rose up into her chest.

Determined not to go downstairs and reveal her embarrassing insecurity, Kellie lay still for another ten minutes, humming softly to herself. Then she threw the comforter aside, swung her legs over the edge of the bed, rummaged through her overnight bag and headed for the shower.

The spray, hot and strong because there were no guests this week, soothed her aching muscles. She stayed under for a full twenty minutes lathering her body, working shampoo and conditioner into her hair, shaving her legs, luxuriating in the steamy blast.

Clean clothes, a warm turtleneck and soft jeans, felt heavenly against her skin. She spent a long time moisturizing her face and hands, applying lip gloss and mascara and pulling out her thick curls into attractive wisps around her face. Surely Claire would be gone by now. She pressed her ear against the door. Silence. She exhaled gratefully and walked downstairs to the kitchen, stopping in dismay at the door.

Claire sat at the table reading the morning paper. She looked up at Kellie and smiled. "Good morning. How are you feeling?"

Kellie manufactured a smile, stopped at the stove to turn on the kettle and sat down at the table across from Claire. "Better, thank you, and you?"

"I'm fine. I was never in any danger with Colin. I've known him for years. He was as pleased to release me as I was to go."

An awkward silence filled the room. "Where are Tom and Heather?" Kellie asked.

"Heather's at school and Tom is out of milk. He'll be back shortly." She hesitated. "You're probably wondering why I'm here?"

"Yes," Kellie said honestly. "I suppose I am."

"I'm leaving for Galway. I've applied for funds to attend the university. My application was accepted."

"That's wonderful," Kellie said sincerely. "Congratulations. Will it be enough to sustain you?"

"Susan said she would help me, but I'm going to find work. She's very kind but I don't want to be dependent on her."

"What about Heather?"

Claire bit her lip. Her eyes were bright and hard. "Heather will stay here. Banburren is her home and I won't be able to care for a child properly, not for quite a while. I'm hoping she'll want to come and stay with me when I have my holidays."

Kellie nodded. "It's difficult for women with families. I don't know how they do it."

"How did you do it?" Claire asked.

"I earned my degree after secondary school. I was very young and had no family to care for."

"What was it like for you?"

Kellie frowned. "I don't know what you mean?"

"Not many women from the Falls attend Queen's. Was it difficult for you to adjust?"

"No. I loved it from the first day. I think you'll find Galway a lovely city."

Claire nodded. "I want to leave the North. There's nothing left for me here, except Heather."

"I hope you're not leaving Banburren because of me."

"Not *because* of you, Kellie, although your presence in Tom's life had some influence on my decision," Claire said honestly. "I want an education. I'd like to do something important in this world. Here, in Banburren, that isn't possible. I'm glad to be going."

"This isn't really goodbye," Kellie said. "After all, Heather is seven years old. Surely you'll come back to Banburren for special events in her life. You should be a part of that."

"Of course." Claire stood. Her smile was brittle. "I'll be leaving now."

"I thought you were waiting for Tom."

Claire shook her head. "I waited to talk to you. Goodbye, Kellie. Good luck to you."

Kellie poured her second cup of tea without milk when Tom walked through the door. He held up the carton. "Sorry I was so long in coming back. I ran into Maggie at the store."

"Claire left," said Kellie tonelessly. "You just missed her."

"I never miss Claire," replied Tom. He opened the carton and poured milk into her teacup. "Did she tell you she's leaving Banburren?"

"Yes."

Tom nodded. "It's for the best. She should have done so years ago. Staying here, marrying me, that was her mistake."

Mean-spirited as it was, Kellie took comfort in hearing him criticize Claire. "It sounds as if her entire life has been a mistake," she prompted.

"So far," Tom agreed, "but she's thirty-three years old. Plenty of time to rectify it, to earn her degree, do whatever she wants with it, even marry again and have more children."

"Where does that leave Heather?"

"With me, thank God." He pulled her out of her chair and held on to her hands. "And with you, if you're willing."

"I'm willing."

"You're sure?" His eyes, blue and serious, were very close. "No more doubts about my loyalties?"

"Not a one."

"Tell me you love me."

She kissed one corner of his mouth and then the other. "I love you."

"How much?"

"Desperately."

"Completely?"

"Unreservedly."

Kellie closed her eyes and met his kiss. Life, she thought, had a way of working out after all.

Susan Whelan, not accustomed to knocking on the door of her son's home, walked into the kitchen and came upon an intimate scene she would rather not have observed. She turned around abruptly. "I'm so sorry," she gasped. "I didn't know—I wasn't—"

"It's all right, Mam," Tom assured her, unembarrassed. "Kellie said yes. We're getting married."

"Thank God," said his mother, her hand still over her eyes. "I think I'll be leaving now."

"That would be best," agreed her son, "and lock the door behind you."